How to Marry an Earl

The Cinderella Society, Book One

Alyxandra Harvey

Dragonblade Publishing, Inc. is an imprint of Kathryn Le Veque Novels, Inc.
P.O. Box 23
Moreno Valley, CA 92556
ceo@dragonbladepublishing.com

Produced in the United States of America

First Edition March 2022
Trade Paperback Edition

ARE YOU SIGNED UP FOR DRAGONBLADE'S BLOG?

You'll get the latest news and information on exclusive giveaways, exclusive excerpts, coming releases, sales, free books, cover reveals and more.

Check out our complete list of authors, too!

No spam, no junk. That's a promise!

Sign Up Here

www.dragonbladepublishing.com

Dearest Reader;

Thank you for your support of a small press. At Dragonblade Publishing, we strive to bring you the highest quality Historical Romance from some of the best authors in the business. Without your support, there is no 'us', so we sincerely hope you adore these stories and find some new favorite authors along the way.

Happy Reading!

CEO, Dragonblade Publishing

Chapter One

S OME LADIES PROMENADED with delicate lace parasols, and some ladies fell headlong into holes.

Persephone Blackwell counted herself fortunate that she had learned the trick of falling a long time ago. She had once gotten stuck in an Iron Age barrow and required a rope, two ladders, and three footmen to get her out. All while her grandmother's pet spaniel Chartreuse ran around the edge barking hysterically. That had been a much bigger to-do. She'd just had word from Henry about the beauty and pleasure of Egypt, from the pyramids to the pillars at Karnak, and it had set her off. She'd marched down into her little British barrow, determined to dig right down until she hit water or hellfire itself in search of her own historical findings.

She'd found two toe bones and a tooth. And she was fairly certain the tooth belonged to a badger.

Which was still more than she had found in her current barrow.

Or, hole, rather.

To be fair, the hole wasn't supposed to be there. She'd explicitly requested a trench be dug several yards further from the square in order for the children to practice their archaeological skills. For this express reason, it had to be said. Anyone might have fallen into a hole situated as it was, entirely too near the walking paths.

Also, it wasn't supposed to be quite so... grave-like. It was meant to be an attraction in the village festival, not a harrowing challenge in one's pursuits of leek pies or lace fichus, or whatever it was normal people did at a festival. Her tastes might run differently than most, but even she could see that. Not at the moment, of course. At the moment, all she could see was dirt, the pale roots of grass, and a slice of sky. This particular hole really was rather deep.

"Hello?" she called out.

A nearby swallow trilled a not-particularly-helpful song.

Never mind, she dug holes as a hobby. She might not find treasures of any historic significance in the village green, but she could certainly dig herself out. She pushed her bonnet back and ignored the twinge of new bruises along her elbow and shin. Her left knee throbbed. She *really* didn't have time for that sort of behavior.

It might be half past seven in the morning, but at any moment someone was bound to come along on some errand or another; a constitutional, the chasing of a dog, a turnip cart. She wasn't keen on having this added to the litany of stories told about her. Honestly, she could have written her own gothic novel. Not a terribly good one, but still. Fueled by the promise of new humiliation, Persephone launched herself out of the hole.

Well, not precisely *out* of the hole.

More like *at* the hole.

There was no denying she was short. And the hole was… tall. She slid down the side, dirt dropping into the sleeves of her spencer, and down the top of her dress. It was cold insult to injury. So was the dirt currently sticking to the back of her throat. She choked out a cough.

A new tactic was clearly required. She dug the toe of her boot into the side of the hole, trying to burrow it into the shape of a foothold. She lifted her right foot a little higher and did the same. She shoved her hands into the earth, searching for roots to hold onto. She could do this.

The earth, too soft to support her, crumbled away.

She landed with a jolt and an expletive best suited to gaming halls and pirate ships. The trouble was, she was accustomed to proper tidy trenches that sloped gently into barrows. This felt more like a trap from that same gothic novel she could now write.

Enter a handsome and mysterious gentleman.

"Lady Persephone?"

Splendid.

Not just any gentleman, but *this* one in particular. Of course.

Conall Hunter, Earl of Northwyck, future Marquis of Ashton.

He was aptly named – he put Persephone in mind of a hunter, not an earl. Tall and lean, with dark hair and grey eyes that tracked everything around him. They were currently fixated on her.

Stuck in a hole.

She had not seen him for several years. Not since she had ruined herself thoroughly enough that he would either not recognize her or else greet her with one of those insufferable smirks men seemed to reserve for ladies such as herself.

"Lady Persephone, it *is* you." He inclined his head. Not a smirk in sight.

"Lord Northwyck, good morning." She found herself tongue-tied. "Y-you're back!"

And I'm in a hole.

She curtsied quickly. A clump of mud fell from her sleeve. Honestly, who curtsied while stuck in a hole in the ground? Even silhouetted against the sun, he was entirely too handsome for his own good.

"Are you hurt?"

"Only my pride," she muttered.

"Let's get you out of there then, shall we?"

"Yes, thank you."

People always said they wanted to be swallowed by a hole in the ground. She wouldn't recommend it. Even if the sight of Conall shrugging out of his coat and clad only in his shirtsleeves was diverting. He rolled up his sleeves, displaying strong forearms. Muscles tensed under his skin when he leaned down to offer his hand. "Take my hand," he said.

She swallowed and reached up. His fingers closed over hers

and he pulled her up so quickly the sky tilted. She pushed into a sitting position, trying not to look as dishevelled and awkward as she felt. Her knee twinged sharply. She shifted her weight. "Thank you."

"You're welc—"

"Oi, miss, are you hurt?"

Persephone glanced over at the man hurrying their way. "I'm all right, George."

"Oh, it's you, my lady." The alarm in his gait faded to his usual amble. The local blacksmith was accustomed to her. She'd once begged him to teach her how to make an iron buckle like the one she'd found under the plum tree. She'd dated it to the fourteenth century and her father had agreed. She'd dined on that pride for a week. Until their next discovery.

"Who else would it be, George?" She smiled wryly. She stood up, wobbling slightly when her knee gave another protest. Conall's hand was suddenly at her elbow, steadying her.

George touched his cap to Conall as it was clear by the shine on his boots and the starch of his cravat that he was a gentleman. Not to mention the silver threaded waistcoat. She remembered him as a solemn and shy young man. Clearly, he'd outgrown his shyness and adolescent awkwardness. By miles. Leagues, even. "Sir." George blinked at the hole. "Rather spooky, that."

"Indeed." She discretely wiped her cheek. Mud had a habit of traveling in all directions. "Though I suppose being buried is better than having your brains pulled out through your nostrils."

George blinked again. "Your ladyship?"

"It's how they buried their dead in Ancient Egypt. Stuffed full of salt, with their internal organs preserved in tidy canopic jars."

"Aye?"

"Never mind." She was used to that particular expression. At least George didn't scare easy. He only looked mildly alarmed. He'd become accustomed to her.

"Are you hurt anywhere?" Conall asked.

"Fit as a fiddle," she assured him. "This is rather deeper than I intended," she added to George. "Can we have it filled in some, please? It's meant to be a much shallower trench, for the children to practice digging for treasures."

"Of course, your ladyship."

"Excellent. Have Mrs. Hastings give you luncheon when you call at the house. I have a feeling it's going to be a busy week."

"Thank you."

"Bring your boys too, I happen to know the duke's cook made a batch of treacle tarts. She's too fussy to serve them above stairs as the pastry cracked, but they taste divine. I had two yesterday."

"I'll do that. And I'll set to filling the hole right away." He hurried away in search of a shovel.

Persephone tucked a lock of hair back into its pins. There was more dirt on her pelisse, it had to be said, than in all of the fields of Little Barrow. Just as she liked it. Usually.

The mist was burning off the fields and the main road of the village was currently home to more pigeons than people.

Also, just as she liked it.

It was so much easier to get things done without an assortment of the local gentry—busybodies—looking down their noses at her. Not that she wasn't accustomed to it. Truly, she hardly noticed any more. But sometimes they messed with her excavations or jostled the artifacts, and that, she could not tolerate. Not from an earl, not from a duke. Not even from her own grandmother whom she adored. She'd been accused of being a trifle autocratic when it came to her antiquarian pursuits. Actually, her grandmother had likened her to a donkey.

She'd been accused of worse. And all of it true.

Luckily, the only duke she knew was Lord Atticus St. James, the Duke of Pendleton, and he was rather more autocratic than she was, and this was all his doing, anyway. The Little Barrow Antiquarian Festival had been his idea. She was its first devout acolyte.

"Do you routinely invite people to the duke's house for treacle tarts?" Conall asked, sounding amused. He lounged against a nearby tree in that way rakes always lounged, as if the weight of their own charm was simply too much strain on the spine.

"I do when they use their valuable rest time from their crops to help him with his festival," she replied. "Thank you again for your assistance. I'll be on my way." She curtsied again. *Ouch. Shouldn't have done that.* She walked away, trying to hide her slight limp. More bruises sparked to life with every step.

Conall walked up behind her, leading his horse. "You *have* hurt yourself."

"It's nothing." She tried for a breezy smile and picked up her pace.

"Let me take you home."

"Thank you, no. I'm not going home. I'm sure Mrs. Hastings will have a cold compress for my knee."

"So, it's your knee, is it?"

"Really it's nothing." Didn't he know better than to be seen with her? The village folk would all be at the windows by now, judging the weather for the day. Judging her. Of course, he was the charming and dashing earl and could do no wrong. He might survive her. Best not to risk it. Anyway, what did dashing earls possibly have to say to her? Or she to them? Even if she had known him since childhood. Even if she found she had missed him, now that he was back. Odd.

"As it happens, I'm on my way to Pendleton House," he said smoothly. Everything he did was done smoothly, like thick cream to coffee. "Let me see you there because I'm not about to let you hobble off on your own. My mother would disown me." He smiled a smile that ought to have been outlawed. She paused. She didn't like this new smile and she couldn't think why.

But he'd find it odd if she kept fighting him and then she'd have to explain herself, and she'd rather tumble back into the hole. And if they hurried, no one would see them. A rooster crowed. A back door slammed shut. And her knee did hurt more than she liked. She could *not* afford to be hobbled for the next week. That made up her mind. Scandals came and went, but ancient scarab beetles brought from the pyramids themselves were rare.

"Certainly, let's go." She grabbed the side of the saddle so abruptly that Conall had to rush to help her. He grasped her around the waist, and she felt a small thrill race up her spine at his touch. His breath ruffled her hair. Pain lanced through her kneecap, effectively ruining the moment. It was just as well. She had no business being distracted by the strength of his arms or the tilt of his now amused half-smile. She liked that one. It seemed real.

Perhaps she'd hit her head when she'd taken the tumble. Her brain was veering off into the strangest places.

She had a festival to organize and the promise of history about to share ancient secrets—there was nothing better. She ought to concentrate on that. Several distinguished fellows from the Society of Antiquarians had been invited to attend. As no one easily declined an invitation from a duke, it promised to be quite the event. Persephone had been working on the details for weeks now; from the children's displays where they would dig up treasures she would hide in smaller, safer holes—to tours of local sites of historic interest, to having enough teacakes at the series of lectures scheduled for the assembly rooms.

The anticipation thrummed through her, even buried under the mundane details her grandmother thought beneath the attentions of an earl's daughter. It was one thing to dig up bronze brooches or pieces of broken Roman mosaics from the back hedges, and quite another to be afforded a true glimpse of canopic jars from Ancient Egypt. All her life, she'd dreamed of such collections. Her visits to Montagu House in London only fanned the flames of her obsession. She considered it her *field*, not her obsession. Well, not *just* her obsession. Even she had to concede that she likely ought to feel this kind of excitement over the handsome scholars about to descend on the village, instead of their broken artifacts.

But artifacts were so much more interesting.

Usually.

Conall's chest pressed against her gave her pause. He smelled of cedar and rain. His arms wrapped around her to hold the reins and she couldn't help but watch the tendons flex in his wrists. She couldn't remember the last time she'd been so close to a man. Actually, she could. But he had been a lad, young and green. And a pragmatic means to an end. "So, am I to assume Pendleton roped you into his festival?" Conall's voice rumbled in her ear. It was intimate, husky. And it sent a march of embarrassing and inappropriate goosebumps along her neck.

"I was happy to volunteer."

"Were you?"

"Of course. Do you know how rare it is to be able to exhibit the kinds of artifacts that are even now on their way to Little Barrow?"

"Hmm."

She wasn't sure how to read his non-reply, only that it spoke volumes. "If you're not interested in history, why come here? Especially now?"

"I never said I wasn't interested."

"You are not an antiquarian."

"You seem very sure."

"Not a speck of mud on you, to begin with," she pointed out.

He smiled down at her. "There's enough in your hair for both of us."

She considered being mortified then decided there was no point. There was usually mud somewhere on her person. It would be exhausting if she were offended every time it was pointed out. "But you wear it like jewels," he murmured in her ear.

She twisted slightly to arch an eyebrow at him. "Really."

"You don't sound convinced." He sounded downright amused.

"You needn't flatter me, Northwyck," she returned, briskly, despite the warmth she felt in her cheeks. He had no business knowing he'd affected her. He was obviously too used to ladies melting into puddles at his feet.

"Is that what I was doing?" he murmured.

"You've known me too long to think I'd believe you anyway."

"Is that so?"

"'Tis."

"And have I been away so long that compliments offered to pretty ladies are no longer the thing? Even here in Little Barrow?"

She absolutely would not blush. He was teasing her, playing the polite Society games she used to know how to play. "So why are we digging holes for children to fall into, exactly?" he asked when she did not reply.

"They are meant to be excavation trenches, barely as deep as a washing basin," she explained. "It's somewhere for them to practice their techniques, to foster a curiosity about the past and the search for artifacts that tell us about our forefathers."

"You do sound like the duke."

"He's a kindred spirit."

"Indeed."

She glanced at him again. "Why are you here then, if not for the festival?"

"Visiting family," Conall replied. His voice really was entirely too delicious: rough and smooth at the same time, like whiskey.

Something about it burned a path through her, just as that whiskey would have.

THE DUKE OF Pendleton lived on the other side of the village, in an estate roughly ten times the size of Little Barrow itself. It was well situated with rolling hills and pockets of woodland and access to several ancient barrows and a single desolate stone circle. The walk up the drive alone usually took Persephone half an hour to complete. She was grateful that she did not have to do so today. Conall's horse was a massive brute, with very gentle manners and a smooth gait. He snorted gently at the stableboy who darted out to take the reins.

Conall steadied her as she slipped out of the saddle. She slid along his body, far closer than was polite. It flustered her and she tripped on a cobblestone. Assuming it was due to her knee, his hand closed over her shoulder. "I'll carry you inside."

"*Absolutely not.*" She'd blurted out. He looked at her curiously. She forced a smile. "I mean, I'm perfectly able to make it to the door."

If he carried her inside it would cause a hullaballoo and she'd had a lifetime's fill of being stared at. She limped ahead with a determination generally reserved for unpleasant appointments with the dentist. She'd have hopped like a rabbit if she'd thought it would get her inside faster. She didn't trust him not to scoop her up anyways. He was exactly the sort.

Instead, he kept pace quietly beside her, his hand near her lower back, not quite touching her. More respectful than the shape of his eyebrows. She'd never considered that eyebrows could have a moral slant, but his were decidedly wicked.

The house was a renovated abbey dating back to the Reformation and the Dissolution of the Monasteries. One of the Duke's ancestors had evidently performed some valuable service for King Henry the Eighth and was subsequently well rewarded. The abbey was built of gold-hued stones that glowed in the morning light. She had always loved it. And not just because of the rings of ancient barrows tucked behind the back woods which she coveted.

The duke welcomed her into his gold house and so he expected everyone else in the village to follow suit. They complied because he was a duke and in return, she did not pay any awkward social calls which might require a reciprocal visit. And so, the delicate balance of social life was protected. Until the festival, that was. Because now Persephone had call to be everywhere and as no one wanted to be left out of the celebrations they must give way. They still had opinions, of course. A lot of them. Right down to the duke's butler, Basil.

He was too professional to say so outright, but not quite professional enough to suppress the quivering of his nostrils. It was a dead giveaway. Had she thought that he would stoop to play cards, she would have warned him about his tell. As it was, she only smiled cheerfully when he answered the door. "Good morning, Basil."

"My lady." He bowed smartly to Conall. "My Lord Northwyck. The duke will be so pleased you've arrived."

"Thank you, Basil."

Persephone handed him her bonnet, slightly squashed from her tumble. His gaze flickered to the mud flaking off her hem onto the marble stones of the foyer. She winced. "I'm sorry, Basil. There was work to be done in the village."

"Indeed."

She fancied explorers into the artic had faced less frigid waters. When he seemed transfixed with the mess at her feet, Conall's voice went sharp. "Is His Grace in the breakfast room, Basil?"

Basil jumped. Persephone had never seen him jump. "Yes, my lord. He's expecting you."

"Good. Let's not keep Lady Persephone on her feet. And have Mrs. Hastings bring up a cold compress immediately."

"At once, my lord."

She hobbled through the yellow drawing room, the music room, and a hall of ancestral portraits. Expressions suggested backbones of steel, aristocratic arrogance, an obsession with spaniels, and frankly, what had to be at least one uncomfortable case of gout. She remembered similar portraits in her father's hall, especially a young child in a lace ruff that still occasionally haunted her nightmares.

"Percy, there you are," the duke bellowed before Basil had a chance to announce her. He might have passed his seventieth birthday, but it had done nothing to quiet his voice. As always, his shock of white hair was tamed into a queue fashionable when he was a younger man. She curtsied and a clump of dirt fell from her sleeve onto the pristine white tablecloth.

"You've been in the fields," he said approvingly. "It's never too early for a true antiquarian, is it, my girl?"

Conall shook his head with a grin. "And I thought you were bad, Pendleton."

"Conall, my boy, it's good to see you! It's been too long."

Persephone had to hide a smile to hear a man such as Conall referred to as a boy.

"Where's your sister?"

"Priya follows in the carriage. I imagine she'll arrive within the hour."

"Good, good."

"I didn't think she was coming." Persephone perked up. She hadn't seen Priya in months. They wrote letters of course, but it was so much better when they could see each other in person.

The duke's goddaughters were famous—well, infamous—for their quirks. Having a duke for a godfather, especially one that encouraged eccentricities and was perfectly happy to support a veritable tribe of ladies so they did not have to marry if they did not wish it, perplexed society and thrilled his goddaughters. A man with any lesser title would never have been able to get away with it half so well. As it was, they were often referred to as the Cinderellas. And as the Cinderellas stuck together, most of them cared not a whit for Persephone's ruination.

"All my goddaughters will attend to me," the duke preened. "Why wouldn't they, for our triumph?" His sharp gaze snapped at Persephone. "Why are you listing to the side? It's making me feel seasick."

"She had a tumble in the village," Conall explained before she could wave it away.

Persephone slid into the nearest chair. "I wrenched my knee. It's nothing."

"Tut," Mrs. Hasting said, bustling through the door with a basket of medical supplies and a cloth full of ice from the icehouse. "We'll have you right as rain in no time."

"Thank you, Mrs. Hastings," Persephone replied. "But I don't need the ice. His Grace will need it for his guests."

"Hang the guests," Conall interrupted, taking the bundle of ice and dropping it unceremoniously into her lap. Gone were his city manners and devilish smiles. "Go on."

Persephone's own smile wilted at the edges. Everyone was staring at her. She wasn't about to fling her skirts up over her head with Conall standing so close. She might not have much of a reputation left but she probably ought to safeguard what remained of it.

"Conall, you'll embarrass the girl," the duke barked. "Have some coffee and let her be."

Conall held Persephone's gaze for a moment. Her cheeks must be as red as the day she'd gotten burned digging too long without her bonnet. She was used to staring, at least from displeased aristocrats. She wasn't used to *this* kind of staring.

He was very, very good at it.

Something flickered in his eyes.

And he knew it.

"The ice will do you more good than it will in someone's lemonade glass," he said, as if there wasn't some other conversation going on silently between them. She wasn't sure what was being said but she was fairly certain it was inappropriate. He had heard about her, then. She looked away, hiding her disappointment. It was absurd to be mad at the rain for being wet. What was, was. She was ruined and therefore Society had different rules for her, plain and simple. It was hardly a revelation.

"He's right, dear," Mrs. Hastings agreed. She turned subtly, blocking Persephone with the widths of her skirts. Persephone propped her foot up and slid the ice bundle over her knee. She made a little sound of relief. Conall's jaw tightened.

"Breakfast?" the duke asked him.

"I'll wash the road off before I sit down," he said. He bowed to Persephone. "Lady Persephone."

"Thank you for your assistance, Lord Northwyck."

"So formal," the duke sighed. He expected it for himself, but it did seem to irritate him and please him in equal measure between his godchildren. "You've known each other too long for that nonsense."

"It's been years," Conall said. "I wouldn't have recognized her if she hadn't been down a hole."

Persephone wrinkled her nose. The duke laughed. "That's my Percy. Did you know she is single-handedly going to make my festival a success? Fairweather can choke on it."

The rivalry between the duke and the Earl of Fairweather centered mostly on a rare sarcophagus. Or was it a cuneiform tablet? Truly, no one could recall.

"I'll leave you to your work then."

When Conall had left and Mrs. Hastings had taken her basket of supplies away, the duke nodded to Persephone. "Have some coffee," he ordered. "I know how you love it."

"Grandmaman will be scandalized," Persephone teased, leaning over to kiss his cheek. Behind her, Basil stifled an apoplectic sound at the casualness of her greeting. He had returned with the morning newspaper, freshly ironed. "Ladies are meant to drink tea."

"Your grandmother is not scandalized, my dear, but rather *scandalizing.*"

As there was no sense in arguing with truth, Persephone let a footman bring her a cup. She smiled her thanks and added a dollop of cream from a dish painted with violets. The sun came in through the wide windows, touching china, silver spoons, glass carafes and endless bowls of white roses from the gardens. It also found stacks of books, shards of rusted iron dug from some barrow or another, and a disconcertingly full-sized statue of Anubis, the jackal-headed Egyptian god of death. Most of the footmen refused to look at it directly. Persephone thought it beautiful in the most covetous manner.

Artifacts never sneered at the smudges on her sleeves, or the state of her hem. They didn't look down at her, or whisper behind their hands when she passed. They only sat patiently while she teased hundreds of years of stories from shards of pottery or twists of glass beads. A crystal egg might have belonged to a Saxon princess, the rusted pommel of a sword to a Viking warrior. A farmer might have dug up that enamel pin only to turn it under again in order to plant his peas. The possibilities were endless.

She was doing it again.

Obsessing.

Her father had passed his joy in digging up the ancient barrows and stone cairns in the surrounding countryside to her. He'd bought a manor house in Little Barrow solely because it afforded him a place to pursue his studies. As it wasn't entailed, Persephone had inherited the country house and her second-cousin Eustace had inherited the earldom and everything else. He'd declined to follow her father's wish of setting her up with a hefty annuity and dowry. And legally, he was not required to comply.

Luckily, she vastly preferred the country estate pockmarked with excavation sites and mysterious grassy ringforts to Town. It was no secret that she also preferred dirt to debutante balls. But a lady, even one with her own modest house, was afforded few opportunities to travel abroad to interesting locales such as Cairo or Athens. She could read about them and visit the Elgin marbles, but it wasn't quite the same.

But now, famous antiquarians would bring their private collections practically to her backyard.

Only a few more days.

The duke smiled at her, as if reading her mind. "It won't be long now, my dear."

She wondered once more if she ought to tell him about Henry. He was a duke, after all, he might be able to help. Surely, he had connections at the War Office? And it didn't take a genius to know that her oldest friend, Henry Talbot, was in a heap of trouble. And when Henry was in trouble, Persephone got him out of it. He was kind and funny but not particularly bold. He looked to her for direction, mostly because his father only cared to provide any at the ends of his fists.

She'd been in paroxysms of fear when he first sailed off to fight Napoleon. A thin boy of barely twenty-one with a knowledge of books and fields and odd neighbour's daughters who liked to dig up bones. What did he know of muskets? Or sailing with the Navy? Or whatever it was his commission had brought him. His father, the Earl of Culpepper, had been so proud. His son had finally done something for him to boast over. Persephone had cried, privately. Publicly she'd toasted her friend, promised to write him weekly letters, and shot glares at his father until her eyeballs ached.

And then a year later, she'd ruined herself. Henry had been so annoyed. He'd written her his shortest letter yet: *I'd have married you, you pea-brain.*

A kindness she wasn't about to repay with an acceptance. Why on earth should she ruin his life as well as her own? She'd said as much. His reply was caustic, at best. He'd been gone for years now. Even with Napoleon finally defeated and sent packing in June, and three months later, still no sign of Henry.

Only that one letter.

"Are you well, Percy?" The duke asked in his booming voice. "You look peaky. Have some more herring."

Persephone forced a smile. "I'm perfectly well."

Best to keep Henry's secrets a little longer.

Chapter Two

PERSEPHONE SPENT THE rest of the morning attending to the myriad details caused by the imminent arrival of dozens of priceless artifacts, not to mention the early influx of the Ton arriving for several house parties preceding the festival. One of which started in a few hours and was the only reason she was heading back home to Halcyon House.

She wished dearly that she could avoid the party, but it was being held by their neighbour, Henry's grandmother, Lady Culpepper. Lady Culpepper barely tolerated her, and only for her grandmother and Henry's sake. As it was more than she felt was necessary given their connections, she expected Persephone to attend as the only female antiquarian. She could finally be an *interesting* novelty, like a strange beetle in a naturalist's collection.

The duke had insisted his carriage see her home and she suspected, had ordered the driver to slow down as he passed through the village so that all of the gossipmongers might catch a glimpse of her. At any rate, she was glad to be home, if only for a respite.

The red stone building sat in a patch of bright sunlight ringed with oak trees, hawthorn, and wild gardens. Down the hill behind the herb patch was the hermitage, a space of her own for her work. She hadn't had a chance to visit in days. She missed it as much as she missed Henry. A friend was a friend, after all.

She thanked the driver and climbed up the front steps. Her

knee barely protested, to her great relief. It would not stop her from excavating her own trench this afternoon. Lady Culpepper had invited the few antiquarians with impeccable bloodlines or, at the very least, considerable fame, to exhume the barrows and ring fort in the fields of her estate. Little Barrow was aptly named, surrounded by such curiosities.

Persephone frowned when she stepped into the front hall and Mrs. Bell, the housekeeper, was nowhere to be seen. Usually, she had a preternatural sense of Persephone's arrival. There wasn't even a footman in sight. Even her grandmother's spaniel, Chartreuse, was hiding.

Dread iced her stomach.

She took a tentative step forward. There was only one reason why the staff would have deserted their posts as one. Only one reason behind this sort of silence.

Mr. Erstwhile Asher.

Just the name sent a foreboding shiver down her spine. She didn't consider herself particularly prone to psychical warnings, but facts were facts. Erstwhile Asher was here.

Not only here, but running naked down the stairs, the chandelier rattling over his head.

"Gah!" Persephone slapped a hand over her eyes so fast she nearly put one of them out entirely. "Mr. Asher!"

Mr. Asher paused, blinking owlishly. He wasn't even wearing his spectacles. "Matilda, is that you, my dear? I thought you were going to hide with the cupcakes."

"*Grandmaman!*" Persephone wailed in response, peeking between her fingers. "I told you I'd only be gone for the morning!"

"Miss Blackwell!" Mr. Asher said primly, as if she were the one naked on the Turkish carpet runner. "I say!"

Lady Matilda Blackwell, dowager countess and thirty-seventh in line to the throne of England, stood in the doorway to the main parlor wearing nothing but her own considerably wrinkled skin and her best wig. It towered like a giant pink cake with roses made of buttermilk silk frosting accented with spangled birds. "Persephone, you're early."

"I'm not! You're naked!"

"Yes, dear."

"Again!"

"Yes, dear."

"You *promised*."

Matilda shrugged unrepentantly and sighed up at her devoted squire. "The children of this generation are terrible fusspots, aren't they, Mr. Asher?"

Mr. Asher bowed, jiggling alarmingly. Persephone fixed her gaze very firmly on the crown moulding, suddenly manifestly interested in the plaster grapes and cherubs. She'd always found them cloying and pedantic. They were positively beautiful to her now.

"I remember when I was your age, Percy, women welcomed men into our boudoirs to help us dress, just like Marie-Antoinette."

"Grandmaman," Persephone said, torn between a laugh and a shout. "*Go away.*"

She waited until the sound of footsteps retreated, then a few more minutes to be safe, before daring to look away from the fat cherubs. The one on the left had a chipped nose.

"Oh, Miss Persephone, thank the Good Lord you're home again," Mrs. Bell said fervently, bustling down the hall from the kitchen. "I expect you need some tea."

"Yes, by all means, fortification." She paused in the parlor doorway. "Is it safe, do you think?"

Mrs. Bell attempted to look unflustered, dark dress straining proudly over her ample bosom. "There is marzipan tucked into *that* statue and champagne spills in the green parlor, Miss. But I don't think your grandmother was long in this drawing room."

Persephone grinned. *That* statue was as close as Mrs. Bell ever came to admitting there was a stone relief of a dancing satyr, minus the fig leaf, in the house. "Tell the servants they shall have a bowl of punch tonight and make sure they have an especially good dinner."

"My pleasure, Ma'am. I'll speak to Cook. Perhaps tartlets?"

She loved custard tarts and the Cook loved her. Other households repeatedly tried to lure him away with promise of higher wages for his tartlets alone. But as long as Mrs. Bell stayed at Halcyon House, so did Cook.

Needless to say, they ate a lot of custard tarts.

Between Persephone's decor and her grandmother's antics, the tartlets might be the only thing keeping Mrs. Bell here. "Perhaps a double batch," Persephone suggested prudently.

Equipped with a cup of strong tea and lemon biscuits, Persephone raised her teacup in salutation to the statue of Nemesis she'd had set between the two banks of windows. If she'd been born in ancient Greece, she might have left offerings of barley cakes and olive oil. Which only made her think of the marzipan offerings to the satyr and what he might have seen. He did look a bit shocked. She hastily drank more tea and tried to think of less harrowing things.

Like Conall.

She might have hoped the passing of several years would somehow make him less interesting. He'd become more polished, even more distinguished. He'd always been handsome, but he clearly wasn't shy any more. There was a gleam to his gray eyes. And if the stories were true, he had spent the last couple of months flirting with widows and dancing and drinking champagne until dawn. He's grown stronger now, wider in the shoulders. She could well imagine the strength of him whirling her around the dance floor in a waltz.

"Your cheeks are pink. You're not turning prudish on me, are you, Percy?" her grandmother interrupted.

She knew full well she wasn't turning red because of her grandmother's antics. She was made of sterner stuff. "What if I'd been the vicar?" she asked.

"Serve that pompous windbag right." Her grandmother reached for the last biscuit. "You don't like him either. If I recall, you littered the church with pagan human bones."

"I was ten years old." And deeply upset that the old vicar had left for a new parish. She hadn't cared for her mother's explanation of old men retiring to be nearer to their families. She'd found bones in a barrow and when her father said they were of no particular significance, she'd used them to decorate the church. "And all the same, you're frightening the servants."

Only her grandmother could bring out that particular prim tone. She didn't care for it, but nor did she care to ever see Mr. Asher's flabby buttocks again.

"Pah. Mr. Asher's most embarrassed. Have a care for his sensibilities, won't you?"

Persephone would wager he wasn't embarrassed enough not to repeat the entire process the very next time she found herself in the village for a few hours.

"You interrupted a most enjoyable afternoon, you know. 'Twas very rude."

"I beg your pardon," Persephone returned drily.

Her grandmother patted her hand. "Never mind. We'd run out of cupcakes anyway."

Persephone shuddered.

"I saw that, my girl," Lady Matilda accused.

"I am sitting in a draft," she replied. She loved her grandmother and in fact thanked God daily that she had cupcake capers to deal with instead of a family who clung too tightly to Society, but there were limits.

She'd rather like to be able to eat cupcakes again one day.

"I suppose I ought to get ready for the afternoon's festivities," Lady Matilda said. "Make sure you wear something cheerful, my dear."

"I will," Persephone said. She was lying, of course. They both knew it. No one did sartorial cheerfulness like the Lady Matilda. It required a certain visual fortitude.

"You so rarely go into society, you want to be noticed, don't you?"

She really, *really* didn't. She'd had enough of that to last a lifetime. Three lifetimes. She'd rather live in that hole. "Yes, Grandmaman," she said dutifully. Her grandmother wrinkled her nose before heading off to her chambers.

Persephone was on her second cup of tea and contemplating ringing for cake when Mrs. Bell entered with a letter on a silver platter. "For you, my lady. It just arrived."

Persephone leapt for it with enough enthusiasm that Mrs. Bell jumped. "Goodness!"

"Who brought this?" she asked. The letter was still sealed but worn and creased and slightly water-damaged. Her stomach soured.

"A boy from the village," Mrs. Bell answered, snatching her hands back as if she was afraid she might get bitten. "It fell off the mail coach and was only now found in someone's garden hedge."

Persephone tore into it, even as she broke into a run for the privacy of her own bedroom. "Thank you!" she shouted over her shoulder.

Mrs. Bell shook her head. At least the younger mistress of the house kept her clothes on in the parlor.

THE LETTER WAS not from Henry.

Frustration and worry sizzled in Persephone's belly. She'd been hoping he would send word that he was back in England, if unable to come home directly. Or better yet, share with her the evidence that had put him into this predicament in the first place. But he wanted to protect her. It was maddening.

According to his previous—and far more regular—letters, Henry and a fellow soldier, Peter Oliver, had accidentally discovered a traitorous plot between one of his commanding officers and a peer of the realm. It centered in Egypt where Henry was stationed. That was not a lot to go on.

And instead of telling Persephone more, he hid letters in forgeries on their way to British parlors—and likely, the duke's festival. They were randomly placed to avoid detection as he feared he was being watched. He planned on reaching England first, with his tale to tell, and have the letters as security, as assurance that should something happen to him, the truth would still be told.

Which would have been an entirely more reasonable plan if he'd told her where the bloody letters were hidden. She knew how to spot a forgery from a mile away, after all. Artifacts were her life. As was the festival. And just as soon as he was safely home, she planned on bashing him in the head with something heavy.

She'd written him reams of paper for months now, telling him all about the festival. Any collector worth their salt would be sharing their treasures with the Duke of Pendleton. And the others would covet an invitation, likely publicly enough, that she could convince them to extend her an offer to tour their home displays if necessary. It was hardly a foolproof plan, but it wasn't bad as far as panicked last-minute secret plots went, especially without any help from Henry. She hoped desperately that her plots would not be necessary at all. They were meant as contingency plans in case Henry didn't make it home.

He should have made it home by now.

Fear for him scraped inside her chest, like iron. It wouldn't do him any good if she flew to pieces. She had to stay calm. She read the newspapers regularly enough to know that the soldiers' return home could be delayed for any number of reasons, even when that soldier was an earl's son and even if he had nothing to report to the War Office. His ship could have missed the tide, could have been taken off course by the winds, attacked by pirates. Anything.

She could not save him from the vagaries of the sea, but she could damn well save him from being wrongfully accused and convicted of a crime which resulted in the death penalty.

It would have been easier if his father, the Earl Culpepper, could have been depended upon to help. But the earl had a volatile temper, and a runaway mouth when he drank brandy. And he drank enough brandy to cause a drought in the French court, even when such spirits had to be smuggled into England. Henry's grandmother, Lady Culpepper was certainly daunting but making debutantes cry was hardly helpful under the present circumstances.

And so, it was up to Persephone for the foreseeable future. She would take a tally of every single item in the assembly hall, inspect them carefully for hints they might be forgeries, and then continue on to the crates which were even now being delivered to the duke's ballroom. If the other letters were in Little Barrow, she would find them.

She *had* to find them.

It was as simple as that.

THE SUN CAME out in full, proving that even the English weather was mildly terrified of Lady Culpepper.

The garden party was in full swing by the time Persephone and her grandmother arrived. For a lady who insisted on parading through the parlor naked, the Dowager Countess Blackwater also insisted on unique fashions. She wore a dress in pale aubergine with yellow trim and a turban of silk flowers so tall it resembled a marzipan hedge. "One must be cheerful," she reminded Persephone adding another flower to the lacing of her bodice. "You can't wear dark brown all of the time, darling."

Persephone had only escaped similar decoration because she would be descending into her barrow. She wore her usual riding habit she had altered for ease of movement. It was smart enough that Lady Culpepper sniffed in surprised approval. Besides, dark brown hid dirt the best. The pink ribbon at the bodice was in deference to her grandmother.

"Darling Adelle," Lady Blackwater bent to kiss Lady Culpepper's cheek, then thought better of it when her hair piece wobbled.

"Matilda, do sit down and have some cake."

"You know I shall." She joined a collection of older ladies at the table dripping with lace cloths and groaning under silver platters of iced cakes, biscuits, and delicate pastries decorated like colourful baubles. Ribbons of frosting looped between them, scattered with violets and sugared rose petals. The ladies were equally festooned in ruffles and ribbons of mint green, lavender, and every shade of blue. Pale flowers twined around the supports of the painted tent that shaded them from the attentions of the sun. The entire tableau might have been at home in a confectionary's display window. Everything around Persephone might have been mistaken for a cupcake. It was beautiful.

She itched to be in the dirt.

She curtsied politely. "Lady Culpepper."

"Mmm."

The other ladies paused in their conversation, exchanging glances over their china cups. Lady Culpepper had issued the invitation to the house party, but her personal welcome would dictate the way the others received Persephone.

"My Percy designed that dress herself, isn't she clever?" Matilda asked, sounding as frothy as champagne. "The duke himself commended her on it."

Frothy champagne still had a kick.

"Indeed," Lady Culpepper replied. She might be snobbish and sharp, but her affections for Persephone's grandmother were true. And being a Duke's goddaughter did offer Persephone *some* protection, after all. "Lovely. You may join the others at the barrows."

"Thank you, Lady Culpepper."

Persephone fled before anyone could say anything loud enough that she couldn't pretend not to hear them. Whispers boiled behind her.

"*That's* her?"

"I thought she'd be much prettier, *considering*."

"What an odd riding habit."

"How singular."

IT WAS ONE thing to find ancient bones in a barrow-grave, and it was quite another thing altogether to find *old* ones.

Old bones were not 'ancient'. They were just *old*. And it only figured that Persephone was the one to discover them. The others had the good fortune to be digging inside proper barrows. There was a cluster over the hills beyond the carefully kept formal gardens. The Culpepper gardeners had been opening them up for days in preparation. They were neat and tidy enough, mostly because Persephone had snuck over one afternoon and suggested methods less likely to damage any findings. They weren't digging for turnips, after all, or planting wheat. It was a different thing altogether and equally life-affirming, if you asked Persephone. Which no one ever did. Except for the Duke and he was not attending the dig. Much to Lady Culpepper's pique.

Lord Darrington had already found several elf-arrows and

part of what might have been a bronze torc. Persephone found three coins barely older than she was and likely shoved into the ground by her own hand when she was little. She'd run over the barrows with Henry, making up stories and leaving 'treasures' to be found one day by famous barrow-diggers. Or pirates. Henry was always fonder of pirates than barrow-diggers. She supposed it served her right for tampering.

She didn't want to call for the others, it would only reinforce their belief that she was merely playing at the science. Never mind that the British Museum called her in regularly to examine newly acquired artifacts. In point of fact, Persephone had examined several pieces from Darrington's own collections and once saved him considerable embarrassment before he could display a forged Etruscan urn. The same could be said of several of the collectors here, though they had no idea. Lord Snettisham nearly spent several thousand pounds on a bust of Aphrodite made by a clever worker in one of the Wedgewood factories. Lord Fairweather had better luck, but then he funded more expeditions than everyone else combined. He was quite as obsessed as Persephone would have been, had she access to the same money and power. She envied him in a way that was doubtless unattractive.

There wasn't much to see, the jagged edge of bone, dirt, a decaying slipper with dainty blue heels. A man's dancing shoe.

"Found something, have you?"

Persephone jumped at the interruption, turning to find Conall crouching at the edge of her trench.

"Whose body is that?"

"Regrettably, that isn't the way archaeology works, my lord," Persephone replied. She was pleased that she sounded perfectly normal, and not at all like a girl who had to be hauled out of muddy holes on a regular basis. "Bones don't come neatly labelled."

"More's the pity."

"Where would be the fun in that?"

"It looks more recent than the others."

"It is." She didn't ask him how he knew with such a cursory

glance. She had to smile. She knew exactly who the leg bone belonged to and what it was doing here.

"I've never seen anyone smile at bits of a skeleton quite like that."

Doubtless true.

"This is the very exalted left leg and foot of the eighth Earl Culpepper," she said.

"Exalted, is it?" Conall sounded amused, not at all put off.

"He lost it to illness, regrettably. But he claimed it was the only leg that danced at all well and gave it a proper burial and wake."

Henry had told her all about it when she was nine. His great-grandfather had survived the sawbones coming to take the infected foot turning black and fetid. No amount of vinegar rinses or spider's web and honey poultices had helped. Even the maggots set inside his bandages weren't quick enough. He decided to inter the leg once he was recovered enough to be wheeled about in an embroidered chair. He'd buried his best shoe with it and hired a piper to pipe a lament. She'd been in London with her parents and deeply, deeply miffed that she hadn't been able to attend.

"That's not a story you hear every day. I'm surprised the duke never mentioned it."

Persephone nodded, fighting back a sudden wave of fear and sadness. Thinking of Henry made her stomach churn. Where was he? Why hadn't he arrived home yet? Where were his letters? "I'm not sure he was invited. It was a family event." Even saying Henry's name seemed dangerous, as if it might call more bad luck to him.

She wiped her hands briskly. No more maudlin woolgathering. She wouldn't save Henry by weeping over his great-grandfather's foot. She peered up at Conall. He watched her carefully, as if she was interesting. Curious. Well, she was a curiosity hereabouts, there was no denying.

He probably ought not to be talking to her in public. She wasn't entirely sure what to say that didn't involve dead bodies or treason. He probably didn't want to hear how the Egyptians used to pound strips of soaked papyrus into paper or how Cleopatra had herself delivered to Caesar rolled into a carpet. Naked. Actually, considering what she kept hearing about Conall's escapades, he might be interested in that last bit. But she was meant to talk about the weather and other dull topics. She only liked to talk about the weather if it was threatening a dig. She was desperately out of practice.

The other unmarried ladies of the party drifted closer. They gathered around Conall, like honeybees at the hive. When Lord Darrington, also unmarried and reasonably handsome, joined him there was practically a stampede. "What have you got there, Lady Persephone?" Lord Darrington asked, his shadow falling over her.

"Nothing. It's—."

"These bones aren't ancient," he said loudly, and condescendingly enough that she longed to poke him with her trowel. "I'm afraid you've been duped."

"No, I—."

"Understandable, of course. You lack our experience. It's nothing to be ashamed of."

She gritted her teeth. "I realize—."

"Where's the rest of it?" He slid into the trench, even though he had his own perfectly good trench on the other side of the barrow. His required a ladder and went deep enough to be of proper use. The least he could do was leave her to her own shallow grave.

"Mind your boots!" she snapped when his heel dislodged one of the toes, snapping it like tinder. One of the girls giggled behind her hand. One didn't speak to earls in that way, especially not ruined girls such as Persephone Blackwell. But then one did not go tramping through a dig site like that either. Honestly. She rather hoped Henry's grandfather's ghost wandered by to slap him on the back of the head.

Lord Darrington wasn't listening, he was too busy calling for Sir Reginald Barton, who led most of Fairweather's very successful expeditions. They squeezed into the trench beside her, knocking her back onto her heels. Someone trod on her skirt.

Someone else nearly broke her finger when she curled over the rest of the leg bone to keep it from being splintered. It might not be much of a find, but it was hers. And Henry wouldn't want it getting damaged. It was the least she could do.

"That's enough," Conall interrupted. His voice sliced between them like an arrow. "You're stepping on Lady Persephone," he added stepping into the trench, effectively silencing the men. They stared at him, as surprised as Persephone was. "*Move.*"

Sir Baron nearly lost his footing in his haste to eject himself from the grave. Lord Darrington wasn't as easily cowed, seeing as he was also an earl. He did eventually move. He might be an earl, but he wasn't nearly as wide in the shoulders.

"Lady Persephone, you were saying that these bones are too recent to have been buried at the time the barrow was built?" His eyes were dark and calmly calculating, as if he saw through her. People *looked* through her all of the time, but no one had yet to see through her with a single piercing glance.

She nodded, not enjoying this much attention. "The grave is too shallow," she said finally, quietly. She wondered why she suddenly felt like blushing. She turned her attention back to the bones and the things she actually understood—earls, especially dangerously attractive ones, not being one of them.

One of the ladies giggled. "You truly are the Bone Lady."

And there went her first public social interaction with a handsome man.

If you didn't count falling in a hole on the village common.

It had been a rather trying day, come to think of it.

Persephone brushed dirt back off the ankle bone, dislodging it carefully. The four remaining toes squirmed. Lady Louisa Edgeworth gasped theatrically, clutching Conall's arm. Persephone rolled her eyes before she could stop herself. Conall's mouth lifted in a half-smile. "He's dead," Persephone told the other girl bluntly. "He's not going to hurt you. Or rather, his one solitary leg is unlikely to."

"What about his ghost?" Miss Holly Carter, asked, eyes wide as teacups.

"Very true," Persephone nodded briskly. "Best step back. No telling what might happen."

It gained her a little bit of space, enough to breathe again.

She continued to work both her trowel and brush as they chattered excitedly. Lord Darrington puffed up his chest though she had already stopped listening to his prattle. There was something else buried with the body. It looked like some kind of decanter, the stopper tilted inside the broken neck. Prying it loose from the packed earth too quickly would shatter it. She angled herself so she was blocking the discovery. She wanted a moment before the other antiquarians swooped in again.

All sorts of pottery might be found in graves; rounded, beaker-shape, filled with ashes of the dead, or imported olive oil. Canopic jars, used by the ancient Egyptians to store internal organs during the mummification process. But this was a cut lead crystal decanter, painted all over with delicate curlicues of gilt. There was wine sediment in the bottom, thick and muddy. Henry's grandfather had loved his claret.

She needed more time to bury everything back up properly. But if the footman suddenly standing over her was any indication, she wasn't likely to get it. The ladies were being summoned to change for dinner. And her grandmother would keep sending footmen until there was a battalion of them in their white hose and curled wigs.

Conall winked at her, before drawing the others away toward the house. She watched him for a long moment, before realizing he'd successfully distracted her from her work. She couldn't remember the last time that had happened. Actually, she could.

And look how well that had turned out.

"Did you hear?" Holly asked Louisa. "He's looking for a wife."

As it happened, he was looking for a murderer.

But he could pause long enough to eject a few pompous lords from a trench. Conall never could abide a bully. And a handful of aristocratic bullies descending on a young lady who looked for all the world as through she'd rather be left alone to play in the dirt, was more than he was willing to overlook. It was curious that no one else had come to her defense. It was common courtesy and Lord knew, he had a current deficit to begin with, under the polished manners he put on. There'd been the usual intelligence and curiosity in her expression, but the wariness was new. He'd been gone for a long time. Something had clearly happened to her.

He wondered if she was the one he was looking for. It seemed unlikely, but after years of gathering intelligence for the crown, he knew perfectly well that "unlikely" was not the same as "impossible." Persephone Blackwell might very well be a traitor.

She was clever enough.

Even if she didn't seem the type.

"Well?" he asked of the woman hiding behind the oak tree.

Priya emerged from the shadows, annoyed. The sun glinted off her dark hair, so much darker than his own. He had their father's nose; she had her mother's colouring. Priya was his half-sister, born to his father's second wife, a lady he met in a palace garden in India. "You can see through trees now?"

"No but the shadow of a tree isn't usually trimmed in lace."

She glanced down at her hem, making a face. "Blast."

"Did you find anything?"

She shook her head. "I searched all of their rooms. Darrington keeps brandy bottles under the bed but nothing else. Fairweather is so tidy it makes my teeth hurt."

"Barton?"

"Ugly coats and delusions of grandeur. Nothing out of the ordinary." She fell into step beside him as they returned to the house. "He owes markers at three gaming hells in Town, but again, that's hardly noteworthy."

"He's here," Conall insisted. Or *she* is. "I can taste it." He had that tingle in his hands, as if he had just shot a musket.

"I'll keep searching," Priya promised.

He didn't like to involve her in his work, but sometimes she was insistent. And helpful. And too much time spent in her gardens was turning her into a recluse. Surely one of them ought to behave like a normal healthy member of Society. Especially considering the exaggerated rakehell he had been playing at lately. It was tiresome. But effective. "You've done enough."

"Hardly," she scoffed. "Isn't that why I'm here instead of in my greenhouse? To poke about where I don't belong?"

"You're here because you're the best judge of character I know."

She preened. "True." She wrinkled her nose. "Which is why I don't like Society any more now than I did as a girl."

He frowned. "Have they been unkind to you?"

She waved that away. "Of course not. Not while you're here, or the duke. And not to my face. I have entirely too much money for that."

"Not since you dumped your soup on that viscountess, you mean." It wasn't Priya's beauty that flustered the Ton, it was her forthright opinions and remarkable ability to ferret out secrets. Not to mention her supernatural ability to hold a grudge.

She smiled innocently. "I *spilled* it. A dreadful accident. I am frightfully clumsy, you know."

"She was very sticky."

"Serves the old cow right. I hope she stank of lobster bisque for days." She nudged him. "They'll flutter at me all through dinner," she added. "Your being here is tantamount to a declaration of war."

"War? Hardly."

"You know nothing about matchmaking Mamas. They truly think you truly mean to shop the Marriage Mart."

"Better that than the truth."

"Have you really thought this through?" Priya shuddered. "Debutantes and shifty-eyed fathers, and all that sighing."

"Sighing?"

"Oh, Lord Northwyck, you're so *clever*, you're so *handsome*. The rain is like needles, the grass is too green, the wind smells like cow, save me, save me."

He couldn't help a laugh. "You are cracked, dear sister."

"Yes, and it's all because of my brief three weeks on the Marriage Mart."

He changed the subject before she could launch into another one of her tirades. The war against Napoleon might have ended sooner if someone had put Priya in charge. "What happened to Persephone Blackwell?"

"Why?"

"They whisper behind their hands. They never used to."

"They are idiots."

He'd have to watch her carefully. He didn't think it would be a hardship. She was as lovely as she ever was, in her own quiet, serious way, even with dirt smudged on her cheek. Perhaps *because* of it.

"There was a scandal while you were in France being heroic."

He had to force his jaw to unclench, his shoulders to relax. Heroism was not what he'd call it. "Persephone? She doesn't seem like the type."

Priya snorted. "Neither did I, if you'll recall."

He snorted back at his little sister. "You were *always* the type."

Chapter Three

MUD AND BONES were always better than being stuck in a drawing room full of Society's finest.

Persephone loitered, hoping the other antiquarians would leave once the rain started but instead her grandmother sent another footman down to fetch her, as predicted. She was, perhaps rightly, terrified Persephone would show up at dinner dressed in her mud-stained field apron.

"Grandmaman, what do you know of Lord Northwyck?" she'd asked, as soon as she was safely back in their shared sitting room. She'd lectured herself all the way up the stairs that she shouldn't bother. Men like Conall didn't look twice at women like her. He probably didn't even remember her, not truly. She was one of the duke's many goddaughters, the faceless Cinderellas. She was setting herself up for disappointment. She knew better.

But here it was, the very first thing out of her mouth.

Her grandmother was preoccupied in a plate of jam biscuits. "You're dripping, dear," she sighed. "Adelle will murder me if you get mud on her carpets."

"The earl of Northwyck," she repeated even as she told herself to *stop talking.*

Her grandmother looked up, sufficiently diverted. "Do you have designs on the earl?" she asked eagerly. "Oh, splendid, Percy. It's past time you married like other girls."

Persephone burst out laughing. "Grandmaman, earls don't marry ruined girls. I only ask because he's changed." She remembered the quiet young man who played the violin at every opportunity. His music had filled Pendleton House over many a holiday. She found she missed it.

"Pshaw," her grandmother waved that off. "An indiscretion. You were young. Your biggest problem is that you were caught."

She'd meant to be caught. And had been grateful for her tattered reputation every day since. Every day until today.

"The Northwycks have always been a trifle eccentric," her grandmother admitted.

If that wasn't the pot calling the kettle black.

"But he fought the French," she continued. "Allowances must be made."

"Did he sell his commission?"

"He must have done."

"Was he a captain? A lieutenant?"

"I'm not sure what his role was, but I am certain he was very dashing. He is an earl, after all."

"He never used to be a rake." Persephone squeezed water out of her hair. He'd always been handsome but there was a leashed power in him now. A confidence that had nothing to do with his title or his wealth. It sent a thrill through her despite her internal lectures on earls and expectations. "Is he as wicked as they say?"

"Best hope so," she winked. "I'll make inquiries."

"Grandmaman, *no!*" she said, horrified. The last thing she needed was for everyone to think she was setting her cap for him. A woman could only shrug off so much humiliation.

"I'll be discreet."

This from the woman wearing a gown in such an aggressive shade of tangerine that she may as well have been wearing marmalade. Persephone kissed her cheek. "Don't you dare. I'll go and get dressed."

"Wear something cheerful. You want to be noticed, don't you?"

And so here she was, wearing a dress accented with virulent lime green ribbons because her grandmother was persistent if nothing else. At her pointed glare, Persephone shifted closer to the group of women chattering with several of the antiquarians over champagne flutes. She'd promised to socialize, even though her grandmother would never understand that it wasn't a matter of trying harder. Sometimes trying harder made it worse.

Lord Fairweather smiled at her. "Ah, Lady Persephone. Do tell us what you think of this piece."

The group turned toward Persephone blankly, as if she'd materialized out of nowhere. Sweat immediately began to gather under her stays. She did not enjoy the attention. Not from anyone but especially not from the very same people who had turned their backs on her at her last Society ball. Years did not erase that kind of humiliation and anger, even when you were prepared for it. The whispers and snickers, the shoulders turned her way as she moved through the glittering crowd. The sniffs of disdain and then the eventual silence until she had fled, despite her determination to be brave and resolute.

She turned her concentration very deliberately onto the Egyptian funerary mask in question. It was painted black and old, the profile eye inset with a diamond that glinted menacingly as it watched over the ballroom. She knew exactly what she ought to say: it's lovely. Or, judging by the faint shudder of distaste from the gentleman beside her: it's ghastly.

"It's a forgery," she said instead.

Barton, who led Fairweather's many expeditions, sucked in a breath.

"You insult our host," Fairweather said gently, as though she was an ill-disciplined child. He had no idea that she had already saved him from the embarrassment of displaying forged artifacts in his own collection.

Louisa sniffed. "Just because Henry is your dearest, or should I say *only,* friend, doesn't give you the right to cast aspersions on the Culpeppers, Persephone Blackwell."

"Lady Culpepper is already aware," Persephone replied calmly. She had learned not to let them see her react. Holly looked mortified enough for all of them, shifting from foot to foot, cheeks red as beets. Miss Ivy Jones was pressed to the wall as though she thought she might blend into the silk paper. "She decided she liked it enough that it did not signify."

Barton was frowning as though his own personal honor had been called into question. "You must be mistaken."

"Egyptians did not inlay with diamonds," Persephone replied. "Furthermore, that type of crown is meant to cover the nape of the neck."

"She's quite correct." Fairweather bowed in her direction, suddenly impressed. She answered with a tiny curtsy of her own. That small acknowledgment was better than any declaration of love, no matter what her grandmother had to say on the subject. It was better than chocolate.

"Do tell us about your adventures," Lady Louisa stepped in front of Persephone calculatingly enough to trod on her toes. Hard. "Digging in the backyard is so provincial next to your own exploits."

Persephone eased away. Funny how she never felt alone with a pile of dirt and abandoned bones. And she was better dressed then too. She was likely to blind herself if she caught another glimpse of the horrid lime ribbons. She went back to waiting for supper to be announced, trying to surreptitiously work the ribbons free. She'd said she'd wear them, she never said for how long.

"Well done," Priya said as Persephone shoved the offending ribbon behind a cushion. "Those are particularly hideous. Your grandmother's outdone herself."

"She means well."

"I know," Priya said drily, untying a yellow and magenta striped ribbon from around her neck. She was stunningly beautiful, with her dark eyes and hair and a penchant for daring necklines and sharp retorts. "She accosted me in the stairwell."

Persephone chuckled. "Of course, she did. How long have you been hiding in the ferns?"

"Barely a quarter of an hour but, as usual, it's the best place to survive an interminable evening."

"You still don't enjoy a house party?"

"Not one full of condescending prats." Persephone choked

back a laugh. "It seems worse than usual," Priya added.

"It's the festival," Persephone said. "Everyone wants to be seen and heard."

"I'm sorry I didn't come sooner but you know how I hate to leave my gardens."

"Almost as much as I dislike London," Persephone shrugged. "We're together now so that's what matters. Not that you give a fig about artifacts or museums."

"I really don't," Priya agreed, cheerfully. "But this seems a lark. I haven't seen you in an age and besides that Conall asked me to come."

"So, it's true, then? He's looking for a wife?" Persephone asked, surprised. Even more surprising was the small twist of disappointment behind her ribcage. She had no right to be disappointed. She barely had a right to be politely interested.

She peered through the leaves to where Conall leaned against the silk-papered wall in his black evening attire, a predatory alertness to him. Ladies circled him in a froth of white silks and pretty ribbons. There was a hunger to their circling that made Persephone uncomfortable. He may as well be a rabbit loosed to the hounds. She was glad to be off the Marriage Mart. It seemed a dismal way to decide the rest of your life.

Even if this particular rabbit had more of the hunter in him. Oh, he bowed and laughed warmly when lady after lady whispered in his ear. He greeted debutantes pushed forward by eager parents. His smile never wavered, except the one moment he looked up and Persephone could have sworn he was looking straight at her. "Why do I feel as though your brother can see us even through the ferns? And knows that we are speaking about him?"

"He probably can," Priya shrugged. "It's an infuriating talent he has. You know what a dreadful big brother he was growing up. He always knew when I was up to something."

"And me."

He raised his glass in her direction with a barely perceptible nod of his head. Persephone felt like blushing again, for no earthly good reason. She hoped she wasn't coming down with the ague from digging in the rain. She didn't have the time for illness.

Or whatever it was she was feeling.

Let's call it illness.

She wondered how no one else seemed to notice the way he held himself, as alert as Atlas preparing to shoulder the world. His eyes tracked every guest, lingering, cataloguing, noticing. His reputation had changed sometime during the war, though earls were hardly called to battle. She wondered how Henry might have changed. Conall had always been friendly, but somewhat reserved, quiet. Now, from all accounts, he was invited to every soiree, every dinner party, every ball. To host the Earl of Northwyck was a great coup. He never shunned a wallflower or a dowager. He danced the quadrille instead of disappearing into the cards room. He didn't smoke cheroots or take snuff. And he left countless blushes in his wake.

"Why were they were pinching their bony noses at you, this time?" Priya asked.

"I pointed out one of Lady Culpepper's forgeries."

Priya laughed. "I'm sorry I missed it. I do love watching them realize you know more than they do."

"You're the only one who does. And to be fair, most of the earls and viscounts prefer to fund the expeditions rather than actually join them." She'd have given her left foot to join an expedition.

"Never mind them, they are dull as cold tea. Why else would I prefer hiding in the shrubbery?"

"You've been out of society for a long time, perhaps you've lost your touch," Persephone chuckled.

"Bite your tongue," Priya said, rising to the challenge. It wasn't her manners she was proud of, but her preternatural ability to ferret out secrets. "Sir Avon has a tiny poodle he brings everywhere. She eats roses and pate and bites everyone. That's where he got that scar, though he tells everyone he got it fighting off a cutpurse. And that lady over there in the corner is determined to prove she can swim across the Channel. I can't think why."

Persephone darted in for a quick hug. "I've missed you."

"And I you. Where are the other Cinderellas?"

There were eleven goddaughters at last count, but only five unmarried or still in England. One was a hermit who had not left her house in years. "Just you and I, I'm afraid," she said. "Meg and Tamsin ought to be here any moment, I should think."

"And Clara?" Priya wrinkled her nose.

"Tomorrow."

"Pity."

"Perhaps she's mellowed."

"Doubtful."

Clara was rather high-strung, it had to be said. She was the only Cinderella obsessed with manners and deportment and sharp about it. The others generally enjoyed the softer edges that came with ducal connections. Priya was not out much in Society, but she prided herself on knowing everything about everyone. The patronesses at Almack's begged to have her and her secrets in their ranks, but she refused every time they asked. She was particular on how she weaponized her talents.

"I knew we'd find you back here," Tamsin exclaimed, poking her head through the ferns. Her red hair caught the lamplight as she dragged Meg behind her.

"Speak of the devil," Priya grinned as they exchanged hugs.

"Our carriage broke a wheel," Tamsin explained. "Or we would have been here much earlier."

"It was kind of Lady Culpepper to invite us to dine," Meg added. Her eyes were a startling blue, her smile quiet but heartfelt.

Priya narrowed one eye in her direction. "She's only looking for the duke's approval."

"Still."

"You're too thin, Meg. I hope you plan on eating her out of house and home tonight."

"That's what I said!" Tamsin interjected. "Skin and bones. And paint, of course."

Meg wrinkled her nose, rubbing at the dab of paint on the edge of her sleeve. "You said no one would notice."

"You're always covered in paint," Tamsin shrugged. "So no

one will."

"Is your uncle not feeding you?" Priya demanded. The glint in her eye was clear. Here was a possible secret. And one that might be causing her friend harm. Meg threw a pleading look at Persephone. Sometimes bearing the brunt of Priya's affection took reinforcements.

"Tamsin, have you added anything new to your collection?" Persephone asked, changing the subject.

Tamsin's face brightened. "I have. Oh, nothing distinguished enough for your lot, of course. But I'm well pleased."

It was a noted side effect of being one of the Cinderellas: when your godfather the duke was enamored of all things antiquarian, you tended to be brought up exposed to such pursuits. Even if you didn't live in Little Barrow like Persephone. Tamsin's own interests lay in the more unique and macabre. Her entire house was a cabinet of curiosities full of tarot cards, bones, and crystal balls more suited to a traveling circus. She didn't care for provenance, only stories, the stranger the better.

"I've located a Hand of Glory," she continued, excitedly. Meg sent Persephone a grateful smile. "I'm sure it's not authentic but it is frightfully gruesome," she added, cheerfully.

"Dare I ask what a Hand of Glory is?" Priya inquired drily.

"It's the left hand of a hanged man, dried and pickled."

"Revolting." Priya made a face. "Serves me right for asking."

"Why would you want it?" Meg asked.

"They're very rare."

"I should hope so."

"They *are* part of our history and our folklore," Persephone added. She couldn't help but come to her friend's defense. She might not care for the grislier items, but people regarded her interest in mummification practices with the same expression. Collectors of odd items needed to stick together.

"They say if you light a candle made from the fat of the hanged man and place it between the fingers of the hand, you can render anyone within sight motionless," Tamsin added.

"With nausea, no doubt."

"They were used by thieves."

The dinner bell rang.

"And on that disgusting note," Priya said. "Let us eat."

The procession line came together like an army drill, executed under Lady Culpepper's sharp gaze. Persephone had never met her escort and he offered his arm without a word or a single glance in her direction. He offered the bare minimum of courtesy, as everyone did, because they were scared of Lady Culpepper and the duke. But nothing more.

Except for Conall, who was still leaning against the opposite wall. He watched her as she passed by, with a kind of intensity that left her strangely breathless. No one stared at Persephone.

Not like that.

SHE COULDN'T HELP but be aware of Conall throughout the many supper courses. She tried not to look at him over bowls of white soup, reminded herself not to stare over the steamed endives, and gave up entirely by the time the lamb was served. He was unlike any of the men of her limited acquaintance. Even those who considered themselves adventurers didn't have his presence. He was a burning coal in a field of dry wheat.

She'd always had a fondness for him, but it had never before made her aware of the back of her knees or the heat gathering in her thighs.

The ladies at his side vied for his attention, both debutantes with large dowries. She wasn't sure who had engineered the hopeful seating, Lady Culpepper, or their mothers. The countess had no doubt received many fine gifts from all the parents of unattached girls present. Persephone couldn't help a fond smile at her own grandmother, blissfully ignorant as she skipped the meat course in favor of trifle.

Conall's eyes met hers, the next time she lost the battle not to glance his way. She was as bad as the others. He held her attention effortlessly, while replying to some question asked of him by the lovely pale girl on his right. Persephone had never been pale a day in her life; she spent far too much time in the digging pits. She was freckled.

And ruined, mustn't forget ruined.

Best to think about the festivals and the crates which would start arriving on the morrow. Not Conall's lazy sharp grace, a contradiction that made her feel entirely too warm. She vowed not to eat any more hot soup. Back to barrows and graves.

She was glad of the distraction when Lady Culpepper announced that it was time for the fireworks display. She followed the others through the portrait gallery and out to the main terrace. Before she could locate her friends, the river of guests carried her out into the summer night. The servants were already on the back lawn, setting off blasts that flashed into the sky like exploding stars.

The crowd surged forward; heads tilted back to watch. Someone bumped into Persephone and her arm scraped the stone balustrade. Smoke wafted toward them, stinging the warm air. The fireworks continued, each louder and more impressive than the last. She couldn't help a small worry that they were too close to the barrows and might endanger the excavation sites. She forced herself to focus on the flashing colours like a normal person. Until she was jostled again, this time more violently.

No one heard her yelp of surprise or saw her fall over the rail.

It happened too quickly; she didn't even have time to catch herself. The fireworks spun like wheels above her as the crowd clapped and exclaimed. She was going to land on the flagstones and break something important. Like her skull. She was falling too fast to feel real fear.

And then she landed in Conall's hastily outstretched arms.

"What the devil?" His hands clamped around her, her skirts frothing over his arms.

Relief and a sudden surge of adrenaline made her giddy. She had the inappropriate urge to giggle, especially at the expression on his usually composed face. Her pulse fluttered madly like a runaway horse caught inside her ribcage. He was close enough that she could see the portion of muscled chest where his cravat had gone askew. She hadn't thought a peer, even a dangerous one, would tan in such a way as to suggest he often went around without a shirt. The image was strangely arresting. Something inside her tingled.

This was no time for tingling.

"Thank you," she said, after clearing her throat.

He didn't seem inclined to let her go. He smelled of bergamot and woodsmoke. She probably shouldn't be noticing that. Certainly not while the other part of her brain was trying to decide if she was safe yet. She still felt as though she were falling.

"Where did you come from?"

"I fell over the railing," she explained, feeling like an idiot. Who fell off balconies? On the same day she fell into a hole.

"Do you do that often?"

"No, of course not."

All evidence to the contrary.

"I had no idea societal conventions changed so much when I was on the Continent. Do they routinely physically launch girls onto the Marriage Mart now?" He released her, and she slid slowly down the length of his body.

She cleared her throat again. "I stumbled, is all."

He tensed as the sky exploded behind him. The brightly coloured light showed the fine sheen of perspiration on his brow and the tightening of his knuckles around his flask. He took a deep draught. "I'm sure you can find a better vantage point to watch the spectacle," he said tightly.

She recognized the tension in his voice. She'd heard it a number of times when her grandmother was beset. "Are you quite well?" she asked gently.

He took another swallow and nodded. Another volley of fireworks exploded, and he jerked, spilling whiskey on his cuff. "It's the noise, isn't it?" she asked.

"It's nothing." His jaw clenched.

"You were on the Continent during the war."

"What of it?" The red light cast his features into sinister shadows.

"I imagine the fireworks sound like musket fire or cannons." She stepped closer, until she could smell the whiskey on his sleeve and see the fine tremble of his muscles as he strove to appear unconcerned. "My grandmother was in London when the riots broke out in the '80s. She was trapped in a carriage for several hours while the mob pelted it with stones and refuse. Even now she can't abide a crowd or a carriage. It sends her right back to that day. And it's been thirty-five years."

"I am not an old lady."

"Nor was she, at the time." She slipped her hand through his and his fingers tightened around hers. "We all have ghosts," she added softly. She stepped closer still, until she had to tilt her head back to meet his eyes. They glinted in the flashing lights, gray as ice and smoke.

"If I can catch my breath, it will pass."

"Perhaps if you concentrate on something else, it might not trouble you so."

"On what do you suggest I might concentrate?"

She didn't think he realized he was still holding her hand. His breathing seemed easier. At least until she replied. "Me."

He paused, breath stilled. "I beg your pardon?"

She swallowed. "Look at me," she said. "Nothing else." Oh dear, this would work better if she were a diamond of the first water. But it always calmed her grandmother to stare at her spaniel, Chartreuse, or eat a plate of cupcakes. Since neither were available, Persephone's face would have to do. "Breathe when I breathe."

She inhaled slowly and held it before exhaling. "Again." She thought he looked less pained, but she couldn't be sure.

And then the fireworks reached a crescendo that even she found disruptive. He shuddered, visibly trying to restrain his reaction. His breath stalled and he pressed back against the stone wall under the terrace. Persephone did the only thing she could think of.

She rose up on the tip of her toes and kissed him.

His pulse pounded so hard she felt it through his jacket, through her fingertips when she touched him. His kiss burned with whiskey and desperation, and something else she couldn't understand. His mouth was open against her as he struggled to control his breath, and then it was lips and tongues and heat. She was the fireworks now; and when he deepened the kiss, a fuse she had no idea could be lit fired her with colors and light. It was both gentle and primal and the combination made her knees weak.

It took her far too long to realize that the fireworks had ended, and he was no longer panicking. Not in the slightest. He was too busy drawing her up against this body, one hand fisted in her dress, the other in her hair. His lips slanted over hers, tasting her. No not tasting, tasting implied polite nibbles. He was feasting. And she'd had no idea of the hunger inside her own body. She drew back, gasping. It was her own heart now that raced too fast. "I'm not on the Marriage Mart," she blurted.

"And yet I am officially diverted." His eyes caught on her lips. They tingled as if he was still kissing her. His thumb brushed her mouth lightly and she felt it everywhere. "Are you not betrothed then since I've been away?"

"Of course not."

"Why, of course not?"

Wasn't being knocked off a balcony bad enough for one ball? Did she also have to be humiliated? "I have no great fortune, and no great beauty," she forced herself to say. But she apparently had a great capacity for ruining a moment, as well as herself. She really ought to stick to digging in the dirt. She bobbed a quick curtsy and then fled into the gardens.

He watched her go.

"Are you still really what you seem, I wonder?" The sky was a bowl of smoke and light behind him. "I hope so, for your sake."

Chapter Four

PERSEPHONE BORE THE rest of the evening as long as she could after Priya, Tamsin and Meg returned to the duke's house. Which, to be fair to her grandmother's irritated glare burning the back of her neck, wasn't very long at all.

But standing on the edge of conversations was depressing. She'd quietly listened when blatant historical inaccuracies were bandied about (which was as difficult as suddenly learning to fly). Shoulders were turned her way again and again. She'd made this particular bed and she would lie in it for the rest of her life, despite what her grandmother thought. And she wasn't particularly sorry. Her infamy had granted her the only thing she'd truly wanted: independence to pursue her studies. She would take the snubs and the cold dismissive glances, but she wouldn't dine on them. Not when there were so many more important things to do, like find a way to absolve Henry. Why hadn't he arrived home yet? Where was he?

She couldn't afford to be sidetracked. Not by discourtesy, and certainly not by sudden kisses in the dark. They threatened to erase everything else in her brain. She eased out of the drawing room and then into a dash to put as much distance between her and the others as she could before someone caught her.

Unfortunately, someone else had the very same idea. A young woman hurried down the hall from the back terrace doors, glancing behind her.

They crashed spectacularly.

It was a fumble of lace and ribbons. Persephone skidded on her leather-soled dancing slippers. They toppled, arms flailing. The other woman somehow got her feet under her and steadied them both. "I beg your pardon," she said with a nervous smile.

"It's my fault, I'm sure," Persephone caught her breath. She was manifestly dreadful at this spying business. She who was usually so unnoticeable. The irony of it was annoying. "I was galloping like a camel."

"Not at all."

"Ivy!" A red-faced man bellowed from the drawing room doorway.

The lady, Ivy, flinched. "I must go."

Persephone took the stairs two at a time, pausing on the landing to glance down. She caught a glimpse of another gown, trimmed with violets coming from around the same corner. Lady Culpepper would not be pleased. She did not hold with unchaperoned ladies and her halls were on the way to becoming a proper thoroughfare.

Persephone darted across the landing and up the rest of the steps. Instead of turning toward the guest rooms, she went to the family quarters. The guests would be busy for a couple more hours at the very least. There were card games to be played, brandy to be drunk, inappropriate flirting to be had. Especially with Conall.

She ducked into Henry's bedroom where the mint green coverlet and silver tassels bordering the canopy were so familiar, tears burned in her throat. They'd read contraband books under that blanket, since Lady Culpepper didn't approve of novels in general and gothic novels in particular. They'd shared pots of chocolate and secrets and dared each other to do foolish things like climb too high in the apple trees or chase down snakes in the cowshed. She bought him that ridiculous bear figurine when they were eleven and he'd been determined to sail to Canada to fight bears. Or ride them into battle.

Persephone froze at the creak of floorboards outside the door.

Instinct had her rolling under the bed, beads popping off her hem. The frame dipped in the back; they'd hidden there when playing hide-and-seek. She didn't fit as well as she used to, and she had to pinch her nose against a sneeze when dust wafted up around her.

She was probably overreacting. It was no doubt someone seeking a private place for an assignation. And yet she stayed where she was, peering through the tassels at the moonlight falling over the floor. Heels tapped loudly, cracking glass beads against the floorboards. Black gentleman's trousers blocked the moonlight. Persephone held her breath.

The man crouched, the tassels swinging as he reached under the bed. For what exactly, Persephone didn't know. She couldn't see his face. His evening wear could have belonged to any of the men at the party and he wore no distinguishing rings. He brushed the edge of her hem, and she shrank back further against the wall.

She wasn't technically doing anything wrong, but she didn't want to be questioned in a gentleman's bedroom. Even if it was just Henry's.

And was the man framing Henry for treason? She wanted to see his face.

She tried to contort her neck in order to catch a glimpse but there were only shadows and polished shoes such as any of the guests might wear. There was the sound of desk drawers opening, of a wardrobe being inspected.

Something was definitely afoot. It was too much a stretch of the imagination to think Henry's missing letters, Henry's missing person in fact, and someone investigating his room were not connected. She'd promised Henry she wouldn't launch her own investigation or search party. She'd lied, of course.

Still, it seemed a bad idea to give herself away.

She inched close to the edge of the bed frame. There was an impatient huff and then footsteps stalking out of the door and into the hall. Persephone shimmied free as fast as she could, which was not as easy as it might have seemed. By the time she had sprinted to the door, the bedroom was empty and so was the hallway. The flame of an oil lamp flickered but it was the only indication someone might have passed this way. She brushed herself clean, annoyed, and worried in equal measures. If she was going to save Henry, she was going to have to start doing a better job of it.

She did not see the shadow watching her from the darkness of the servant stairs.

It was no surprise that Persephone couldn't sleep. Scenarios chased through her head, each more dire than the last. Her grandmother was always pointing out Persephone's morbid turn of imagination. But she felt justified in this case. Treason was punishable by hanging, followed by being drawn and quartered. Up until last year before the laws had changed, he would have been drawn and quartered while still alive. And his body parts would have been boiled in salt and cumin to keep the birds from eating them when they were displayed on the street.

Her penchant for researching and gathering details was not always helpful.

Either way, she wouldn't see Henry hanged, not for any reason, but especially not as a falsely accused scapegoat.

As the house settled into quiet and darkness, Persephone decided she may as well get up. She knew which steps creaked, where the footmen were likely to linger, and where the kitchen cat tended to curl up when he escaped. She made her way to the library out of long habit. A small fire still burned in the grate, glinting off gilt lettering painted onto leather book spines and off silver candlesticks. She picked up an arrow from a display niche, testing the rusted tip with her finger. A notecard with faded ink claimed it was shot at the house during the Civil war.

"I'm not sure I believe that," Conall remarked.

Startled, she threw the arrow at his head.

He caught before it pierced his eyeball like a fork in a bowl of fish-eye stew. A horrified giggle escaped Persephone before she could stop it. Really, what else was a girl to do when she kept making such an utter cake of herself?

Conall blinked carefully, as if making sure he was still able. "I see I shall have to keep on my toes with you."

"I promise I am not doing it on purpose," she squeaked between horrified giggles.

"I can scarcely imagine the destruction if you were."

"It would be biblical, I assure you."

He set the arrow down on the table. His sleeves were rolled up, displaying strong forearms. She tried not to stare at the play of muscles under his skin. She tried even harder not to remember how those arms had felt around her, or his lips on hers.

"I admire your sense of humour, Persephone." She hadn't given him permission to use her name. Something about the way he said it sent a delicious shiver through her. "Many a lady would take to their beds after a tumble over a balcony railing."

She shrugged one shoulder. "I'd never get anything done if I had the vapours every time something untoward happened." And it was the least surprising thing that had happened to her that night. This is what came of being surrounded with live people rather than dead ones. She really ought to consider staying home from now on.

At least he hadn't mentioned the kiss.

Why hadn't he mentioned the kiss?

Conall half-smiled, but there was something untrusting about it. As if he knew her secrets, if she'd bothered to have any. She hadn't before Henry. Surely, he wouldn't know anything about Henry's predicament? It would be too risky to ask. Wouldn't it? "I'm almost afraid to ask what you are doing down here at such an hour. Some harrowing antiquarian ritual with the leg bone of a dead man?"

"Hardly," she admitted. "I'm looking for a book to read."

"How disappointing."

"Maybe I'll find something suitably gothic."

"That would be a start."

"Are you feeling better?" Now why had she gone and asked that? She could see that he was fine. And now the memory of their kiss burned between them. She swayed closer, feeling an unnatural pull.

"You are as reviving as tonic water."

The lovely swaying feeling stopped abruptly. She was earth and stone and mud again. "Oh. Good." She turned back to the bookshelves. What did that even mean? Had she forgotten how to kiss? It wasn't as if she'd had that much practice to begin with.

He watched her trail her fingers lovingly over the spines of history books. "What drew you to antiquarian pursuits? I've never asked you."

Of course, he hadn't. He'd spent most of his time playing the violin and hiding from the Cinderellas when they were younger. Well, they had teased him rather mercilessly. One couldn't fault him an expedient retreat.

"Aside from the duke, you mean?" she asked. Most of the Cinderellas had a penchant for history nurtured by ducal birthday presents. Also, it had to be said, parents who encouraged any common interests their offspring might have with a duke. It wasn't the only reason for Persephone's studies though. She was raised in Little Barrow after all. Such pursuits were practically grown in the soil.

"My father was obsessed," she admitted. "I suspect I inherited it, like the shape of my nose or my dislike of jellies." She didn't mention she'd also learned early that it was the best way to get his attention. Watercolors or walks in the woods had never stood a chance.

"And have you travelled much since? To Egypt perhaps?"

"During the war?" She scoffed. "My father was not *that* obsessed, Northwyck."

"He must have wanted to see it. It's positively swarming with antiquarians and treasure hunters."

"I suppose it must be." Just ask Henry.

He was watching her closely, in that way people did when they thought they were being subtle. She'd spent too many hours at the edges of ballrooms watching those same people to be fooled. She lifted a hand to her hair, wondering if it was falling out of its braid. "Anyway, he and Maman died long before the war ended. And everyone wants to go to Egypt, surely. Have you seen this house? Even Lady Culpepper is *au courant*."

"I suppose it's become the fashionable thing to do, hasn't it?" His tone hardened. "Almost as fashionable as visiting the battlefields at Waterloo."

Persephone wrinkled her nose. "I admit I am not keen for that kind of exploration; it seems rather ghoulish to me."

"That's one word for it."

"I am envious of those who visit Egypt, though," she admitted. "How wonderful to dig through the sands. I shall have to content myself with the festival exhibits. Have you been?"

He inclined his head, strangely reluctant.

"Tell me everything," she insisted.

"It was hot."

She stared at him, before huffing a sigh. Devilish kiss or not, that would not do. "Conall, *really*."

There was a telltale twitch at the corner of his mouth. "You want to hear that the Berber nomads wear indigo headwraps, that yogurt tastes better with cinnamon, and that sandstorms are as elegant as they are deadly."

"Yes, exactly."

"Camels spit."

She rolled her eyes. "With such a streak of romance, clearly, you weren't down here looking for novels. You'll make me quiver with jealousy over your adventures."

"I could make you quiver."

She felt the hoarseness of his voice like his hands on her skin. She swallowed. He leaned back against the shelves as if he'd never spoken. He looked faintly bored. She was on fire, and he looked *bored*. She suddenly longed to hit him with a shovel.

"The deserts did smell like sunshine," he admitted. "You smell like roses. And incense?"

"Frankincense," she explained. "With cardamom and cinnamon. All ingredients used in Ancient Egyptian perfume."

"You are thorough."

"History isn't only objects found in the mud. And they say Cleopatra washed the sails of her ship with so much perfume that Marc Antony could smell her from the shore." She bit her tongue. "Sorry, I do go on."

"As you smell delicious, why should I complain?"

Heat moved through her at the compliment and the knowledge that he was standing close enough that he could smell her perfume, close enough that she could see the way his hair brushed over his collar even in the dim light. She realized then that he wasn't wearing a waistcoat, or even a cravat. His throat was the exact colour of honey. "You're cold," he said, misreading her tiny shiver. "Come by the fire."

She knew better. She shouldn't be alone with him, not at night, and certainly not in her nightrail and bare feet. And yet she let herself be drawn closer to the hearth, like a moth about to burn her wings. In the uncertain light, his eyes were like barrow shadows, full of stories and the glint of treasure. He looked down at her. "You're staring."

"I'm sorry."

"You're not like the others, are you?"

She sighed. Not only was snorting not generally considered ladylike, but she was so accustomed to bones and skulls, she could barely carry on a proper conversation, even without the improper setting. "I'm afraid not."

He leaned closer, his gaze catching on her lips. Warmth trickled through her until even her knees were tingling and he wasn't even touching her. "I wasn't complaining," he said softly.

This was the new Conall she had heard so much about. Flirtatious, delicious. Tempting as chocolate truffles. She was certain he was going to kiss her again. She started to meet him halfway, but he drew back sharply, suddenly.

"Excuse me. I must bid you goodnight, Lady Persephone."

The air drafted in the unexpected space between them. He offered her a simple, severe bow. And then just like that, the charming rake was gone. He was all hard lines and serious eyes.

Even more appealing.

And marching away, the library door swinging shut behind him.

She most definitely wanted to hit him with a shovel.

IT WOULDN'T BE right to kiss her again.

However much he wanted to. He could still taste her, could feel her pressed against him. She was more dangerous than traitors and pistols at dawn, more dangerous than the hangman's noose. He had to investigate all the antiquarians, even her. Because ladies did not fall off balconies.

Correction: *innocent* ladies did not fall off balconies.

And it was natural to wonder about her. It was his duty to wonder. It had nothing to do with her self-deprecating smile and clever eyes. Or the way she marched over the fields like a tiny general leading an antiquarian battle. He wondered if she would be as energetic in all aspects of her life. At night.

Especially at night.

He also wondered if the men in this part of England were blind.

He hadn't missed the way they glanced away from her, all pinched-mouthed disdain. Or stared too long, as though common courtesy wasn't required. Something very close to anger prickled under his ribcage at the thought.

He was getting distracted. And that was unacceptable.

He had a traitor to flush out of hiding. It was the only thing keeping him here at this ghastly house party with the debutantes and their parents eyeing him like meat at market. He'd been telling the truth when he told his sister it was his best cover, but he didn't have to like it. He didn't object to marriage, but the societal circus attached to the institution was tiresome, to say the least. His time abroad had eaten away his admittedly thin patience with that sort of thing. He'd seen too much blood, and his sister had seen too much hypocrisy. And now the girls fluttered at him, dreaming of being a countess.

Except for Persephone who had only warned him away. Curious. Even though she had no other particular prospects. Even after kissing him to distract him from his panic.

He hadn't expected the fireworks. It wasn't so much that they sounded like gunfire as she'd supposed. It wasn't the sound of the bullets and the canons. It was stumbling over the dead after the battle had ended. It was the blood staining his boots, the stink of rot and opened guts. The lingering acrid bite of smoke. It was all of those unseeing eyes, seeing him. He hadn't been able to stop it. He should have been able to stop it.

And Persephone, an overlooked girl with no prospects, had

stopped the shivering, sweating panic before it could clamp down on him.

She was clever and kind. Definitely dangerous.

Because here he was thinking about her again.

A glance at the clock reminded him he had other places to be. He went out to saddle a horse, using the light of the rapidly waxing moon to see him to the village. Some of the gentlemen had decided to host themselves a Hellfire Club night and he reckoned he'd waited long enough that they would be too drunk to realize he wasn't drunk at all. Men who were foxed on wine and women had loose tongues. With any luck, he'd make progress on the investigation.

He followed the directions he'd been given, leaving his horse at the Druid's Sickle pub and walking down the hill behind the building, past the well. Behind a line of trees was an opening lit with torches. The flickering light lent it a more dramatic cast, making it feel as if he was descending into a secret sacred space and less like a hole dug into the side of a hill that might collapse at any moment. The sounds of revelries well under way welcomed him: a badly played drum, tambourines, laughter, giddy shrieks. He'd have preferred violin music, truth be told. He'd had enough of this sort of entertainment in the previous three months to last him a lifetime. He pasted on a carefree, arrogant smile, the kind that was expected.

He ducked his head and followed the uneven steps into a grotto that was far better preserved than he would have thought. Water trickled from some underground spring, filling a stone basin lined with broken mosaics A statue of Venus stood alight with candles, the dripping wax the only hint of clothing. On the other side, a mask of Bacchus was painted on the cave wall in various shades of ochre and black. More candles burned in every available nook and cranny, illuminating women in transparent Romanesque chitons dancing with their hair swaying loose down their backs. Two men wearing not much more than loincloths and masks joined them, one beating a drum, one also dancing. Oil gleamed on an impressive amount of bare skin.

"Not bad for a small backwards village, eh?" Darrington

asked. His eyes were already faintly glazed over. He'd long since lost his cravat and waistcoat, and likely soon his balance. Behind him, Barton and Snettisham were gambling with dice, two ladies, and very little clothing left between them. "These Roman ruins are nothing to Egypt, of course. But what can you do?"

Conall's attention narrowed. "Egypt?"

"It's all a Bacchanalia tonight, of course. But I'd have liked to have seen some dancing girls in the Egyptian style." He shrugged and nearly fell over.

One of the dancing women approached Conall. 'I'm Desdemona." She trailed her fingertips across his chest, aiming perilously south. "So strong, my lord. So handsome."

He caught her wrist, amused. "Thank you, no."

She pouted. "But the other gentlemen are nothing to you. They're foxed enough not to be able to find their own peckers with both hands." She tilted her head. "Would you prefer Archimedes?"

He was fairly certain Archimedes was Arthur, the son of the blacksmith. "I'm curious about the painting, actually."

She sighed. "Oh, you're one of those antiquarians." She shuddered at the Bacchus painting, and Conall couldn't help but think Persephone would have already marched everyone out onto the grass so she could inspect the mosaics more closely and preserve them from damage. She'd have told him all about Bacchus as well, he imagined.

And what was wrong with it that it sounded like a better way to spend the night than dragging clinging half-naked women around the place in a drunken stupor?

"That horrid thing," Desdemona said. "With that gaping maw, he could eat me whole." She dragged a finger between her breasts. "Bet you could too, my lord."

He chuckled. "You're a fine woman, Desdemona. I wish you much success in your pursuits." He bowed.

She smiled. "Such a charmer, my lord."

"I'll take you on," Darrington draped his arm around her shoulders. She had to plant her feet so they both wouldn't topple.

"I suppose you're handsome enough," she allowed. "But can

you dance?"

"Like a satyr."

She led him away without a backward glance at Conall. "My heart, Desdemona," he called after her.

"My empty purse, my lord," she called back. Archimedes joined them.

"Fais ce que tu voudras," Fairweather stepped up beside him. His hair looked gold in the half-light. The dancing women tracked him hungrily. "Do what thou wilt," he explained. "The motto for the original Hellfire Club. These aren't quite as distinguished as Dashwood's caves in Buckinghamshire, of course." He offered Conall a bottle. "Drink?"

Conall accepted and took a swig that looked far more impressive than it was. "My thanks. You were saying?"

"Oh, only that these are actual Roman ruins," Fairweather replied. "Better preserved than most but not extensive enough to claim our own river Styx such as Dashwood's. It does well enough for a little country diversion though."

The wine continued to flow and platters of food, more aphrodisiac than historical, circled. There were oysters, strawberries, chocolate. Smoke hazed the air, lending a picturesque quality to what was essentially a tawdry tableau. Conall found a seat and leaned back, keeping his expression faintly bored and his eyes half-slitted so no one could see him cataloguing everything he saw. Men laughed together, gloating. Between the liquor stains on the makeshift table, they used charcoal to sketch out artifacts they claimed to have discovered: scarab beetles, an Isis statue with gold wings, an unhealthy number of mummified corpses.

That the traitor might be here even now, laughing, kindled a cold rage inside of Conall. That a man could pass information such as troop locations and possible ambush plans to the French army in exchange for access to Egypt's artifacts was unconscionable. It wasn't words on paper or clever codes cracked over coffee cups. It was the two dozen men he had seen, strewn about where they had fallen, like discarded paper wrappings. Blood and feral dogs and crows. The butchery. The unnecessary, unexpected butchery of it.

His hand tightened around his goblet. He'd find the bastard. He'd made a promise that day, with blood on his boots and soldiers weeping and retching around him.

But it wasn't a matter of who the traitor *might* be.

It was a matter of too many possibilities to choose from.

At least he was in the right place.

As Persephone approached the barrow the next morning, she felt a happy thrum, even with the light rain pattering down on her. Maybe especially because of the rain, as it meant she would have the site to herself for an hour or two. Shovels and buckets of dirt lay in the cheerful clutter of open dig sites. Thick strips of peeled grass scattered like giant dragon bones around the openings, lantern glass gleaming like eggs. She wondered what Conall thought of it.

She should scold herself for thinking about him. It wouldn't do her any good. But it wouldn't do her harm either, if she remembered that he wasn't for the likes of her. He was singular for an earl, and it had nothing to do with his chiseled jaw hair and lean muscles. He'd stood up for her and she couldn't remember the last time anyone had done so. And he didn't have the affectation of ennui she was so accustomed to; instead, he had a dark kind of energy, a singular focus and a confidence she found entirely too appealing under those knowing smiles.

Appealing enough that she was standing inside a centuries-old grave daydreaming about the shape of his mouth.

Really, that was too much.

Her cheeks burned even though there was no one to know she'd been wondering what he could do with that mouth.

She hurried to the steadying work of digging out a new trench. Better that she spend her time with the bones of the dead than wonder too deeply about Conall. As ever, the work of brushing dirt away from buried secrets had her cheeks cooling and her breath steadying.

The antiquarians had damaged the toes when they stampeded through her site and dislodged the ankle bone. She fumed over it. Her grandmother always said her passions ran too high, along with her morbid curiosity. She couldn't seem to care about the things other people cared about and couldn't pretend not to love what she loved. And Henry's grandfather deserved better.

She was letting herself get turned about. None of this was new, she was well accustomed to it, but Conall had somehow turned everything foreign inside her own mind. History, trowels, dirt. They mattered. They didn't care about her lack of fortune or her past.

She tossed dirt back onto the earl's leg bone. It was then that she noticed the fine crystal decanter, worth as much as a village pony, was missing. Not that he would miss it. But it was the principle of the thing.

Someone had bloody well stolen her find.

Fury prickled through her like a sudden fever. She brushed harder, digging her fingers under the shin bone, in case the jar had been loosened by the rain and merely sank down further. She found pebbles, a startled earthworm, and nothing else. She pushed to her feet, grinding her jaw so tightly pain shot through her back teeth.

Perhaps someone had moved it to the items taken out of the barrow. A quick look doused that hope before it truly kindled. It might have rolled away and into the barrow. Faint hope was still hope.

She tied her long skirt into a knot between her knees. She had a fleeting wish for the breeches she wore in her backyard digs, but it would be beyond the pale at Lady Culpepper's house, even for her. Anticipation sparked through the anger. She hadn't actually managed to explore the barrow yet. The servants were charged with the heavy digging, and keeping the ladies out, for fear of collapse. She'd reminded them there would be no danger if they did their digging properly, which in hindsight, was not the best way to charm her way past them. They'd closed ranks and bowed and called her 'my lady' and refused to budge. She really had to learn softer manners when it came to archaeology.

That day was not today.

She lowered an oil lamp down on a rope until it sat in the bottom of the barrow, climbing after it carefully. The tunnel was narrow and crooked, dirt raining down the sides when she stepped further inside for a better look. There was a discarded finger bone on the left, no doubt from a skeleton they'd found earlier. They'd tossed the bones out, mostly to give the ladies a shiver. Persephone was entirely certain she herself had shivered for the wrong reason: the blatant disregard for the dig site.

And the tiniest flash of jealousy. She only had a single leg bone, after all.

She crept deeper, smelling the faintly mushroom scent of moist soil. She crouched to examine the imprint of the dagger already removed by Lord Fairweather. There was a curve of darker soil that might hint at a chariot wheel, but it was too hard to tell by weak lantern light. Her pulse danced a happy reel in her chest. She loved this moment; the anticipation, the wonder, the cold damp air last exposed by some ancient Briton over two thousand years ago. She might find anything: a crown, a sword, the chariot of a fallen princess. Her stolen decanter (though she couldn't think why).

Or a gentleman.

Persephone jerked back, startled when a shadow detached itself from the rest of the darkness. The wildly flickering light fell on silver waistcoat buttons, a white cravat, dark eyes.

Conall.

She'd thought of him too much and he had appeared. She found she suddenly had to remind herself that she wasn't the superstitious sort. "My lord!" She straightened carefully, not wanting to dislodge the dirt around her. "Mind your step," she added.

"What the devil are you doing now?"

She raised her eyebrows. "I'm dancing a country reel with the prince. What does it look like I'm doing?"

"Skulking."

"I am an antiquarian, sir. I am… antiquarianing." Oh *why* did all sense leave her when he looked at her with those burning eyes? "You are the one who is skulking."

"Perhaps I was waiting for you," he said silkily, closing the distance between them.

"I doubt it."

"Why?" He halted, genuinely curious.

"You're trying to embarrass me," she said. She wondered who he had really been waiting for. The warmth turned to an ordinary chill. She was a goose to be sighing over him. "You're not waiting for me, anyone could see that. So, you're either waiting for some other lady—" She absolutely would not speculate about that. "Or *you* are in fact, skulking."

He flashed a very brief grin. She had a feeling his true smile was as rare as a true king's barrow. Still, it wasn't enough to turn her into a complete idiot. Not yet, anyway. She slapped a hand to his chest. "And I said, mind your step. The soil and the items inside a barrow such as this one are very delicate."

He looked as surprised as she felt. He probably didn't get shoved by ladies very much. And she certainly couldn't remember the last time she'd pressed her palm to a man's chest. Well, she could, actually. That was the problem. It was nothing like this. Did the blasted man carry sheep around the highlands for sport? How else would he grow muscles like that? Muscles she really ought not be touching. Or thinking about. She snatched her hand away, looking up at him through her lashes. She'd seen the debutantes use glances like this one as a weapon, but hers were always too direct, too dry. Too Persephone.

She narrowed her eyes. "Were you messing about in my dig site?"

He leaned a shoulder lazily against the side of the tunnel. "I beg your pardon?"

"Did you take anything from the trench?"

"I'm not accustomed to being accused of grave robbing."

"And that's not an answer. Show me your hands." She might have made a decent governess with that tone.

He pushed out of his lean so slowly it felt vaguely threatening. She refused to be cowed. Bad enough there was a thief about. He extended his hands, his signet ring catching the flickering oil lamplight. There was no dirt under his fingernails, unlike her, and not even a speck on his cuffs. She felt a little bit foolish. But only a little bit. Antiquarians could be devious.

"Do they pass inspection?" he asked.

She nodded.

"And now what would you like me to do with them?" he asked silkily, closing his fingers around hers. He gave a sharp tug until she was pressed against his chest. He was all heat and muscles. She was suddenly very much afraid she wouldn't even be able to spell 'barrow' right now, never mind unravel its mysteries.

She had to tilt her head up to meet his gaze. It was both hot and unfathomable. She thought once more that he might kiss her, and if not, she was fairly certain she would kiss *him*. A sound above interrupted them before she could truly make a cake of herself. Relief should have been what she felt.

It wasn't.

Light swung over their heads. "Who's down there?"

"Blast," she muttered. "Lord Darrington. What's the good of receiving the cut direct all of the time if people won't leave you alone?" She pushed Conall into the shadows. If they were caught like this, they'd boil together in a scandalbroth. He'd be expected to marry her, if she hadn't been previously ruined. In this case, she'd certainly be asked to leave the house party. It might even interfere with the festival. The famous explorers might refuse to have any dealings with her. At the very least, her reputation would not enhance Conall's. "Stay out of sight."

He paused. "Are you trying to protect me?"

"Of course, I am." His fingers were warm on her wrist. She couldn't read his tone, there was something under the surprise. She didn't have time to excavate. "Now hush."

"Come up here at once!" Darrington shouted.

Persephone tried not to look as irritated as she felt. "Botheration," she muttered, before raising her voice, and trying to keep it polite. "Lord Darrington, is that you?"

He peered over the top of the ladder. "Lady Persephone! It's not safe!"

She smiled apologetically. "I couldn't resist a closer look."

"You might get injured. I insist you come up here at once."

"Are you going to look at his hands too?" Conall murmured.

"Bloody right I will."

His startled chuckle was really just an inhalation, but she liked to think there was something happy about the sound. She climbed the ladder after a stern glance into the darkness where she thought Conall might be lurking. She assumed he had the sense to stay hidden until they were well away. Lord Darrington looked over her shoulder as he helped her over the last rung. "You're not having a liaison, are you?" He chuckled.

Persephone had found the best tactic was to act as though she didn't understand the insinuations. All the while easing out of reach. Just in case. "Do you think there was a king buried down there?" she asked instead, breathless and wide-eyed. "King Arthur perhaps?" A ridiculous suggestion.

"Perhaps." Lord Darrington offered his arm. He was more polite than the others, she had to give him that. And his hands were clean as well. "I suppose one never knows."

One did know, actually.

King Arthur probably never came to this part of England, and anyway it would have been a good thousand years after the rough time period of this barrow. She supposed they could have added him to an ancient monument, but it wouldn't have been a small one in Lady Culpepper's back garden.

"Let me see you back to the house."

She stifled a sigh. "Thank you, my lord."

PERSEPHONE HADN'T ACTUALLY wanted to return to the house but as she had little choice, she made her way to the library to begin her research. She knew the books wouldn't help her figure out why someone had been searching Henry's bedchamber, but habits died hard. With any luck she'd find something she didn't know about, some tiny tidbit of information. Anything.

Luck was not in bountiful supply at present.

"Percy, poppet, I told Lady Culpepper that you wouldn't forget her ladies nuncheon."

Persephone froze in the doorway. The library overflowed with ladies nibbling seed cakes with their tea or sketching the many curiosities displayed among the leather-bound books. Lord

Culpepper had once been famous for his collection although it now appeared as though he collected girls in muslin day dresses. Persephone's grandmother herself was dressed in a thoroughly unfortunate shade of lilac. Persephone bent to kiss her cheek. "Of course not, Grandmaman." She absolutely had forgotten. She'd have hidden in the scullery if she'd remembered. She bobbed a polite curtsy in Lady Culpepper's direction. "Lady Culpepper."

"Mmm." Lady Culpepper's greeting was barely perceptible as always.

Persephone helped herself to cakes decorated with sugared violets. When she sat on the edge of a settee, the ladies angled themselves ever so slightly away from her. Holly gave her a tiny smile of apology but kept herself turned toward the others. Priya, crowded in like a strawberry-girl on the first day of spring, narrowed her eyes at them. Persephone crammed the rest of the cake in her mouth and stood up, as though that was what had been keeping her there. She nearly choked on the crumbs.

She turned her attention to the impressive collection. The usual assortment of flint and arrowheads were augmented with green jade from China, elephant-headed statues from India, hand-painted globes, and even an astrolabe with which to chart the stars. There were coins set against black velvet, some kind of spear, and several Greek urns carved with goddesses. It had been too dark to see them last night. Not to mention that Conall was entirely too distracting.

Ivy, inspecting one of the urns, jumped with a startled shriek.

Persephone paused. "I'm sorry, I didn't mean to scare you."

Ivy forced a laugh. "I beg your pardon, it's my fault. I drank entirely too much coffee at breakfast." She smiled awkwardly and scurried away.

Strange.

But since Persephone generally acted much stranger, she shrugged and continued to wander through the cluttered corners and aisles, but she didn't really know what she was looking for.

Until she found it.

The crystal decanter with the broken neck, placed carelessly between an Etruscan vase and a basket of the "elf arrows" she and

Henry had always insisted on bringing to his grandfather. Lord Culpepper had displayed them proudly, never mind that they were bits of flint or broken chalk. She frowned at the decanter. What on earth was it doing here? Someone must have found it outside and assumed it was part of the collection. She stared at it long enough that her grandmother called out from her chair piled with tasseled cushions.

"Percy, do join us for some marzipan."

She forced a smile on her face. "Of course, Grandmaman."

She *hated* marzipan.

NUNCHEON WENT ON so long Persephone contemplated feigning a swoon. When finally released to their own amusements, a quick glance at the clock told Persephone she had a few hours before dinner was served. It would be a pity to waste it in the drawing room when she could be back in the village, working on the festival. With mere days left, every second counted. And fretting over Henry was not proving productive.

Not to mention that the London chapter of the Ladies' Society of Antiquaries was meeting for tea. She received their newsletter, and their presence here was as thrilling to her as the fact that Mr. Bullock of the Egyptian Hall Museum, also of London, would attend the festival.

Persephone had been keen on joining the Society for years now, but she was so seldom in London. She had corresponded with their president, Lady Kenning, but spots opened up so rarely. She'd been assured that she was at the top of the waiting list. She'd take this opportunity to finally meet them in person, to share tea and conversation where she might not be mocked for knowing the exact composition of ancient embalming fluid. She'd pinned the paper flower she'd made from one of their pamphlets to the left of her neckline, as instructed. They'd all know each other as friends that way.

Village activity bubbled around her, soothing and invigorating. The clop of hooves and the rumble of cartwheels was a cheerful cacophony. Blue and white striped streamers and pennants criss-crossed from rooftop to rooftop, jolly against the grey skies above. There was already an obvious increase of visitors. It boded well. The morning crowd was mostly village folk going about their business, fussing over window displays in anticipation of the visitors. Afternoons were for ladies strolling in their finest walking dresses, pausing to admire books, bonnets, and an enormous replica of the Sphinx made out of bread. The baker had also carved a Roman temple out of sugar and it stood on a dais covered in rose petals. Aside from the idiosyncratic elephant carved from a wedge of cheese, it was stunning.

Persephone crossed to the teashop which was positively frothing with flowers. Violets and roses, lilies, snapdragons and foxgloves nodded at the passersby from huge urns painted with silhouettes of Aphrodite. The perfume of hot tea and chocolate overwhelmed the scents of dust and horses and smoke from the blacksmith's forge down the way. She might have been in some distant temple, gathering flowers for an offering.

Three of the Society's members came around the corner, wearing their paper flowers. Nerves tickled the back of Persephone's throat. But here were colleagues of a sort, friends she simply had not met yet.

"Lady Dorcas?" Persephone recognized her ringlets and square jaw from a drawing in the last newsletter. "It's such a pleasure to finally meet you."

With her were two ladies Persephone did not recognize and Lady Louisa.

"Have we been introduced?" Lady Dorcas asked. "Oh, but I see you wear our flower."

"Lady Dorcas, this is Lady Persephone Blackwell," Lady Louisa jumped in.

Lady Dorcas's smile dimmed. "I see."

Persephone kept her smile in place, but her stomach wobbled, as it did when something large rustled in the bushes late at night. "Lady Louisa, I had no idea you were interested in history."

"I've just joined," she said, her expression darkly gleeful. "Last week, actually. It was ever so easy."

"Well, my dear, we always accept the best," one of the other ladies said.

Persephone blinked. She hadn't been informed that a spot had opened up. "Is Lady Kenning not with you?"

"Not for days yet," came the reply. "She enjoys historical exhibitions, of course, but she is less enamored of country pursuits. And country manners." Lady Dorcas tilted her head. "May I be frank?" She didn't give Persephone any time to reply. Instead, she plucked the paper flower from Persephone's collar. "We have standards to keep at the Society. It is difficult enough garnering any respect as it is. We simply can't welcome ladies who…court scandal." She tossed the flower into the street.

A hundred retorts crowded to the tip of Persephone's tongue, but she couldn't seem to say any of them. She'd expected differently from the Ladies Society of Antiquaries. She'd been a fool.

"Lady Dorcas," Priya interrupted from behind her. Persephone turned her head and was greeted with that sharp little smile she knew all too well spelled trouble. The last time she had seen it glittering in such a way, Priya had knocked a wasp's nest down onto the head of a boy poking a cat with a stick. Then she'd taken the cat home. Galahad lived with her to this day and had become the fattest, most spoiled cat this side of Egypt.

"Priya," Persephone said, quietly. There was no use in this particular awkward conversation. Even having a duke for a godfather couldn't entirely erase one's past. She'd been naïve to think otherwise.

"Lady Priya," Lady Dorcas curtsied briefly.

Priya did not curtsy back, only raised her eyebrow. "Are you still having an affair with your footman? The blond one?"

There was a collective gasp.

"He is rather handsome, I'll allow. But so young." Priya's gaze raked the others while Persephone fought a small smile. Priya spent so much time alone in her greenhouse that people forgot how vicious she could be. That she had fifteen thousand a year helped them forget as well. Persephone's own inheritance consisted of one old house and one slightly eccentric old lady who dressed as though she were fruit.

It was fortunate that Priya had a disregard for other people's opinions which bordered on clinical. "I'm so sorry, I thought we were discussing propriety and respectability. And scandal, of course." She pinned one of the ladies with a pointed stare. "I am sorry to hear you lost your father's best horse on a wager."

"I…"

"Quite." She turned her shoulder. "Persephone, shall we? The duke has asked us to join him for tea. You know how he dotes on you."

The duke had requested no such thing, but Persephone nodded. "Of course."

"Good afternoon," Priya tossed back casually as they strode away.

"Pri, you needn't make enemies on my behalf."

"Bah, what can that fusspot do to me? Anyway, I wouldn't have to defend you, if you'd defend yourself."

"What's the use?"

"They can't be allowed to win, Percy. Not when they flout conventions on a daily basis themselves. They are no better than you. And I won't have them thinking they are."

She shrugged a shoulder. "I was rather public with my lack of repentance."

"I remember," Priya grinned. "It was glorious."

"And effective." She sighed. "A little too effective, I suppose. But never mind," she added in bracing tones. It wasn't her scandal which had truly ostracized her; it was getting caught and then not wilting into regretful obscurity. There'd been no public weeping, because she wasn't sorry. "Self-pity is not productive, and I'd make the same decision now as I did then."

"Never mind that Ladies Society," Priya said. "You have us. The Cinderella Society." Her expression changed, like light hitting the blade of a sword. "It has a nice ring to it, wouldn't you say?"

Chapter Five

BY DINNER PERSEPHONE had changed her gown three times, skimmed through an entire shelf of books, and drank two pots of tea. She was no closer to a plan and not close enough to the water closet.

Dinner dragged on longer than the war against the French, and then there were card games to be played, silhouettes to draw, and a pianoforte to be played. Persephone was exempt from the last, since her playing was as rusty as her social graces. Lady Louisa played so beautifully two gentlemen openly wept. One of the other girls took over so an impromptu dance could be held. The footmen moved chairs and rolled the carpets away as Persephone found her usual corner. She had already claimed her favorite chair, half screened by a potted plant in which she'd hidden a small book, should the evening get desperate.

Priya sat next to her before she could reach for it, cooling herself with a fan painted like a peacock. She wore a gown of deep rose that glowed against brown skin.

"No shrubbery for you tonight?" Persephone asked.

Priya leaned back against the chair's embroidered cushion. "Even I must make an appearance now and again." She grimaced. "And I've a dozen new friends apparently, all so eager to renew an acquaintance that barely existed in the first place. I've a mind to murder my brother for not eloping like a sensible person."

Persephone made a noncommittal noise that she hoped

sounded vaguely sympathetic. The thought of Conall courting one of these perfectly polished girls sat like sour milk in her belly. She accepted a flute of champagne from a passing footman when she started to wonder if her silence was too long, implied too much.

"Are you not dancing?" Priya asked.

Persephone shook her head. "Pri, do I ever?"

Priya watched Louisa and Holly, their gazes on Persephone. "Ridiculous," she announced. She waved her brother over. "Conall, make yourself useful and dance with Persephone."

Persephone nearly choked on her champagne. "That isn't necessary."

"I want to put the cat among the pigeons." She looked positively maniacal in her glee. "Everyone here thinks themselves quite above our Percy and I should like to see them suffer a little for it."

Conall raised an eyebrow. "Is that so?" Heat prickled through Persephone just at the sound of his voice.

Persephone shook her head wildly. "No, really, it's fine." Falling off a balcony was preferable. Or into another hole.

He took the flute from her and passed it to his sister. "You should know by now that Priya always gets her way." He held out his arm and she had no choice but to take it or appear unforgivably rude. The strains of a country dance filled the room, as did surprised glances and whispering. A gentleman like enough to Ivy to be her brother, elbowed her indignantly.

"Now you've done it," Persephone told him wryly, as they faced each other in the line of dancers. "They'll be talking behind their hands about this for the rest of the night."

"Let them," Conall said, bowing. "They could do with a set down."

"I don't need defending." She curtsied sharply.

"Of course, you do."

She stiffened, faintly insulted. He chuckled, taking her hand for the next turn. She felt the heat of him through their gloves. As the dance went on, the music swelled. She caught the way Conall kept glancing at the musicians.

"It's the violins, isn't it?" she asked when the steps brought them together again.

He looked surprised. "The violins?"

"I remember how well you played. How thrilled you were when the duke had one made specially for you on your sixteenth birthday."

His smile was brief, nostalgic. "My parents were not pleased. It's not a suitable pastime for an earl."

"Do you still play?"

"No." Something changed in his expression, something that came and went too quickly to name but still had her wishing she could offer some comfort.

"You must miss it."

The dance took them away from each other again, turning them hand to hand with the others, and circling them back together like stars on the same trajectory.

"I wasn't implying that you can't defend yourself before. Priya has quite disabused me of that notion, believe me. But one doesn't always protect a person because they aren't capable, but instead because they are worth protecting."

She concentrated on the steps because she found she didn't know what to say. This wasn't his easy flattery, his practiced flirting.

"Anyway, you tried to protect me from the fireworks, and again in the barrow this morning, didn't you? I'm quite in your debt it seems. Why?"

"If you're truly looking for a wife," she absolutely would not choke the words out like bitter medicine, "Being discovered with me would not exactly help you."

"Nor would it help you, I imagine."

"I suppose not." She sounded exactly as concerned over the possibility as she felt. That was: not at all. Adding more salt to a dish too salty to taste in the first place hardly mattered.

"Surely there is someone here who has designs on your hand?"

She shot him a look out of the corner of her eye. "Are you trying to be witty?"

"Not at all. I am merely assessing the competition," he replied, bending to press a kiss to the back of her wrist, right at the edge of her glove. She felt it burn through her. He escorted her back to her chair. Persephone knew she was smiling foolishly as she retrieved her book from the palm tree, mostly for something to do with her hands that didn't involve pressing them to her flushed cheeks.

"You know an earl can't marry a girl with your reputation," Holly said from the next chair. She said it gently, kindly even. She wore the debutante white, spotless, and gleaming with silver beads. "You'll break your own heart."

Persephone shook her head. "You don't have to worry about my heart, Miss Carter."

She was worried enough for the both of them.

"OH, THERE YOU are," Tamsin said as Persephone entered the Pendleton ballroom. She sat on a padded bench; her violet silk shoes abandoned on the parquet floor. The small table next to her held a tea service and a dizzying array of treats, no doubt for Meg's benefit. Her sweet tooth was a thing of legend. She stood nearby, wearing a canvas apron over her day dress, her black hair in its usual braids woven into a simple and practical coronet.

Persephone stopped to admire her artwork. The duke had decided to partition the ballroom down the center, one side to display his Egyptian artifacts, and the other for Rome. It made for a stunning effect, especially as he'd asked Meg to paint murals on the walls. She fair glowed with the joy of it. "That's coming along beautifully," Persephone told her.

She was working on a floor to ceiling rendition of Atalanta holding a basket of golden apples. The gilt paint shimmered prettily but Atalanta's expression was surprisingly fierce.

"She hasn't said anything amusing in at least an hour," Tamsin complained.

"I'm busy," Meg retorted mildly.

"Too busy for your oldest and dearest friend?" Tamsin teased. "You wound me."

"I shouldn't. You know *Percy* is my dearest friend."

Tamsin lobbed a candied pecan at the back of Meg's head. "She's so good at putting on quiet, docile airs," she said to Persephone. "One can almost forget what she is truly like."

"Not with you though," Meg said, unruffled.

"True. But then I'm a duke's daughter," she grinned. "So, I can do what I like."

Persephone took a turn about the enormous room, examining the shelves of the duke's artifacts which had been brought from all over the house. They would be augmented with twice as many items on loan. Even now though, the collection was impressive. Canopic jars, beaded collars, a scribe's palette. A mummified body propped up in its painted casket.

And a pair of carved gaming dice carved from bone.

Persephone clicked her tongue. "These doesn't belong here." She picked them up carefully. A thousand years ago a Roman soldier had used these to pass the time while on campaign. They were worn and yellowed with wear. She crossed the floor to drop them properly in Ancient Rome. And noticed a cat carved from black stone, small enough to fit in the palm of her hand. "Oh, honestly. This is all sixes and sevens."

As Persephone began a thorough inspection of Roman coins, Tamsin groaned. "I'm not going to get any decent entertainment from either of you now."

It was at least an hour before Tamsin could get any attention at all. By then she was sliding along the gleaming waxed floors in her stockinged feet, as she had when she was little. She could never abide being indoors too long. "Don't tell my stepmother!"

"Especially not when it was your *mother* who taught me how to slide when I was past old enough to know better," The Duke of Pendleton remarked drily as he strode into the ballroom.

Tamsin grinned proudly. "She made a terrible duchess by all accounts."

"Which is why we liked her so much," he agreed. Tamsin's stepmother was not well liked. She was distant and chilly, carved out of diamonds and ice. "All my doves, in one place. Well, nearly."

Tamsin snorted. "Doves?"

"You're doves to me."

Tamsin kissed his cheek. "You're sweet, Uncle Atticus. But I'd rather be a crow."

As a duke's daughter she was comfortable with a far more informal form of address than Persephone would have presumed, godfather or no. And no one dared quarrel with him half so well. Especially when he added, "But who will marry a crow?"

"I don't need to marry," Tamsin said airily. "Isn't that the entire point of being related to so many dukes?"

"You need a good match. Someone steady," The duke insisted. "You all do."

"For my part, no thank you," she said, tugging on his queue of white hair.

He harrumphed. "How goes it in here, you ungrateful hoyden?"

"Persephone is muttering under her breath about coins and Meg won't talk to me at all."

"Despair," he said. "Meg, my girl, your painting skills have grown even more exquisite."

She smiled, pleased. "Thank you, Your Grace."

"I wanted her to paint the lions in the Coliseum. A good maiming always makes for good art."

"But rather less festive for a ball."

"I suppose."

"How's your tosspot uncle?" The duke asked Meg.

"Still a tosspot," Tamsin interjected.

Meg studied her brushes. "He was vexed he did not receive an invitation."

The duke's laugh was sharp and smug. "Good. Never did like the man." He peered over Persephone's shoulder and clucked his tongue in much the same manner as she had. "Who would put that little black cat on the Rome side?" He shook his head. "I may have to ask the staff to attend some of the lectures we have planned."

"I found two Romano-British coins in with the Roman ones as well. Iceni, I think."

"Scandal! What would Queen Boudicca say?"

She grinned at him. "I knew you'd understand."

"Well, you look like you have everything in hand here. I'm off to visit the lecture hall. Where's Priya? It makes me nervous when she's off alone," he muttered, stalking into the hall where the footmen scrambled to attention.

"Where *is* Priya?" Persephone asked.

"Being sneaky with her brother," Tamsin waved a hand. "You know how she is." She tilted her head. "Speaking of which."

"Priya?"

"Conall."

His name sent a bolt of awareness through her. She must never admit to it. Never. Tamsin would be relentless. She kept her eyes on her work. "What about him?"

"He danced with you."

She snorted. "Conall dances with everyone."

"He never used to."

"True."

"And he was different with you," Meg pointed out. Traitor. "Serious. With all the other ladies he's all smiles and charm."

"Isn't that…?" She wasn't sure what she wanted to say. "Proof that the dancing meant nothing? Especially since Priya forced him in the first place?" She shouldn't want it to mean something, but she did.

"Firstly, no one forces Conall to do anything," Meg said, stepping back and wiping her brush on a cloth. "Not when he was younger and shyer, and certainly not now I'd wager. Secondly, it means he was more himself with you. It was obvious."

Persephone shook her head, wondering why her face felt warm. "Surely not." She caught the look Meg and Tamsin exchanged.

"And did he not ask for a tour of your private collection?" Meg asked archly.

"It's an antiquarian festival."

"Conall is *not* an antiquarian," Tamsin scoffed.

Persephone glanced at her watch fob, tucked into her collar. "And he's never late either. I should go for that aforementioned tour."

"We're going with you," Tamsin announced. "I can't be cooped up any longer."

"And you need a chaperone," Meg said.

"I hardly need that," Persephone disagreed. "I'm already ruined."

"What if he is overcome with passion?" Tamsin paused. "On second thought, perhaps we shouldn't accompany you. Are you blushing?" she added, delighted.

"Oh, stop it."

Tamsin laughed. "It seems as though I shall have my entertainment after all."

"CONALL," PRIYA PANTED, half-running to keep up to his longer strides. "It's too early for calisthenics."

"It's noon." The sun struggled to shine between stately trees as Persephone ducked into the oak leaves ahead. Tamsin and Meg followed close behind, not unexpectedly. He kept a sharp eye on her, pretending he hadn't noticed how adorably serious she looked carrying her leatherbound books.

"Let me clarify," Priya added. "It's *always* too early for calisthenics."

"You didn't have to come."

"Of course, I did, since you're set on the idiotic conclusion that Percy is some sort of spy," she snapped.

"I'm hardly set on it."

"I can't believe you'd even entertain the notion for a single moment," she muttered. "Our Persephone. You and I know both know that's bollocks."

"I have to be thorough. And I have to investigate every clue."
She rolled her eyes.

"Either way, I don't want my inquiries to ruin her reputation until I have all of the evidence, so hurry up."

Priya snorted, or would have, had she any breath left. "You're asking one ruined lady to chaperone another ruined lady. I know you were on the Continent for a long time but that's not precisely how it's done."

"If she's guilty, it won't matter."

Priya nudged him hard enough that he had to reach out and steady her when she bounced off his unyielding shoulder. "Ooof." She narrowed her eyes. "Give over, Conall. You can't *actually* think she's part of a treason plot. She's never even left England."

"I admit it's unlikely." He wanted it to be even more unlikely than it was. But anyone with such an obsessive interest in Ancient Egypt had to be a suspect. Even if she smelled like flowers and ink. Even if she made him feel things he'd never felt before.

"Then why are we chasing her across the lawn?"

"Unlikely is not the same as impossible." Priya hadn't seen the fields stained with blood, the crows thick as rain clouds. All because one small piece of information was passed into the wrong hands. By an Englishman. Purposefully. Those soldiers had been ambushed. Many had died waking in their beds. "I have to be sure."

They closed in on Persephone and the other Cinderellas within moments. Persephone looked up in surprise. "Priya! I didn't think you'd come. You hate museums."

"I don't hate yours."

"You hate mine," Tamsin pointed out cheerfully.

"Because yours is disgusting."

"Lord Northwyck," Persephone bobbed a small curtsy, knuckles tightening around her books. He glanced at the titles. Ancient Egypt. Of course. Priya noticed him noticing and rolled her eyes rather aggressively. She might need a poultice later.

"Good afternoon, ladies," he said. He smiled lazily at Tamsin, a rake's charming salute, because he knew it would needle her and she would not take it seriously.

"Oh, cease and desist," she shot back, though she slipped her arm fondly through his. "Before you do yourself an injury."

There were women, he was told, who found him irresistible.

When he mentioned it, Tamsin laughed so hard she nearly did herself an injury.

The oak trees gave way to green fields and a wide creek full of silvery stones. Halcyon House nestled in a valley, ringed with more oak trees. As they approached, gardens of hollyhocks and larkspurs and red roses waved bright blossoms at them. Conall saw Persephone's shoulders visibly relax. She took a deep breath, much the way he imagined she must when casting off her corset at night.

Which naturally led to imagining her casting off her corset at night.

"My lord, are you well?"

He cleared his throat. "Of course." Mortified and shifting uncomfortably in a way he hadn't done since he was a lad, but otherwise fine.

"I can call at the house for tea, if you'd like," Persephone offered.

Priya waved her off. "Don't bother. I've had so much tea this week already I could fairly float home down the Thames. Basil still doesn't think ladies should drink brandy."

The hermitage was a small stone building tucked into yet more rose gardens. The door was arched and set with massive iron hinges, much like a dungeon. It was old and crooked and faintly ominous. Persephone beamed. Conall couldn't help but wonder what a man might have to do to get her to beam at him that way.

She used a key from the chatelaine clipped to her dress and led the way inside. The museum was small and filled with light from the many Tudor-style windows. A wall was painted with Egyptian hieroglyphs in ochres and black, no doubt thanks to Meg. It had the warmth of a well-loved place.

It was also a disaster.

The shelves had been thoroughly tossed about. Flints lay scattered on the floor like rushes in a medieval castle, next to pages ripped from sketchbooks. Spear heads and rotted sword scabbards were jumbled together with delicate faded fabrics and tiny bones. Meg stifled a small gasp. Persephone didn't make any sound at all.

Conall stepped inside, shielding the others. "Wait in the garden. The thief might still be about."

"There's no one here." Persephone crouched to lift the broken halves of a crystal egg. "This belonged to an Anglo-Saxon queen. My father found it in a barrow." She was like a doused flame. Fury made a swift and surprising attack. He felt it in his bones.

"What's behind that door?" he asked, keeping his voice even.

She didn't look over her shoulder. "It's still locked. No one is in there." She rose, still cradling the cracked crystal. Her eyes glittered.

"Don't cry," he said brusquely. "We'll find the culprit." He must already be hunting the bastard. It strained credulity to believe there was no connection with the antiquarian he sought, and a private museum being ransacked.

"Oh, let her cry, Con," his sister said. "She deserves it."

"I am not weeping," Persephone said very clearly. "I am incandescent with rage."

"Good," Tamsin said. "Rage is so much more effective." She was already pacing furiously, hands in tight fists.

Meg stopped to gather the pieces of a broken clay tablet and gently lay them back onto a shelf. "You can fix it, Percy. You're good at putting things back together. And I can help."

"Who would do this?" Priya demanded, staring at Conall as if he should know. Or as if he'd done it himself. Well, she was right about one thing. He bloody well ought to know who was behind this. "Another antiquarian?" Priya pressed. "A cruel joke?"

Persephone squared her shoulders, her chin titled stubbornly, like the Anglo-Saxon queen buried with her crystal egg. "At least nothing is missing."

"Are you sure?" Conall asked, prowling the room. He felt like stew about to boil its lid right off the cauldron.

She nodded confidently. "Quite sure. I know my collection, even when it's on the floor." She frowned. "But that's odd, isn't it? That nothing was stolen? Why else would someone bother to do this?" She scooped up a handful of flints. "Not that there's anything of true value here, certainly not to experienced antiquarians. And not with the kinds of collections we're set to display in the village. Most of this is from my own fields." She shook her head. "I suppose someone heard about the festival and thought they might find some treasures to sell."

The other explanation was that Conall was an ass. He'd somehow led the traitor to Persephone's door. He'd know someone was on his trail, or at least suspect. He might be trying to throw Conall off his scent. Or else he thought Persephone possessed information or some kind of item of interest. Which led to the next question: what was the item?

Whatever it was, Conall would be damned if Persephone suffered one more second over it. "Perhaps the local children dared each other?" he suggested, mostly to put her at her ease. There was no sense troubling her when he would find the culprit and feed him a fistful of iron.

"Still, I'm sorry for this," he said softly.

"Be sorry for whoever did this," Persephone promised, her eyes glinting.

"I heard one of the maids mention a burglary in the village," Meg said. "A few coins, someone's favorite brooch. It sounds like there must be a thief about."

Conall wasn't certain. He surveyed the space as they worked but the traitor hadn't left a convenient calling card. Still, he could assume for the moment, that it was someone nearby. Someone at Lady Culpepper's house party, even. It was a small step forward; but it was something. He made a mental list of the guests. A kind of hunger lifted the hairs on the back of Conall's neck. He was close now. There'd be an outlet for this simmering anger and guilt.

"Con, there's no need to break more of Lady Persephone's collection," Priya clucked her tongue, prying a slightly bent key from his grasp.

"I found that when I was eight years old," Persephone said. "I was so proud of it, my father let me keep it. Technically, he ought to have turned over any antique metal to the crown but neither of us thought the king would mind very much if I kept it. My mother however, minded very much that I used to wear it on a velvet ribbon. I'd have worn it on my debut if she didn't hide it in the chicken coop."

"I remember that," Tamsin said, grinning.

"I won't ask how you found it again," Conall said, amused.

She was such a singular woman. She remained unbowed, even the sunlight showed more broken pieces of her treasures.

"You may as well return to the house," she said, wearily. "I can get everything sorted."

"We can stay and help," Meg offered.

She shook her head. "Thank you. I need a few minutes."

Priya's eyes narrowed. "Don't you dare hide out all day. They'll think they've won."

Persephone forced another smile. "I stopped playing their game a long time ago."

"Then they really will think they've won," Tamsin added. "And that simply won't do."

"The thief is long gone." Conall paused. "But I can stay, if you'd like."

Persephone shook her head. "I'll be fine."

Disappointment was a surprise. He decided not to read too much into it. She was an intriguing mystery, that was all. Especially when she hefted a centuries-old sword pockmarked and nibbled by rust. "Besides, I have this."

He flashed a grin. "Woe to any intruder."

"Precisely."

PERSEPHONE WAITED UNTIL they had gone before she dashed to the locked workroom, fumbling for the key hanging from her chatelaine. The small space was undisturbed, rows of forged pots lining the shelves and her potter's wheel sitting quietly in the center. Etruscan vessels, Roman amphorae, pots scratched with diagonal lines meant to hold the ashes of the dead—they were all hers and all safe. Relief was like a trickle of cold water on a hot day. Fury had made her feel as if she was eating fire. But now at least her workroom was still secret.

She'd taught herself to make her own forgeries, in order to better detect them in other collections. But it would be too easy for this workroom to be misinterpreted. In fact, it could ruin her far more successfully than a tumble with an earl's second son. She cared about her professional reputation far more than her personal status. She'd made her sacrifices and she'd be damned if the rewards would be snatched away. She hadn't exaggerated when she'd brandished her chipped sword. To have her hermitage tossed, her collection scattered. To have it all witnessed by Conall. The sword of some dead warrior seemed like the exact right response.

She shook her head, locking the door again. She allowed herself another turn about the room to calm her anger. She'd get new locks fitted for the doors; and she was seriously considering setting traps. Glue traps, steel leg clamps—even the kind of massive stones said to crush explorers who entered secret jungle temples uninvited. Something suitably bloody in any case.

"Now, there's a smile to frighten Napoleon himself."

She jumped, turning to find Conall leaning against the red bricks of the hermitage. There were rose petals on his boots.

"You didn't have to wait," she said as he fell into step beside her.

"I'm truly sorry about your collection, Persephone."

"It's hardly your fault," she replied. Everything was roses and the scent of his bergamot soap. His strides were unapologetically hungry, eating up the ground. "If you truly mean to marry, shouldn't you be at the house getting to know the young ladies?" Why did she keep bringing it up? Perhaps she needed the reminder, but he certainly didn't. She was worrying at it like a rotten tooth.

"I'd rather be here with you."

She knew it must be polite flirting, but she still felt a thrill, like sneaking cake in the kitchen when everyone else was asleep.

"You aren't going to giggle?" he asked with a sideling glance.

She arched an eyebrow. "You weren't particularly funny."

He grinned at that, a slow happy smile that turned her bones to pudding. Possibly her brain too. "Persephone, you are refreshing." He lifted an oak branch to let them pass into the grove.

"So you've said. Like tonic water," she pointed out drily.

"No." The branch dropped, letting the green swallow them up. "Not like tonic water." His fierce gaze snagged hers like a thorn, all beauty and danger. She could smell roses again. She couldn't move, had no wish to. She could see the flecks of green in his grey eyes, still holding her as securely as his hands might, if he would only touch her. The rustle of leaves receded; the dappled sunlight disappeared. If she took a deep breath, her lips would brush his. His breath was warm on her cheek. It was almost enough.

Never enough.

He swallowed, his jaw tightening. He eased out of the trees, breaking the spell that smouldered between them. He lifted the branches again, as polite as a footman. "If I am refreshing," she murmured. "Then you, sir, are confusing."

"Yes, I imagine that I am." There was sadness under the sardonic tone, quite gone before she could properly excavate it.

Chapter Six

P ERSEPHONE HAD HAD her fill of genteel entertainment.

She rose at dawn the next day, passing more than a few revelers who were only now stumbling back to their beds. She drank a cup of tea standing up at the sideboard, filled a napkin with toasted muffins and sailed past the footman manning the front door. His powdered wig was slightly askew. Lady Culpepper held to the old traditions and she was rather fierce about it. Persephone reached up to straighten the offensive tilt to the curls. The footman jumped.

"Thank you, my lady," he then murmured.

"Our little secret," she grinned. She paused. "Any word from Henry?"

"No, my lady."

She refused to let her smile slip. Henry was fine. He had to be. In her head, she listed the ways he might have been detained. It helped a little. A wagon wheel could have snapped its axle on the way to port, a sandstorm could have landlocked them before they even made it to the ship. And no matter his rank, soldier, captain, general, their time was not their own. She breathed through the anxiety. He had survived Bonaparte; he would survive this. Whatever *this* turned out to be.

She couldn't remember a stranger house party. She was fiercely glad to be returning to her normal schedule, even if that included several hours digging through crates at the assembly hall. She was even more keen to get down to it now; never mind the ancient treasures, she had to find Henry's wayward forgery.

The sun burned away the morning dew and tattered the mists. It was invigorating, cleansing. She had to shake off the secret sneers the guests had tried to hide behind their hands, the mess of her hermitage. Conall's kiss under the fireworks.

The man had no business kissing like that.

How was one supposed to muster defenses against it? Heat snuck up her spine and tingled the back of her knees at the memory. For heaven's sake, he was making her *knees* tingle a full day later. She was outgunned. Entirely. And thirsty for something she could not quite name. Or, more truthfully, had no wish to admit to. Surely, she had enough to be getting on with.

She marched all the way to the village and an hour later, with a wet hem and grass stuck to her boots, finally felt refreshed and more like herself. Kisses were nothing to lose one's head over. House parties were ripe with far juicier scandals. She was on an even keel again. She was Lady Persephone Blackwell again.

"Good morning, your ladyship." John, the Duke's burly footman, regarded her with mild concern when she jumped, yelping.

So much for an even keel.

"Are you well?"

"'Twas an early morning," she assured him, sunnily. "I'm perfectly well." He had been waiting for her outside the assembly hall which was really the second floor of the inn. The duke insisted upon sending his strongest footman to help her, even though he had already sent an army to unpack the crates. John was to be nearby at all times, should she need his assistance. He was kind, quiet and built approximately like a bull. She'd seen ladies with waists smaller than his neck.

"Another three crates arrived," he informed her. "With two more on the way."

"Thank you, John. Won't you take a seat? And some tea?"

Every day she offered the same courtesies and every day he refused them. He stood alert, more like a soldier than any footman she'd ever seen. "I cannot, my lady. Thank you."

"One day, John, you'll take tea and a scone," she teased. "Mark my words."

He smiled but did not otherwise respond.

The hall did not have the grandeur of a proper assembly room in London, of course, but it was lovely in its own way. There was a small card room off to one side, with refreshments procured downstairs in the main inn's dining room. The building dated to the sixteenth century and was still in possession of its original beams, crossing overhead and dark with soot and age. The walls had been recently whitewashed for the event, and the mullioned windows scrubbed until they gleamed. Shelves and tables were brought from the duke's house, as well as begged, borrowed and outrighted commanded from the neighbours.

It bustled with movement and energy, with chatter and shouts and the hammering of nails securing displays. She felt as though her stays loosened. This was important. *This*, the pursuit of history and knowledge, not tossed belongings and scandals and cold shoulders.

Or heated kisses.

Not that she wouldn't take a horsewhip to whoever had desecrated her private museum, because she fully intended to do just that.

But for now, this gave her the space to think and breathe again. To plan. To plot.

The open crates offered tantalizing peeks of pottery shards, broken stone statues, Greek amphorae, Roman mosaics, and Viking glass beads of the sort often found in the hills around Little Barrow. This exhibit had every possibility of rivalling even the collection of the British Museum. And this was only the secondary exhibition, the main display would be set up in the duke's private ballroom.

"Is that a canopic jar?" she blurted out with all the finesse of a child on Christmas morning with a fistful of sugar plums.

The worker currently holding the jar blinked at her. "Don't know, my lady. It came in this crate." He waved his hand. The one currently holding the jar. Persephone charged forward. He froze.

"Please be careful with that," she said, as though he were holding a newborn. Or a wasp's nest. "It's several thousand years old. It might still hold some ancient Egyptian's liver. Or his intestines."

He blinked again, this time far more rapidly. "Blerg."

She was fully aware that not everyone shared her fascination. "Give it here, if you please."

He passed it over eagerly. She pretended not to see him wipe his palms on his trousers. It was in remarkably good condition, only cracked along the top where the lid had crushed down into the jar. It was carved into the likeness of a falcon's head, with a pointed beak. "Definitely intestines," she said. "This is Qebehsenuf, one of the sons of Horus. He was said to protect the intestines. If it was Anubis, it would be the stomach." She stroked the beak. "It's beautiful."

"If you say so, my lady." He did not sound convinced. Queasy, definitely. Convinced, no. But ghoulish or not, it *was* a beautiful piece of art.

And it was a forgery.

Authentic canopic jars were made of pottery, but more often limestone. And the shape of this one was wrong, if only subtly so. It was slightly too squat at the bottom, meant to flare up from a slender base and it was marble, faintly Romanised.

Anxiety thrummed down her arms and into her fingertips. Her skin prickled painfully. Was this one of the items Henry had sent home? She couldn't open it now, not with all of the workers around her and John keeping his careful watch. The itch to lift the lid was painful. It was even more painful to put the jar down as if it wasn't suddenly the most important artifact she had ever held, fake or not. She glanced at the open crate it had come from. "Whose collection is that?"

"A Mr. Bouchard."

She'd never heard of him. In all likelihood, neither had Henry. He'd chosen his unknown deliverers at random, only the destination remained the same. The festival. She'd have to wait until tonight to retrieve the jar and take out Henry's letter. Assuming there was one. And if Henry didn't come home soon, she'd have to find out who to send it to. She hoped not to involve the duke but it might come to that. Until then, she would do what she could on her own. It was too dangerous. Too volatile. Even the Cinderellas could not know.

She reached for the lid. Surely no one would notice a quick peek. It was entirely within character, after all.

"Lady Persephone."

She jumped a foot at the sudden voice behind her, gravelly and delicious.

Obviously, she'd have made a very poor spy, her ability to go unnoticed notwithstanding.

She whirled around. "Conall! That is, Lord Northwyck." Without really thinking about it, she let the hand holding the canopic jar drop to her side.

"Here now," John shouldered between them. "You're not to bother the lady." He glowered at Conall. Conall, in return, only smiled slightly. He didn't look remotely concerned, despite the fact that John outweighed him by two stone. Still, there was something about the way Conall moved that would have encouraged Persephone not to underestimate him. She touched John's shoulder gently. She could barely see over it. He was that large. And she was that short.

"Thank you, John. No need for concern. This is the duke's godson, Lord Northwyck. Lord Northwyck, may I present John Goode."

Conall inclined his head as though footmen were introduced to earls on a daily basis. "My godfather set you here, did he?"

"Yes, my lord."

Conall nodded. "Good man."

John waited a beat before nodding in return. "Sir." He stepped back to his usual position by the door.

Persephone didn't want to let the canopic jar out of her sight, but she also didn't want Conall or anyone else to notice her interest. And Conall noticed everything. She shifted, placing the jar back into the crate and blocking it at the same time. She made a show of peering into the next crate where a slab of broken stone was being unwrapped.

It didn't work.

Conall strode forward in that way of his, all confident ease, and focused immediately on the jar. He lifted it out of the box and then tipped it alarmingly to observe the base.

Persephone squeaked.

Loudly.

He raised an eyebrow at her. "That is a sound generally reserved for irate mice."

She snatched it from his hand. "My lord!"

"What seems to be the problem?"

"Only that this jar is several thousand years old!" she returned sharply. Never mind that what it held inside was priceless. "And it does not belong to you." She replaced it in its packaging, gently, reverently. "The duke has been granted a loan from several well-known and well supplied collectors. All with the promise that the utmost care would be taken at all times."

"I am starting to feel like I'm about to get my knuckles rapped by the governess."

"If I thought it would do any good, I would consider it."

"Would you, now?" Something in his voice made her feel like blushing. Also, she'd threatened an earl. Really, even without her scandal, she was fairly certain she had been destined for spinsterhood from the get-go. One did not threaten earls.

But she'd do it again.

Instead, she turned her attention very pointedly to the slab of stone in the next crate. It was the colour of sand and intricately carved with hieroglyphs. "How marvelous."

"What does it say?" Conall asked, stepping closer. He looked interested, not merely polite. She certainly knew the subtle differences between the two by now.

"We don't know yet," Persephone replied reverently. "A similar stone was found in the Egyptian village of Rosetta by French soldiers, oh, sixteen years ago? Antiquarians are still trying to decipher it. Hieroglyphs remain a mystery and with the war not many Englishmen have had a chance for a proper look." She rubbed the letters softly. The stone was cool, smooth under her fingertips. How she wished she knew what the carvings stood for, the little hawk for instance. Did it signify Horus? Or was it a letter? A symbol from a story long lost?

"Enjoy a good mystery, do you?" Conall was even closer now, bending his head to admire the stone. His breath stirred the hairs on her nape. *That's not all it stirred. Not now, body.*

"I'll enjoy this one even more when it's solved. It's so satisfying, don't you think? Even if you're not the one to solve it."

"I'm not sure I agree," he replied. The tone of his voice was odd, edgy, intense.

She tilted her head. "I know it's frustrating but that's antiquarian pursuits for you. More questions than answers."

"I prefer answers."

"You'd make a terrible historian," she teased. "The very fact that we can even hope to understand hieroglyphs one day is because of a stone very like this one."

"That dusty old thing?"

"Yes. The Rosetta Stone is written in Greek and demotic and hieroglyphs. As we already know how to read Greek, it gets us that much closer to deciphering it. And now that the war is over, the French no longer control our travel into Egypt."

"You can read ancient Greek?"

"Passably," she admitted. "It's not my forte."

"I had no idea the war had such an effect on your studies."

She shrugged. "I admit I'm not likely to travel to Egypt any time soon, but it's nice to let myself dream. More importantly, those who *can* travel there will bring back the most interesting stories and theories." Not to mention proof of Henry's innocence.

"Is that what fills these crates?"

She nodded. "We haven't seen artifacts like these in years. The exhibits are going to be phenomenal. They'll rival the British Museum, and Bullock's Egyptian Hall, if only for a week."

"Your cheeks are pink."

She touched her face. She was always prattling on, too excited by 'dusty old things' as everyone put it. "I apologize. What can I help you with, my lord? You did not come here for a lecture."

"Don't apologize," he replied. "Why apologize for what brings you pleasure?"

Something about the way he said that made her squirm. She cleared her throat. "All the same."

His grin was fleeting, wicked. She narrowed one eye at him in reproach, her cheeks growing pinker. He only laughed and bowed before walking away entirely, leaving her question unanswered.

She decided he was right, after all.

Unanswered questions were a pain in the arse.

SHE WAS HIDING something.

And she was dismal at it.

He knew the signs; the held breath, the determined refusal to glance away lest you glance in the wrong direction. He had wanted to believe she could not be part of the kind of treachery that had cost hundreds of men their lives. But he was all too mindful that her obsession with history and its artifacts were a mark against her. Especially when finding her gleefully knee-deep in ancient Egyptian objects.

He did not believe in coincidences.

Not in matters such as this one.

A cart rumbled by, packed with thick cuts of raw meat from the butcher. From the sheer amount, it was likely headed to the duke's kitchens. The slabs were wrapped but Conall could smell the blood, imagine the red raw flesh. He had to duck into the shadows between the buildings. His body wanted to run, felt like it had already been running for hours, even as he stood preternaturally still. The smell of residual gunpowder, the blood staining the grass. He didn't have to imagine them, but he could imagine all too well the panicked cries of the men as they fell. His breath stuttered and he forced air through his nostrils, held it, released it. He had to get a grip on himself.

Persephone was not here to distract him, both by falling on him out of nowhere and kissing him gently, cautiously. As if she was afraid he might shove her away, when all he wanted was to get closer. He had no business remembering the feel of her in his arms, not now. And his breeches had no business being so uncomfortably tight. This was no time for a cockstand. Not for a woman he was suddenly no longer convinced was not a traitor. Or at least working in cohorts with one.

A pity.

More than a pity. The disappointment he felt was both keen and surprising. He'd liked her. She was clever and funny and had tried to save him and his reputation. He could perfectly call up the scent of her unusual perfume, a touch of roses over something rich and spicy. It soothed him, distracting from blood-soaked memories. She smelled like incense, like something secret. Apt, he supposed.

At least this uncomfortable awareness of her allowed him an edge. He would have to use it to his advantage. Everyone else seemed content to overlook her entirely but he saw the bolstering smile she used to convince herself that it didn't matter. Her self-deprecating humour when she found herself in one unusual situation after another. The way she'd clutched at him when he kissed her back.

The way she swallowed nervously just now when he surprised her.

He knew in his bones she was hiding something. Perhaps it was something innocuous, innocent. Utterly unrelated.

He wished for it fervently enough to surprise himself.

Sneaking out of the house was harder than it looked.

Lady Culpepper had a veritable army of servants, as many as the duke's household. Mostly because she counted the exact number of the duke's staff and made certain she was not lagging behind. Lady Culpepper had *standards*.

She also had a poor footman stationed by the front door in case a guest should have need of him. Currently, he was propped against the wall, eyes closed. He didn't stir when Persephone picked her way carefully across the marble floor. An oil lamp burned low, saving her from a stubbed toe and what would have no doubt been a very unladylike yell.

And at Halcyon House Persephone knew where the kitchen cat, Bast, was likely to be. The Culpepper cat was white and fluffy with a very dashing silver collar. And he scared five years off her life. At home, she knew which of the steps creaked, and which of the windows offered easy access to the terrace instead of a rosebush.

A very thorny rosebush.

Currently taking liberties, one might add.

The cat had startled her so thoroughly while she opened the window that she leapt through the opening before suitably inspecting where it led. Really, it was no wonder she was thoroughly on the shelf. Who would choose to marry a walking disaster? She rolled out of the garden bordering the house, petals in her hair and up her nose. Scratches stung the back of her hands. That, at least, would be easy to explain. An antiquarian's hands were not as soft and manicured as an earl's daughter's hands ought to be. And if worse came to worse, she would blame it on the cat.

Who named a cat Lancelot? Bound to give him airs.

Persephone scrambled to her feet and tried to feel more like a dashing spy and less like a clumsy miss straight from the schoolroom. Or the circus. Of course, an acrobat would never have botched the landing the way she had. It was too hard to stay calm, to still the trembling of her hands. She was off to find that canopic jar, to help protect her oldest friend.

To have an adventure.

She kept close to the house, in case one of the guests chanced to glance outside on their way to use the necessity. Then she darted from tree to tree until she was reasonably certain she would not be noticed. The late summer night was warm, and the moon was bright. It would be full come the festival, as they'd planned. It made it so much easier to dash about the countryside, whether in a carriage or on foot. She'd put on her dark blue digging dress so as not to catch further attention. It was a bit of a walk from the Culpepper estate to the village, but it would wake her up. And the sun would be coming up on her return, so if she got caught, she could claim early-morning exercise.

It felt good to do *something,* instead of writing cheerful letters to Henry and hoping they would not get lost *en route* or that they had any hope of bringing him a moment of peace. It seemed silly to write about the swallows in the barn, the hedgehogs the gardener chased until he was red-faced and puffing, and her own hours in the barrows. Henry said it helped.

She hoped this would help a great deal more.

A meadowlark trilled as she tested the inn's front door. It swung open, revealing the smoky dark interior. It smelled of yeast from beer and bread and decades of stews bubbling away in the kitchen. There was a clatter of dishes from that kitchen and a murmured curse. Someone was up before dawn, stoking the fire and putting the kettles on to boil.

Persephone darted silently up the side stairs leading to the hall. Any guests would use the main staircase from the bedrooms. And the door linking the bedchambers to the rest of the floor was already locked, from inside the hall.

Where at least one footman was already on guard. There would be up to five when the festival truly got underway.

Henry was trying to capture a traitor and hold him accountable; all the while being framed for those crimes. After surviving years of warfare on the Continent. Surely, she could maneuver around a single footman.

It was her duty as a friend. As an Englishwoman.

Suitably bolstered, but still without an actual plan, Persephone hesitated. There was no use in pretending to be a maid, all of the footmen knew her. She crouched and waited for the one currently on guard left to relieve himself. It took far longer than she would have liked, and her thigh muscles were screaming by the time she could risk coming out of her crouch.

She found a small window, easily opened from inside the card room. She'd have to mention it later and make sure it was properly secured. For now, she allowed herself a small smug smile.

The hall was shadowed, with a little light coming in from the window to the back balcony. It gleamed on glass cabinets and silver doorknobs. She crept across the long room, careful not to make a sound.

Even when a hand closed over her mouth.

Especially then. Her yelp was strangled, muffled. She was

hauled back against a strong male body. Her skin prickled painfully with a burst of fear. A burst which disintegrated into something else; into several something elses: surprise, annoyance, excitement. She recognized those arms, that chest pressed against her back.

"Hush," Conall murmured in her ear. The whisper of his voice and his breath on her ear, sent an inappropriate shiver across the nape of her neck. He was warm and solid.

And he had absolutely no reason to be here.

Not tonight.

Not *now*.

She scowled over her shoulder and when he didn't release her, she kicked back with her heel. Mostly because she was seized with the most bizarre urge to snuggle back against him. That wouldn't do. Kicking him was like kicking a horse. He barely moved, but at least his hand dropped away. "What are you doing?" she whispered hotly. She jerked out of his grasp and whirled to confront him. "You scared me half to death."

"This is an odd hour for you to be cataloguing exhibits, *Lady* Persephone."

She narrowed her eyes. "Odder still for you to be here at all, *Lord* Northwyck."

"I expect we're after the same thing."

"I doubt that." She couldn't take the canopic jar while he was here. She couldn't even look at it. She needed him to be any-where but here. He saw too much. "You ought to go, my lord."

"Looking to be rid of me, are you?" His expression was suddenly too complicated to read, and not because of the shadows falling across his face. His eyes glittered; there was a hunter's intensity there, but also disappointment? That hardly made sense. And it hardly mattered. She needed to get to the jar.

Conall did not budge.

Persephone huffed a sigh. "Can I help you with something?"

"You can tell me the truth." His tone was dark, dangerous.

She blinked. "All right."

He waited. She waited. Finally, she shook her head. "I don't understand this game, my lord."

"No, and I'm surprised you're playing it at all. I suppose it serves me right for thinking I understood you. Or any lady, come to that."

"Don't be tiresome."

"I beg your pardon?"

"You're not one of those men who are unkind or discourteous to women merely by token of them being women. It's dull. And not very clever."

His mouth twitched. "And you aren't who you appear to be either, are you?"

She was aware that he seemed to be having a different conversation than she was—especially when he suddenly stalked toward her. She backed up a step before her brain fully registered that her feet were moving. She would have stood her ground on principle, but he was already pushing against her, his hands closed tightly around her arms, until she was pressed against the nearest cabinet. The glass rattled. She nearly snapped at him to have a care for the artifacts, but something stopped her. He wasn't teasing. There was something in his expression that seemed suddenly more dangerous than any weapon he might have brandished.

"I'll ask you again. What are you doing here?"

Her mind raced to find some answer that might satisfy him, even as she vowed to speak to the duke about his autocratic godson. "I was merely testing the security of the exhibits," she said quickly. There. That was plausible. "Clearly, it needs work." She tilted her chin up. He was so close, crowding against her. "How did you get in?"

"Never mind that. I don't reward liars."

"I *beg* your pardon." She attempted to infuse the regal confidence of an Egyptian queen into her voice, the kind Cleopatra would have mastered. Her gaze fell over his right shoulder, to the window to the balcony. It was partially opened. "You didn't."

"Answer me, Persephone. *Now.*" There was a silky menace to his nearness. She'd never seen this Conall before. Heat tingled in her thighs. She was meant to be intimidated, frightened even. And she was. But she was something else too. Aware. Aroused?

He would never hurt a woman. He would never hurt *her*. The resulting thrill that licked up her spine was hot, languid.

How mortifying.

"I can't help you if you aren't honest with me," he insisted darkly.

"I don't need your help." She shook her head, confused. She sniffed discreetly. He didn't smell like he'd been drinking.

"You need my help more than you know." His mouth was so close to hers. His breath was warm against her cheek. She swallowed. He half-smiled. She wanted to ease back but there was nowhere to go.

"What are you doing?" she whispered.

"I don't know," he whispered back. "But I intend to enjoy it."

Her mind whirled; every part of her pulsed with awareness from her blood to her skin to the tips of her toes. His lips brushed the side of her mouth. His hands flattened against the wall on either side of her and his body pressed closer, closer. He was all heat and hard muscles. Her breath caught on an embarrassing gasp when he dragged his lips in an open-mouthed kiss along her cheekbone to her ear. His tongue lightly traced her earlobe, followed by a nip of with his teeth. Someone moaned. Worse and worse. She was gasping and moaning and in great danger of burning up from the inside.

And Conall wasn't.

He was methodical, determined, resolute.

She wanted him to feel what she was feeling. The craving, the rush of heat and disregard for anything but the feel of him under her palms. Was that the faintest inhalation, nearly a groan? He touched her as though it was the most important thing in the world. He nuzzled below her ear, along her throat. "Tell me who you're working with."

He wasn't the least bit overcome.

She was an idiot.

She shoved at his chest for all the good it did her. To wit: none at all. He didn't release her, didn't suddenly apologize for his rakish behavior. Although she wasn't sure if she wanted an apology for the kiss or for the fact that he didn't seem to mean it.

It was clearly in service of some other purpose. Honestly, she was a reasonably intelligent woman. Why was she surprised? Or a trifle hurt, even.

Conall made a sound of frustration and pushed her more firmly against the wall. His hand closed lightly around her throat, pinning her in place. The game had changed again. And she was equally lost. "Do you know what trouble you've got yourself into? Do you have any idea what they do traitors? Even earl's daughters? *Do you know what you've done?*"

She sucked in an offended breath. "I would never—." She cut herself off abruptly. Not her. Henry. This was about *Henry*.

She should have known. Handsome earls didn't dally with girls like her because they were interested.

Oh, honestly, Percy. Focus.

If he knew about treason, what else did he know? Was he searching for the letters? Was he hoping to condemn Henry for crimes he didn't commit? Would he even believe her if she told him? She had to get to the canopic jar first. Before he even thought to look for it. Her entire view was taken up by a frustrated male, all bare throat, linen shirt, muscular shoulders. If she squirmed just so she could see the corner of the cabinet where she had set up the jar. It ought to be on display, with a little handwritten note detailing its provenance. She hadn't mentioned it was a forgery, of course.

Conall stilled. Goosebumps prickled on her arms. He turned his head.

No, no, *no*.

She gripped his arm tightly with some vague notion of distracting him, of holding him back. Even though she knew perfectly well nothing could distract him. Certainly, not her.

"You seem rather preoccupied with this cabinet," he said softly.

"I'm not." She'd meant to say it calmly, like a sane person who didn't give a fig for the cabinet. Instead, she blurted it out so violently her words ran together.

"Did you know that peoples' gazes naturally find the thing most important to them? Particularly if they are trying to assure themselves that it is still where it ought to be."

Persephone swallowed. "Interesting. I'm sure I don't know why it would pertain to me."

"Let's test that theory, shall we?"

"Wouldn't you rather keep trying to seduce me?" There she was, blurting things out again. Honestly, you'd never guess that both her mother and her grandmothers had been the toasts of the *ton*, and not only as debutantes but also as married ladies.

Conall's eyes pinned her in place again. "More than you know," he said quietly. Something fluttered low in her belly. "But alas."

He let her go abruptly and crossed the floor in long, determined strides. She darted after him. She had to get to the letter before he did. Conall perused the shelf of artifacts, the scarab beetles, the blue faience statue. She made a tiny, tiny sound in the back of her throat when his hand closed around the canopic jar. She tried not to, and it was barely loud enough to rival a mouse. But of course, he heard her, infuriating man. He quirked an eyebrow at her. She refused to give him the satisfaction of reacting any further.

Until he lifted the jackal-headed lid of the sandstone container.

And there was nothing inside.

Not shrivelled ancient intestines dried in natron salt, not the fine linen that would have been wrapped around them, not dust.

And not a letter, either.

"Give me that!" she cried out, fury and fear overriding her good sense. He stumbled back a step when she burst like a firecracker exponentially more enraged than when he'd kissed her. "Where is it? What did you do with it?" She turned an accusing eye on him. "*What did you do with it?*"

"Do with what?"

"This time, you'll answer *me*," she flashed, grabbing the jar. It was still empty. She shook it helplessly. "I need the contents of this jar, Lord Northwyck."

"Do you indeed?" He stalked toward her. "*Why?*"

"History," she said.

"Try again." He didn't believe her. Fair enough, she wouldn't have believed her either.

"It's not your concern," she tried instead.

"Oh, I think it is. Treason is very much my concern."

"I'm not a traitor, for Heaven's sake."

There was a sharp, heavy pause. "But you seek to protect one?"

"*No.*"

His demeanor changed. He was just as sharp, just as dangerous, but she felt less like he might turn into a dagger at her throat. Someone else's throat, definitely. "You know who he is."

What she knew was that Henry's letter was *missing*. How had they found it? Who had known to look for it? And had they destroyed it?

Of course, they'd destroyed it.

Aside from Henry and herself, only the actual traitor knew about it. Despair and determination warred within her. She wouldn't let Henry be a scapegoat. She would find the next letter. Somehow.

And before Conall could.

Again, *somehow.* As plans went, it hardly inspired. But surely resolve counted for something. Because as much as Conall suspected her involvement, it was clear he was even more involved. But it was far less clear which side he was on. She couldn't countenance him as a traitor. Perhaps he served the Crown and the War Office. And not to sound like the traitor he'd accused her of being, but damn both the Crown and the War Office if all they wanted was a scapegoat instead of the truth.

"You have to tell me who he is, Persephone," Conall pressed.

He wouldn't believe her, or Henry more to the point. She wasn't going to let Henry hang. He might be a peer, but even peers were punished for treason. She had to get out here. She had to *think.* But Conall was unlikely to let her walk out of here.

"I'll protect you," he promised. She had no doubt he *would* protect *her.* But she wasn't the one in need of protecting. Being rescued, at present, would be nice. She'd have to do it herself. She hit the heel of her boot three times on the floor, loudly.

Conall frowned. "What in the devil?"

Heavy footsteps thudded up the steps and the footman burst in. "Hey, now! Who's there?"

"You little…" Conall muttered.

"Joseph," Persephone called out.

Joseph paused, confused. "Lady Persephone?"

She sailed toward him, out of Conall's reach. He made a sound suspiciously like a growl. "Yes, I came to see how well we had secured the exhibits."

"Oh." He deflated, realizing she and another gentleman currently occupied the locked room he was meant to protect. "I only stepped out to reliev—that is, I was only gone a moment."

"Yes, of course. We will need at least one more footman, I think," she replied briskly, as if her heart wasn't racing. As if Conall wasn't moving in the shadows behind her. "Lord Northwyck came in from the back window. Someone will have to be posted there as well, I should think."

Joseph gulped. "Yes, my lady."

"Have you seen anyone else?" she asked, watching him as carefully as Conall had watched her. "Anyone at all?"

"No, my lady."

Irritation hummed through her at being denied her prey. A feeling she had every intention of sharing with Conall. He would not have his quarry this night. "The duke sent you with the cart, I presume?" she asked Joseph. He nodded. "Oh, good. Because I do feel rather…faint."

She'd never fainted before. Was she supposed to go rigid and tip over? She didn't want to hit her head. And he might need Conall's help carrying her down the stairs which would defeat the purpose. Better to droop, like a tulip in a dry vase. She fluttered her eyelashes, feeling foolish. Joseph darted forward to help support her. "I'll take you home straightaway, my lady."

"Thank you." She only just remembered to take her voice breathy, instead of the usual brisk tone her Grandmaman scolded her over. She shot Conall a glance over her shoulder. "I am certain Lord Northwyck would be more than willing to stay with the exhibit until your return. Just to be safe."

He watched her, frustrated, but also reluctantly faintly amused, as though she'd impressed him despite himself. "Of course."

PERSEPHONE SLID FROM the cart before Joseph could clamber down to help her. The birds were starting to sing in the hedgerows and the light had changed, turning misty and pink. "Thank you, I'm much better!" she announced.

"Shall I see you to the door?"

"No need," she assured him, "And Lord Northwyck is waiting for you."

"If you're sure, my lady."

She nodded and stood there smiling politely like a ninny until he finally drove the cart away, the horse nickering softly. She hoped no one had heard the clomp of hooves or squeaking of wooden wheels. She would be sunk if the butler opened the front door and found her there. Pretending to take a morning walk in the gardens was one thing, being escorted home in a pony cart was another.

She went round the side of the house and the dew was chilly as it soaked into the hem of her dress. She eased through the prickly rose bushes and back through the window she'd left open. She would murder for a cup of tea, but she knew that Conall would hurry back as soon as he could and would demand to speak to her if she wasn't already safely ensconced in her chamber. No tea and none of the crumpets she could smell baking. The kitchen staff was well into their work with the sun easing above the horizon.

She darted upstairs and closed her door softly behind her. She couldn't avoid him forever, but she'd take a few hours to sort through her thoughts. She couldn't ignore the feelings he'd stirred in her either: desire, need, and an unfurling heat she had never felt before, even during her ruination. She might not be able to ignore them, but it didn't mean she had to give them credence. Or feed them in any way. Even if she could still recall the feel of his warm hands on her. And might always.

She certainly still recalled the duke's house being haunted by his violin. The music trailed from room to room, down the long hallways, sneaking into corners. But mostly he liked to play in the bluebell woods with birds and caterpillars for an audience. He'd been shy, calm. She still didn't entirely understand the Conall who danced a waltz and flirted over champagne flutes. The Conall who stood in the darkness of an abandoned assembly hall with burning. The one from this morning was a new version altogether.

She watched him now stride up the laneway, white gravel crunching under his boots. His hands were in his pockets, his brow furrowed, his dark hair tumbling over one eye. He was already unfairly beautiful and the way he moved was unlike any other gentleman she had ever known; he didn't take small steps, didn't let his posture droop as though he were a delicate flower full of ennui. And he didn't stomp to show his strength. Everything about him was leashed, graceful, dangerous.

He looked up then, and it was as if he could see her there, watching him. She stepped back, a warm shiver dancing up her thighs. She heard the front door open and not long after, his footsteps approaching down the hall. She held her breath. For some reason, she had to fight the urge to wrench the door open. She tucked her hands behind her.

His steps paused outside her door, and then finally, finally, he walked away.

If she was warm, it was only because she was overtired.

Overset.

She'd suffered a setback and then been accosted in the dark gallery, after all.

Deliciously accosted.

Percy, stop it.

Overset. That was it. Clearly.

Never mind that she had never been overset a day in her life.

PERSEPHONE'S GRANDMOTHER CAST a critical eye over her as they descended to breakfast. "That shade of blue is not all the thing, Percy," she said. "You need an under-eye treatment. A lemon and egg white mixture perhaps."

"I woke too early, that's all," Persephone replied, fighting a twinge of vanity. What did she care if she didn't look her best? The house party didn't care and Conall was clearly using her company to some other purpose.

Only Henry mattered.

She had every intention of heading straight back to the Druid's Sickle assembly hall to sort through the crates and then onto the duke's, but her grandmother accosted her on the lading and would not be gainsaid. As skipping breakfast would only slow her down when hunger befuddled her, Persephone allowed herself to be dragged along. Holly met them at the bottom of the stairs, her cheeks red. Raspberry jam was smeared over the neckline of her white dress.

"Oh dear," Lady Blackwell tutted. "Never mind, dear. Your maid will be able to get that out before the stain sets."

Holly nodded miserably. "Pardon me." She rushed up the steps as though she were on fire instead of only slightly gummy.

"Here," Her Grandmaman said, glancing at Persephone and pulling a chartreuse velvet rose from her dog's collar. Nestled comfortably in her arms, he barely bothered to open an eye. "This will distract the eye and Chartreuse has not chewed this one yet." She shoved the flower into Persephone's cleavage. It tickled atrociously. Not to mention that it looked like a squashed moldering cabbage. That colour was not flattering on anyone, human or canine.

"It will certainly distract," she allowed. She would have preferred Holly's smear of raspberry jam. Her stomach growled.

"Goodness," her grandmother remarked. "Quickly to the crumpets."

Breakfast had been laid out on the terrace in order to enjoy the fine weather. The gentleman had returned from time in the excavation pits, for which Persephone felt a twinge of acid envy. Priorities, she reminded herself. She'd give up all of her time digging in barrows if it meant saving her friend's life.

Tables were set up against the house, to shade the platters and plates heaped high with food. The Culpeppers kept an old-fashioned breakfast table, with coddled eggs, fried kippers and kidneys, chops with greens and a bakery's worth of baked goods from brioches to biscuits to bread. An army of jarred preserve, apricot, plum, quince, raspberry, and strawberry shared space with three types of honey and herbed butter. Persephone helped herself to toasted bread with nutmeg and butter, eggs, a slice of pound cake and a cup of chocolate. She needed fortification.

She couldn't help but think on what the ancient Egyptians might have eaten for breakfast, likely dark bread with leeks and onions, figs, dates, and beer. Her grandmother jostled her with an elbow. "Pay attention, darling," she murmured before taking her seat to let a footman serve her. "You can't hide in the shadows forever."

In point of fact, she could. It wasn't so bad. For one thing, she wouldn't have to share her pot of chocolate. She turned with a sigh. Lurking wasn't all the thing, not on the Culpepper terrace. The guests drank their tea and ate their food, silver cutlery flashing. There was an empty seat next to Lady Louisa, who would stiffen her spine and sniff as if Persephone's reputation was catching.

Or she could sit next to Conall.

She was surprised at the thrill of anticipation and the tiniest bit of fear. The way he was looking at her was not genteel, not mild. He was angry that she had escaped him last night, that much was obvious. But why was he staring so directly at her, dark eyebrows slashed down in warning. And why was he lunging from his chair, right at her?

Really, that was too much.

Someone shouted. Everything seemed both too fast, and too slow, as though she were moving through honey. An egg slid off Sir Barton's spoon with a plop, his eyes comically wide. Lord Fairweather was on his feet. Her grandmother was strangely pale. Chartreuse barked once, piercingly. There was a sound, like stone grinding on stone. Persephone couldn't place it.

And then Conall reached her, shoving her against the wall and pressing his entire body against her. Her breath caught in her throat as the world whirled around her.

A huge urn, easily as tall as she was, crashed from a third-floor balcony, shattering into sharp shards.

The flagstone cracked. A pot of tea tipped over, splattering the white cloths. Conall caught her stunned gaze. "Are you hurt?" When she only blinked at him, registering the confused and frantic babbling around them, he repeated the question. "Persephone, are you hurt?"

She finally shook her head, taking inventory of herself. A bruise on her elbow perhaps, a few cuts on her leg from the shards. Nothing, all told. "You saved me." She realized he was still covering her and shifted. He stepped back, reluctantly. His hands curved around her shoulders, warm and steady, as he looked her over. He scowled, noting the blood on the hem of her skirts. "Get the doctor," he snapped at a nearby footman, shaking like jelly. "*At once.*"

"It's nothing," she assured him. Chartreuse was barking in earnest now. "A scrape or two." She stared at the broken urn, the mess of stone and dust and spilled tea. It would have crushed her if Conall hadn't been so quick. She swallowed, feeling odd.

"Percy!" Her grandmother was trying to stand up, but she was flustered, too pale.

"I'm all right, Grandmaman," Persephone called out, making her tone as cheerful as she could, under the circumstances. She turned to Conall. "Are *you* well?" She could see a rip in his sleeve. "Your coat!"

He shrugged. "I have more coats."

"I was more concerned with the bruises underneath," she pointed out, drily as the others converged upon them. Someone was chattering hysterically. Several ladies clutched at Conall, running their hands down his arms and over his shoulders to see if he was hurt.

Conall ignored them, meeting the eyes of the stunned butler over their heads. "Secure the room and the balcony where the urn came from. No one goes in or out but myself."

Lady Culpepper fanned herself violently, the lace trimmings flying with enough speed to do her eyes permanent damage if she flicked her wrist any harder. "An accident," she said. "I'll have the responsible maid or footman turned out immediately."

"I should like to speak to them first," Conall said darkly. "I don't take kindly to an accident that might well have killed my fiancée."

Chapter Seven

PERSEPHONE WAS REASONABLY certain that another urn was not currently falling from the sky, but it rather felt like it might be.

Time stopped again. Everything went slow and treacly, and the expressions of the people gathered around her were just as shocked. Possibly, more so. She was known for getting into scrapes but rather less well known for catching the attention of a gentleman. Especially an earl. She blinked at Conall. She ought to say something, but he narrowed his eyes at her warningly and anyway she had no idea at all of what one said to celebrate one's fraudulent engagement. After being nearly crushed by garden pottery.

"Oh, Percy," her grandmother sighed. "I'm so happy you've made your announcement. As if there could be any doubt after that romantic kiss under the fireworks."

She might look like an oddly decorated confection, but her grandmother was still sharp as she'd ever been. "Northwyck, do take her inside." She winked at the astounded guests. "There are enough windows in the drawing room there that you shan't need a chaperone. I've my tea to finish."

Conall bowed, reluctant amusement behind his eyes. "As you say, Lady Blackwell." His amusement dropped like an anvil when he looked at the butler. "Gather the servants, I'll interview them first"

"My lord." The butler scurried away.

"First?" Lady Culpepper echoed, trying to decide if the unfolding drama would enhance her house party or detract from it. "You can't mean to interrogate my guests!"

"I merely wish to ascertain what I can," Conall assured her smoothly. "There's many a sharp eye here."

"Hmph."

"I'm sure Lord Northwyck is being overly cautious," Persephone rushed in. He had no idea how miserable they could make his life if these people were peeved, earl or not. "'Twas an accident."

Conall's smile had more in common with the curve of a scimitar than any expression of gentility. Persephone curtsied for the both of them. Her knee twinged as she hobbled back toward the house. She was fairly certain she could not tolerate another minute of everyone staring at her with their mouths open and their brains chasing the best way to tell the story, without screaming. Conall's hand slipped under her elbow, supporting her. "Let me call for the doctor."

"It's not necessary. It's my knee again. I'll be fine once I sit down a bit."

"And the shock. Tea?"

"Thank you."

"And brandy?"

"Better and better."

He led her into the blue drawing room, where everything was the colour of blue Wedgewood pottery. She'd read about blue scarab beetles of a similar shade and hoped to see one in the crates awaiting unpacking. She really must get to it. But her knee, under the achiness, felt a little like jelly. She'd take a moment to catch her breath. "I promise I am not usually this exciting."

"I find that hard to believe." He handed her a glass of brandy after having pulled the bell for the tea cart. He crouched in front of her. His eyes were clear as glass and just as sharp. He fairly thrummed with energy, with contained fury. She knew then and there that he could be as deadly as any scorpion, despite his reputation for carousing. But with her he was gentle, careful.

Even when a few hours ago he'd been angry with her and was likely still. "Are you sure you're well?"

She nodded, taking the smallest sip. "You saved my life." She touched his arm. "Thank you." She noticed her fingers were shaking, and then her teeth. How odd.

"You're in shock," Conall murmured, helping her steady her glass and tipping it up to her mouth. "Have another sip, it will help."

"I'm fine," she chattered. "Barely a scratch on me." She took another swallow of brandy, this time a proper mouthful. She hissed at the fiery sweetness but the warmth that spread into her ribcage was soothing.

"You are indomitable," Conall said.

"For someone who falls in holes and off balconies."

His brows lowered. "Yes, about that." He searched her face. "Have another sip, first."

"Are you trying to get me soused?"

"If only it were that simple."

She made a face at him but took a last drink. "I'd rather have a crumpet. I never got my breakfast."

His smile was quick but blinding. She might have thought she'd imagined it. "My god, what a woman."

"Because I'm hungry?"

"Because you're you."

The warmth that spread through her had nothing to do with spirits.

"I'll have them bring you as many crumpets as you'd like. But first, do you remember who was nearby when you fell over the balcony?"

She shook her head. "There was a bit of a crowd, guests, servants." She paused. "You don't think it was an accident."

"Once is an accident," he said grimly. "Twice is something else altogether."

"But who would—?" she cut herself off. Although she wanted to believe he was over-reacting and being overly cautious, she had to wonder herself. Treason was a powerful motive, and a dangerous transgression to hide. Such a person would stoop to any means to protect themselves. And it was not a secret that she and Henry had grown up close as siblings. It would be a reasonable assumption to think she knew more than she did. Henry had never disclosed the name, he'd want to protect her as much as she meant to protect him.

"I can see it in your face, Persephone," Conall said quietly. "You know something. And I can't protect you if you don't tell me what it is."

"It's not your duty to protect me." But oh, how she wanted to lean into him. "And if you're right, it would only put you in danger."

"I can look after myself."

"As can I." Probably.

"How about we look after each other then?"

There was no question she needed help. She couldn't dodge garden urns and learn to fly in case she was shoved off a higher balcony all while doing the work that needed doing. No one else was half so good at spotting a forgery. Henry needed her. And she wanted to trust Conall, despite having no specific evidence that she should. Well, other than the fact that he *had* saved her life.

He waited patiently though she could see that it cost him. He wanted to be hunting, cornering his prey. Her prey. She did need him. And he didn't know it yet, but he needed her too. He'd never find the forgeries without her. Not half so fast.

Still.

She hesitated. Not just for Henry's sake, but for Conall's. An earl searching for a suitable wife was hardly prepared for treason. Not that he was prepared for finding a wife either, since he had declared he had already found one.

She was betrothed.

"We'll have to call it off, of course," she blurted out.

"I beg your pardon?"

"The betrothal. I don't know why you said it in the first place. You must have been addled from the accident."

"I am not addled," he said, very deliberately. "But I can keep safe you much better with the protection of my name and my house."

"But… you were looking for a wife."

"One crisis at a time, Percy."

It was the way he said her name that decided her. Gentle, frustrated, a tiny bit desperate.

"I shall cry off as soon as this business is done," she declared, ignoring the small flicker of *something* in her belly at the thought. "Your reputation will survive, you are an earl, after all."

"And yours?"

She waved that away. "That ship sailed a long time ago." Her hand dropped, fingers twisting together.

He smoothed his fingertips over her strained knuckles. "Tell me, Percy."

"Are you really sure you want to know?"

"I need to know."

"I suppose you *were* in the war." There was a flare in his eyes, like a hound finally at the mouth of the rabbit burrow. She swallowed. "It's about Henry Talbot."

He exhaled. "Is it?"

"He's being set up as a scapegoat for treason."

"You mean he's not the traitor?"

"Of course, he's not!" she declared hotly. "This is why I didn't want—. Wait." Her eyes widened. "How do you know there's a traitor in the first place?"

"It's why I'm in Little Barrow."

She narrowed her eyes. "You're not hunting for a wife at all, are you?"

"No."

"Oh." She sat back, mind whirling. There was too much to sort through, like a barrow filled with broken beads. She needed to put the pieces together. "Did the War Office send you?"

"In a manner of speaking."

"And they think Henry is a traitor?" She was offended all over again. And scared. Desperately scared for her friend.

"Henry's name has not yet come up."

Relief hit her like the brandy. She felt light-headed. "Thank God for that at least."

"Tell me what you know."

"You must promise not to accuse Henry."

He stood. "I can only promise to see justice brought to a traitor."

She eyed him carefully. He looked stern, aloof, holding back the ferocity inside. She nodded once. "As Henry is not the traitor, I accept those terms."

The corner of his mouth quirked.

She told him what she knew, about Henry's letters, the forgeries, the fact that he was still not home and ought to have docked with the other members of his party. Conall listened intently, without interrupting. "I'd like to see the letter he sent you."

Persephone nodded. "Certainly. She glanced over his shoulder where Lady Louisa loitered at the window, her nose practically pressed to the glass. "Never mind the traitor, I suspect there is a line-up of debutantes waiting to do me in."

"No one is going to do you in." He sounded very sure. She decided to believe him. It made the fear prickling through her limbs abate somewhat.

"You don't know debutantes and their mothers."

"I do actually."

She snorted. "You think you do. You've only seen their society masks. They've been told to be pleasant in order to find a husband. Without one they've no recourse to make money of their own, even if they had some kind of skill beyond a country dance and could legally control their own funds. And once their fathers pop off, they've nowhere to live, each to a one." She shook her head. "And so many men lost to Napoleon on top of that."

"The men of England are currently outnumbered; I'll grant you that."

"It makes it all so much more frantic. It might look like a pretty game, all that flouncing and curtsying, but you don't know the kind of desperation underneath."

"I suppose not." He raises a brow. "Not that I am not sympathetic, but I am much more concerned with the traitor's desperation at the moment."

"Right. Stand right there," she said. "Don't move."

He did as she asked, only quirked an eyebrow. She turned her back to him.

"I can't imagine what you're doing now." He sounded amused, despite himself.

"Good." She slipped her fingers under the edge of her bodice and her stays. She could just reach Henry's letter, tucked against her skin for safekeeping. She wriggled slightly. Conall made a strangled sound in his throat. She wriggled again, held her breath and success! The edge of the paper was soft from being folded inside her dress. She turned, smiling. "You did say you wanted to read Henry's letter."

Conall blinked at her. He was at a loss for words that even snatching her out of midair or saving her from falling urns hadn't managed to accomplish. He took the letter from her, and she was suddenly acutely aware that it was warm from her body heat. From being tucked between her breasts. She absolutely refused to blush. Ladies who hunted down traitors with handsome accomplices did not blush. "I had to be sure it would be safe," she explained.

"I see." He didn't sound dignified or amused any longer. She liked the slight catch in his voice, making it faintly hoarse. He skimmed the letter. "May I keep this?"

She didn't want to let it go but she'd already made a copy of it. It was currently tucked in her shoe. One couldn't be too careful. He didn't have to know about it. "I suppose."

"Thank you, Persephone." That intensity was burning in him again. "You've helped me and the War Office more than half the men I know."

She might have preened a tiny bit. Recognition and admiration were not often offered in her direction.

"Have your maid pack your things," he added. "You'll be Pendleton's guest. No one will attack you in a duke's house." He paused. "But I'll hire more footmen. I've a few in mind who can travel down from London on the next stagecoach."

"I couldn't impose."

"It's not an imposition. Nor is it a request."

"You do have a dictatorial streak, don't you?"

"It's been said," he murmured. "And of you, as well, so this should prove interesting." He didn't look displeased about it. "We shall have a betrothal supper, to cement our alliance. I want word to get out."

"I don't like lying to the duke. And anyway, if I *am* in danger—"

"You are. You can't pretend otherwise. You were attacked twice, and your hermitage was tossed."

Fury simmered again, instantly sparked at the thought of her broken artifacts. "If that's true, then I am most certainly not leaving my grandmother unattended. Or bringing that kind of hazard to the duke's doorstep. The man is seventy-two."

"I wish I could say no one would think of harming your grandmother, but I can't be sure. I've seen the result of this traitor's selfishness." His jaw clenched. It was a visible effort for him to unclench it to speak again. "Your grandmother will also come to the estate. There's a festival, after all, a string of house parties, and a betrothal to celebrate. No one will think on it. And the duke is well protected. Not to mention that your grandmother's dog is possibly the best protection there is."

"Chartreuse?" Persephone said doubtfully. "She's a spaniel obsessed with cheese."

"But she will alert any footmen I station near your grandmother should anything go amiss."

She relaxed slightly. Chartreuse was not shy about using her voice. "That's true."

Have you told Henry's father?"

"Definitely not."

"Why is that?"

She hesitated, realized there was no point in keeping it from him. It was common knowledge, after all. "The earl is not a...sympathetic man."

He raised an eyebrow. "Not even when it involves his only son and heir?"

"Especially then."

"I see. I do remember something about that, now that you

mention it."

"I once filled all of his snuffboxes with pepper," she confessed. It was after Henry had sprained his wrist "falling" from a tree. She'd never been so angry and so filled with vengeance, even at thirteen.

Conall flashed her that grin, the one that made her belly tingle. "Remind me never to get on your bad side."

"I've never seen anyone turn that shade of red, not before and not since." She probably ought not to find such satisfaction in it, all these years later. But she did, there was no denying it. She'd do it again.

"Pack your things," Conall said. "We'll go as soon as possible, and I won't be leaving your side until then."

"They'll never believe us, you know."

He raised his chin. "And why not?"

"Earls do not marry ladies like me, Conall. You know it was well as I do."

"Ladies like you?"

She rolled her eyes. "You cannot pretend to not know that I am ruined."

"Gossip." He dismissed it.

"And yet."

"I won't have anyone denigrating you," he said. "Not even you."

She smiled at him. She had to.

"What?" he asked.

"You're really rather sweet, aren't you?"

"Leave off."

She was almost certain his ears were turning red. Adorable.

Conall caught sight of Lady Louisa, still spying through the glass. Holly had joined her, in her new dress, sans raspberry jam. "Well then, we'll have to be convincing, won't we?"

Conall raised her hand to his lips. She wasn't wearing gloves as she'd been about to eat breakfast. His mouth was warm, barely grazing her skin. Goosebumps snuck up her arm. He looked up at her and she felt his faint smirk against her knuckles. He knew exactly was he was doing.

She snatched her hand back, fighting a blush. "I believe you promised me crumpets, sir."

"I believe I did." He offered his arm. "A feast before battle is traditional, after all."

As her skin tingled, she hoped not to have to battle herself alongside the real enemy.

If goosebumps could have laughed, they would have laughed right at her.

Loudly.

THE LAST TIME Persephone had been on the roof of the Culpepper country house was when she was eleven and Henry was ten. They had evaded his tutor and a battalion of nursemaids in order to hang over the balustrade and throw raisins down on the guests arriving for a winter ball. They'd managed to elude capture until a raisin had struck an elderly man in the eye. He'd been so incensed he'd hit the guest standing next to him with his cane. That man had landed in a pile of snow, shrieking. At the time it had been entirely worth the scolding.

"The terrace is over here," Persephone said, leading Conall to the scrolled stone edge. "I didn't even know Lady Culpepper kept pots up here. Only Henry and I ever bothered to climb all those stairs on a regular basis."

Conall walked to the edge and looked down. "None of the balconies line up right so it has to have been from here. It's quite a distance." His jaw hardened as he noted the angle of the roof and the terrace below. "This was no jest. Nor an accident, not with the weight of the urn. It wasn't windy enough by far and I've never heard of a squirrel big enough to move something like that."

Persephone stepped up beside him, looking over the edge. She had just enough time to take in the guests still eating their breakfasts, the footmen carting away shards of clay and clumps of potted dirt before vertigo gripped her. Her knees went watery, her stomach wobbled. Conall's big hand caught her around the waist. "I've got you."

She wanted to lean into the heat of him, the strength of his arms. She didn't allow herself to give in. It would set a bad precedent. And if he grew concerned that she might forget their engagement was a sham, the humiliation would do her in far more effectively than any traitor. Never mind the urn, she'd jump.

"This seems like an awful lot of trouble," she said, dubiously instead. "To create an accident that doesn't look terribly accidental after even the briefest investigation."

"As you can see, no one else is investigating."

"True." She turned her head. "That's the other reason you announced our engagement," she accused. "You want to draw the fire onto yourself."

He didn't look sorry in the least. "The traitor might be getting desperate.

She swallowed. "I gather that's not a good thing."

"It might well be," Conall said. "It could mean we're closer than we think."

"Closer to a murderer," Persephone said blandly. "Splendid."

IT TOOK AGES to get out of the Culpepper manor house and ages more to be settled into Pendleton House.

First, Persephone had to navigate a swath of entirely insincere congratulations. Had the engagement announcement been made earlier, she would not have put it past some of the mothers to have pushed the urn onto her. Conall was in high demand and she was…not. The whole thing was ridiculous. She gave it hours before it fell apart all around them. She'd have to put every moment of those hours to good use.

First, she helped her grandmother pack while Conall stood in the hallway and interrogated everyone he could get his hands on. He wouldn't let her out of his sight. Lady Culpepper was both affronted and pleased to have such drama at her house party. Her grandmother was proud as punch. "Why, Percy, you sly thing," she teased as Sarah hurried to fold dresses into trunks lined with lavender bundles. "You only asked about Northwyck a couple of days ago."

Persephone caught Conall's eye when he turned to glance at

her through the doorway. An eyebrow raised. As if the man's ego needed to know she'd been asking about him.

She turned to her grandmother and forced a smile. She wasn't sure if she ought to lie to her about the betrothal. It would go easier on her when the inevitable parting came to be, but if Conall was right, she might be in danger. She wouldn't trade Henry's safety for her grandmother, nor the other way around. She'd just have to save them both.

And her grandmother would worry. She'd make herself ill over it. Add to that, she would do the cause more good if she truly believed Persephone and Conall were going to be married. She would chatter and plan and generally fuss, drawing attention away from more serious matters. It was settled, then, Persephone told her uncertain belly. She pressed a hand to it, trying to calm her nerves.

"We'll have to go home first," her grandmother was saying. "I haven't packed for a visit with a duke."

Conall shook his head slightly. The footman he had been interviewing scurried away, eyes glistening suspiciously. Persephone returned his forbidding expression with one of her own. He couldn't go around making the household staff cry. The lot of them had enough to be getting on with, between the party and Lady Culpepper being, well, Lady Culpepper.

"I believe the duke is expecting us, Grandmaman," Persephone turned back to her grandmother. "We can send Sarah to gather the rest of your belongings."

"I suppose you're right." She turned to Sarah, narrowing one eye. "Mind you bring the pink satin."

Sarah's shoulders drooped slightly. It was difficult to get a name for yourself as a lady's maid when your lady's favorite ballgown made her look like a frilly grapefruit. But a happy grapefruit. Sarah curtsied. "Yes, your ladyship."

After that they took their leave of the party, endured another round of sympathy and felicitations, and climbed into the pony cart as Lady Blackwell flatly refused to ride inside a carriage unless there was rain or ice or the four horsemen of the apocalypse on the horizon. The very near horizon.

The duke welcomed them with surprise but true happiness, making Persephone feel guilty all over again. Grandmaman went to lie down, and Persephone hovered until she threatened to throw a shoe at her granddaughter. When Conall sent a footman to stand guard outside the door, Persephone finally allowed herself to leave.

She stole a moment to herself in her guest chamber. It was decorated in shades of plum and pink, with silk paper on the walls and peonies and grapes painted over the ceiling. There were roses on every table, offset with mint to freshen the air. A maid had already unpacked her dresses and was working on her dancing slippers. Persephone felt her smile slip its mooring, but she forced it back in place. "I can manage from here, thank you." She paused.

"Bethany, my lady," the maid supplied helpfully.

"Bethany, thank you."

"Yes, my lady. Would you like a tray? Tea?"

"No, thank you."

"I can have a bath drawn."

She swallowed. "No, thank you. I just need a moment." Her voice was tighter than she'd have liked, but still not as strained as she'd feared. Bethany finally curtsied and left the room.

Persephone sank onto the edge of the bed and gave into the tremors that had been gathering in her hands and shoulders. She'd have liked another sip of Conall's brandy but never mind. She only had a moment to get a hold of herself. She wasn't entirely sure how one was supposed to feel after escaping death and being launched into a make-believe engagement with a man one found entirely too tempting. Usually, she'd have talked to Henry about it. They'd have found a way to make light of it, somehow; they always did.

She didn't think Conall would approve if she told the Cinderellas the truth, either. More pressing, it might not be safe. She struggled to slow her breathing. Being overset was perfectly reasonable under the circumstances but it would incite more questions, more stares, more *attention*. She took a long deep breath, then another. The trembling in her fingers eased. Mostly.

The knock at the door undid it all. She yelped with a sudden jump that was not only undignified but also violent enough to topple her onto the floor.

"Persephone Blackwell," Tamsin announced from the doorway. "You are a sneak." She tilted her head. "What are you doing on the ground?"

"Nothing." She scrambled to her feet as Meg followed Tamsin inside.

Tamsin closed the door firmly. "Tell us everything," she demanded. "Immediately."

"There's nothing to tell."

"Liar."

Meg pinched her. "Give her a chance."

"Where's Priya?"

"She's cornered her brother," Tamsyn replied. "Don't think you're not next. She hates when she's not in on a secret."

"It wasn't a secret."

Tamsin scoffed. "You pretended not to know he cared for you."

"It's not…." She desperately wanted to tell them the truth. "I wasn't sure, that's all."

Meg reached out to squeeze her hand. "Well, clearly there's nothing to worry about."

"And everything to celebrate!" Tamsin pulled a small bottle of brandy out of her reticule and a box of decorated chocolates. "I'm not sure I'd care to be married to someone so pretty, to be honest, but if you wish it then I'm happy for you." She poured brandy into crystal glasses waiting on a tray by the door. "And even happier for him. He's the lucky one."

Persephone felt better after minutes with her friends. She couldn't repay that by putting them in danger. She toasted them with the kind of smile she hoped a newly engaged woman might make.

One not up to her ears in intrigue.

Meg raised her glass. "To the Cinderella Society!"

THE DRUID'S SICKLE was a comforting cacophony of voices,

hammers hammering, crates dragging to and fro. Dust hovered in the air. It was a better balm than any warm bath or the lavender sachets her grandmother insisted calmed the nerves. They made Persephone sneeze. Though after a night of strange dreams where she dug through raspberry bushes until her arms bled from the thorns, a lavender sachet might not be a bad idea.

The cabinets and shelves had been thoroughly cleaned and the glass doors set with sturdy locks. There were glass beads, chipped arrowheads made of obsidian from South America, a blue faience lotus cup from Egypt, a carving of a nymph from Rome. The collection grew hourly. It sat waiting for her, like an old friend with stories to tell.

She consulted her notebook, bristling with notes and careful lists of each artifact on loan. Everything seemed to be in order.

"What's this piece about?" Conall asked, stopping in front of a stone mask of a face with horns and crowned with leaves and grapes. His beard was all intricate loops and curls. "He looks cheerful, if a little manic."

"Dionysus," Persephone explained. "The god of wine and madness. So, you're not wrong."

"How can you tell?"

"By the grapes and the horns. And here, that little pinecone. It's called a thyrsus."

"And this rather impressive thing?"

Conall pointed to a gold lozenge far bigger than her hand, glimmering with secrets. Lines etched on the surface, echoing the lozenge shape.

"That was found At Bush Barrow near Stonehenge only a couple of years ago by Sir Richard Hoare," she replied. Her voice took on an awed tone, as though she were in a church. She couldn't help herself. "It was in a barrow grave, with a belt buckle and several daggers. But we only have the gold plate on loan. It's Bronze Age. Not quite as old as the Egyptian pyramids, though Stonehenge is older. Can you imagine what it was like to build them?"

"The Pyramids?"

"That too, but I meant Stonehenge. They used mostly stone

and wood tools, I reckon. Maybe some antlers." They would have eaten fish from the nearby river Avon, berries, birds. Their diet might not have been so very different from a farmer's diet in the same place today.

"You've gone away again."

She winced. "I apologize."

"Don't." Conall glanced at her, noticing the softening of her shoulders. He was good at noticing things. "Better?"

She nodded once. "Better."

She knew he had encouraged her to prattle on in order to calm her. As ever, a moment lost in the wilds of history had done her immeasurable good. She tapped her lists. "We'll start here."

"I had no idea you were so terrifyingly organized."

"These items are priceless," she reminded him sternly. "And they were entrusted into our keeping."

"Do you have a list of the guests who have passed through the Culpepper house this week?"

"I can have one by dinner time."

"Yes, I believe you can."

She felt better able to concentrate on the exhibit, with her brain no longer circling like a rabid ferret. Her grandmother was safe. She had help clearing Henry's name. A large garden urn had not, indeed, fallen on her head. All in all, it was in hand.

She noted the first cabinet on the left, checking off each item from her list. She had already inspected them and knew them to be authentic. Nothing to help Henry there, though plenty to help the festival. "Can you tell a forgery at a glance?" Conall asked.

"Sometimes. Certainly, upon careful examination." She lifted her chin, too accustomed to this particular conversation. There was a reason she helped the British Museum anonymously. "I'm very good at what I do."

"I'm not doubting you."

A refreshing change, that.

After an hour's work she had sorted through what felt like bushels of faience beads. She stopped in front of a painted pottery urn with traces of gilt put together so clumsily it made her back teeth hurt. Not a forgery but an affront all the same. She plucked it off the shelf with care. "Honestly, why bother at all if you're going to make such a muck of it," she muttered.

She glanced inside for good measure, just in case. Nothing. Well, not nothing. There were gloppy dried bits of glue.

"That bad?" Conall asked, amused.

"Worse. I could hamstring the—." She stopped abruptly.

A piece of white marble had caught her. It was new.

And Egyptian.

Conall followed her gaze. "Found something?" he asked quietly.

"That wasn't here yesterday," she murmured, glancing over her shoulder to see if anyone was paying attention. John stood alert by the door and the other workmen were occupied taking apart an empty crate.

The artifact was skillfully carved into the shape of a duck, with its head turned to look over its back. Ducklings and leaves were scattered over her, and her feet were cleverly tucked to the side to give the whole piece more stability. There was a large crack over the top end, nearest to her neck where a lid slid open to reveal the concave belly. It would have held cream or ointment at one point and nothing at all now.

Persephone shook her head. "It's empty." She ran a finger over it, and then turned it over as carefully as if she'd been lifting a baby. "It's Roman Egypt, not the usual subject matter," she explained. "But not a forgery."

"We'll find it," Conall promised her, eyes glittering.

She nodded because he was right. She wouldn't, *couldn't*, countenance anything else. "Still, it's not here."

"Is this everything?"

"Is anything amiss, my lady?" John asked, frowning. "His Grace set more footman to guard the hall after the burglaries."

Persephone sent him a sunny smile. "Not at all, John. Merely taking inventory."

"All of the other crates have already been sent ahead to the duke."

"Of course. Thank you, John."

"That ought to make things easier," Conall murmured.

If it wasn't for the scores of the Beau Monde she would soon have to navigate, Persephone might have agreed. With a last longing glance at the long gallery empty of people and full of treasures, she followed Conall outside.

Chapter Eight

A BETROTHAL, EVEN a pretend one, was not enough to turn Persephone into the type of person who preferred a party to a crate of dusty old artifacts.

Especially when those crates were mere meters away in the ballroom, waiting for her.

She was wasting precious time and there was nothing she could do about it. Playing the part meant joining the others for a congratulatory afternoon tea ordered by the duke and held in the Avenue. At least she wasn't trapped inside. And the Avenue was her favorite place on the entire estate, barrows included.

It was set in the center of the terraced gardens, wide gravel paths meandering between roses and larkspurs and feathery bushes. Pedestal columns rose at measured increments, crowned with marble statues gleaming white. Diana with her moon circlet, Apollo with his lyre, Mercury and his winged sandals. Between them, busts of unknown Roman citizens with curled hair, veils falling from carved diadems. A gentleman was missing an arm, a lady a nose. It did not detract from their beauty one bit. Persephone could easily mistake a stroll down the Avenue for a stroll in some Roman temple, or the Forum even.

Her grandmother presided over the tea table, smiling at all of the guests; both to rub it in their faces that her granddaughter was marrying a future marquess but also because the duke had no hostess. His sister often helped him in that regard, but she had refused to travel back from Paris for a festival of "the dusty and the dreary".

There was walnut cake, scones with clotted cream, a mountain of cheese, sandwiches with salmon and cucumbers, macaroons, plates of lemon slices for tea and, also, champagne. And because her grandmother was her grandmother, sherry and brandy, despite Basil's disapproving sniff.

"Are you catching a cold?" she demanded of him. "Have a care not to sneeze on me, Basil." She never gave a fig about the rules governing the spirits which ladies ought to drink. "They only want to keep the whiskey for themselves," she announced, accepting a delicate sherry glass filled with that same whiskey from the only slightly disapproving Basil. "Thank you," she smiled. "It's so much prettier in crystal, isn't it? Instead of those ghastly tumblers."

"Yes, your ladyship."

"Good man."

The party was relatively small, for which Persephone was thankful. Lady Culpepper had her own guests to tend to and the duke was mostly interested in the other antiquarians who had begun to arrive. He had set aside guest rooms for the ones he admired most; three of whom had arrived that afternoon.

"Well, you look miserable," Priya joined Persephone at the feet of a rather impressively muscular Jupiter.

"I'm not miserable," she protested. There was a raspberry floating in Priya's champagne flute. Something about it distracted her. The color perhaps. It reminded her of something, but she couldn't say what. It tickled at the back of her mind.

"And you're a terrible liar," Priya said, smiling wider. "I've always liked that about you. You'll make a fine sister-in-law."

Persephone hesitated. Had Conall told his sister the truth? Priya lowered her voice. "I know."

She relaxed, relieved. "You do?"

"Yes, it's why I'm here in the first place. We are all looking for the same traitor."

Persephone eyed her consideringly. "You work for the War Office too?"

"They should be so lucky. I work with my brother occasional-ly, when his great fat head will allow him to see reason."

She grinned slightly. "Ah. I might have guessed."

"Allow me to give you a small piece of advice, Percy. Do not let him get his way all of the time. He will be insufferable. And don't let him take himself too seriously."

"Priya, we're not…."

"Yes, yes." Priya waved that off. "We'll see." She smiled at Meg, who joined them, carrying a plate of orange jam biscuits decorated with candied violets. "There you are."

"These taste like perfume," she complained, biting into a biscuit. "But I can't seem to stop eating them."

"They match your hair."

"Lady Blackwell insisted she had just the ribbon for me."

Persephone winced at the bright orange ribbon now woven through Meg's black hair. "She does like a bit of colour."

Meg smiled. "Even if it does clash horribly with my dress."

"Take it off," Priya suggested. "She'll never notice."

"Oh, I couldn't. It might hurt her feelings."

Persephone laughed. "Meg, every potted plant in every house in the county has been home to discarded ribbons at some point or another. I have a chest full of them at home. You can tie it around Jupiter's ankle. We'll say it was an offering."

She shook her head. "It was kind of her to think of me." She touched the ribbon. "I can use it with a different dress."

"I do like this one." Meg wore a white gown with a tulle-overdress in burgundy. Pink strawberries were embroidered from neck to hem, accented with spangles.

"I remember the dress," Priya said. "But not the strawberries. Did you stitch them yourself?"

"I did."

"It must have taken an age."

"It did," she agreed.

"Your uncle still refuses to buy you new gowns, I see."

"Priya," Persephone said when Meg's smile tightened.

"She's not wrong," she said softly. "But I don't mind. I like to embroider."

"I mind," Priya muttered under her breath. Persephone nudged her with her elbow.

"I want you all to know I did not push Sir Eugene Jones into the blackberry bushes," Tamsin announced, joining them. "Even though he is odious."

"And he's coming this way."

Tamsin groaned. "Do you see the trouble that comes when I restrain myself?"

"Jones is convinced that his sister Ivy ought to be Countess Northwyck," Priya told Persephone. "She's over there pretending to be one of the statues."

"Wonderful."

"Never mind him," Priya said dismissively. "He's afraid of me."

"And now me as well," Tamsin put in helpfully.

"Is he?" Persephone couldn't imagine anyone giving Priya or Tamsin the cut direct or making snide comments about them behind their fans. She couldn't imagine either of them caring one bit, more to the point. Persephone didn't care as much as the Ton wanted her to, but it was still mildly humiliating to know the comments Conall would hear about her.

More gentlemen followed after Eugene, a collection of white cravats, arrogant smiles, and polished Hessian boots. There was nowhere left to hide.

Conall scanned the area, his gaze lingering when he spotted her. He smiled warmly and bowed to her from the other end of the Avenue. He looked happy to see her. She knew it was part of the act. The tingling sensation suddenly warm in her belly, did not.

When he moved toward her, a blush crept up her neck. She couldn't help it. She'd never been the center of that kind of attention, of that kind of smile, full of secrets and private amusements. She knew the only secrets between them were state secrets, but the others saw more. Amused whispers swirled. Before Conall could reach them, the duke called him over. He sent Persephone a wink, barely there. She tried to hide her answering smile.

Eugene trotted toward them, breaking the eye contact between Persephone and Conall. She probably shouldn't dislike the poor fellow on that account.

Not when he presented so many other reasons to choose from.

He bowed smartly to Priya, while snapping his fingers at his sister to attend to him. Having no sense of self-preservation, he did not notice the matching narrowing of the eyes as Priya and Persephone looked up at him. "Ladies, a pleasure."

"I'm sure it is," Priya said with the kind of sweetness that ought to have warned him, but only succeeded in setting his shoulders back proudly. When he hovered, Priya sighed loudly. "Lady Persephone, may I introduce Sir Eugene Jones. Sir Jones, Lady Persephone."

"And Ivy Jones," Priya added when his sister reached them, looking dreadfully uncomfortable. "Hello, Ivy. It's lovely to see you."

"And you," she replied softly. She was lovely, pink cheeks, dark hair, all curves.

"I hear congratulations are in order," Eugene said with fake joviality. "Nabbed yourself an earl, did you?"

Ivy physically winced.

"Jones, don't be a bore," Priya said.

"What? We're all friends here, aren't we?" He smirked at Persephone. "You could give my sister lessons, eh?"

She blinked, momentarily astounded at his manners. Then she smiled gently at Ivy. "I am quite certain your sister does not need my help."

Ivy looked as if she might very much like to crawl under the carpet, thank you very much. Eugene nudged her with his shoulder and sent her stumbling a foot.

"But I should be glad to get to know her better, of course," Persephone said tightly.

"That means go away, Jones," Priya added. She turned her shoulder and refused to look at him again until he slunk off, ears red but with a laugh thick with bravado.

"Mind you don't use *all* her tricks, sis," Eugene tossed loudly over his shoulder. "Rather risqué, wouldn't you say? For a lady, I mean."

Persephone jammed a *petit four* into her mouth, sparring herself the need to answer. She had no wish to be ungrateful for the duke's celebration, truly, but if someone else asked her about Conall in that arch, knowing manner, she might stab herself in the ear with a fish fork.

ONE MORE WORD about Persephone in that tone and he was going to plough his fist into some blighter's face.

She sailed between their comments as if she barely heard them, as if they were utterly boring. But he saw how they affected her, noticed the tightening at the edges of her mouth, the tension in her shoulders. She never defended herself.

It was making him feel quite feral.

He clenched his teeth at Lady Louisa's arch comments, mostly because he couldn't toss her into the fishpond as he longed to. She was saved, though she did not know it, by the duke. He stood up, and there was a pause in the conversations, even the birds in the oak trees seemed to quiet. "Where's my god-daughter and my undeserving godson?"

Conall inclined his head from where he was leaning negligently against a thousand-year-old marble. He'd long ago learned that the trick to being considered a proper rakehell involved kissing a lot of ladies' gloves and leaning against the furniture. No Corinthian worth his salt stood straight. It was bloody annoying. But effective.

"A toast," the duke said.

Conall knew the exact moment Persephone realized she could escape the attention of the guests. She stood straighter, her spine rebelling. He envied her that. Her smile was genteel, calm. A lie from end to end.

He moved through the crowd with exaggerated languidness, to draw more of the attention. He felt like a proper idiot, but the slight softening of her shoulders was worth it. When he reached her, he extended his arm with a flourish. "Shall we?" Someone sighed, a fluttery envious sound.

"Do I have to?" Persephone muttered under her breath.

"I'm afraid so." He grinned at her. She had no idea how adorable she was. He would take her honesty and her reclusiveness and her slightly obsessive determination over any other lady of his acquaintance ten times over. Perfumed, drowning in pearls and diamonds and polite pretty smiles; they were nothing compared to her muttering and usually muddy hem. What a thing to realize, while being watched by dozens of gossips and possibly one murderous traitor.

"I didn't mean it like that," she said hastily, apologetically, as her hand closed over his sleeve.

"I know. It'll be quick, I promise."

"I'm sorry. It's ridiculous that you have to do this. With me, I mean."

"Percy," he said, firmly enough that she actually looked at him. Good. "There's no place else I'd rather be."

She fought a blush even as her smile turned wry. "I can see why you have the reputation you do," she said. "You're very good at all that smoldering."

He wanted to argue with her, to set her straight but this was hardly the time or place. "I practice in the mirror at least an hour every day," he said instead.

She snorted a little laugh, and he felt an unreasonable amount of pride that he'd made her do so with so many eyes upon them. The duke smiled at them both as he lifted his glass in a salute.

"Congratulations to you both on this very fine occasion," he said. "May you know many years of love and happiness. You have my unwavering love and support, as always." His gaze rested pointedly on the well-known gossips. "And Northwyck, I know I can rely on you to take care of Lady Persephone, who is like a daughter to me."

"Oh, well done, Pendleton," Conall murmured. She now had the protection of both his name but also the duchy, clearly and publicly. He lifted his own flute. "She is a true treasure. May I endeavour to deserve her, Your Grace."

"Oh honestly," Persephone said through a stiff, polite smile starting to rust at the edges. A lady behind them sniffled into her handkerchief.

"Too much?" he whispered back to Persephone, smiling the same smile he generally reserved for violins.

She only rolled her eyes at him.

"I'M SORRY FOR my brother," Ivy said later as Persephone rejoined her friends. The guests continued to mill around the statues, parasols fluttering in a kaleidoscope of colors, like giant flowers on stems. Persephone had forgotten hers, of course. Mostly because she did not own one. And refused to borrow her grandmother's lace monstrosities. Her parasols had nothing on her wigs and her wogs rivaled every confectioner's creation ever made.

"I'm often sorry for my brother as well," Priya grinned. "Although not like that. You don't really want tips, do you?"

"No, thank you."

Persephone was deeply relieved. She had no tips to give. "Try to get yourself the attention of a traitor and murderer" seemed dodgy at best. "This hunting is awful business," she said instead. "I feel badly for everyone involved. No one wants to be quarry."

"Speak for yourself," Priya snorted.

"You wish to be quarry?" Persephone asked, dubiously. "That is a surprise."

"Certainly not, but I hardly feel *sorry* for them. Once they wed, they get a wife's dowry or inheritance. What do we get?"

"Love?" Persephone suggested.

Priya laughed loudly. "Hardly. We no longer have what little legal access to our own money, our own bodies. Our own decisions. It's a nasty business."

"I take it your marriage was not…welcome?" Ivy asked.

"Actually, it was. My husband was a lovely honourable man. He insisted on saving me from a fortune hunter. Conall was away, you see." That was for Persephone's benefit, as if she did not want Persephone thinking ill of Conall. As if they were truly engaged. It was a brief moment, lovely in its fantasy. Persephone reminded herself not to hold on to it.

"But even he could not change hundreds of years of tradition and law," Priya continued. "Instead, once he realized he was ill, he bought me houses and jewels—as much as could be bought with funds that were not entailed. I am well cared for." She shrugged one shoulder. "I'd rather care for myself, but there it is, I suppose. Better to be seated above the salt even if they are only serving tripe and moldy old cheese."

"There it is," Ivy echoed.

Priya laughed again, a softer sound. "I've gone and changed the mood. I apologize. I am out of practice when it comes to polite conversation. I should have talked of the weather and the pretty teacups."

Persephone grinned. "As am I. But I *can* tell you that Cleopatra used ground carmine beetles to color her lip salve."

Priya wrinkled her nose. "Splendid." Ivy was quiet but smiling. "And you?" Priya added. "Can you save our atrocious attempts at polite conversation?"

"I'm afraid not."

"Oh good. That's a relief."

Priya's grin was positively wicked when she turned to Ivy. "By the way, I have just the thing to add to your brother's tea when he is being particularly tiresome."

Ivy might have looked like a delicate rose, all pink cheeks and silence, but the answering gleam in her eyes spoke entirely of thorns.

PERSEPHONE AND CONALL had the honor of opening to dancing for the evening.

An honor Persephone could have easily done without.

"Steady on," Conall whispered when she curtsied and managed to step on her own train.

"I'm sorry," she muttered. "I'm not good at this."

"You are perfectly fine," he said, clasping her waist. She felt the heat of his hand through the silk of her gown. "It's everyone else that's the problem."

She smiled up at him briefly. "If only that were true. But I know that they are thinking: we are too different to be a match. I knew this wouldn't work."

"Oh ye of little faith. We are far more alike than you assume."

"How's that? People stare at me and never actually see me."

"They stare at me as well."

"Because they *see* you."

He shook his head with a crooked smile. "That's where you're wrong."

The music cradled them and swept them around the room in a cocoon of warmth. Conall's movements were powerful and simple, he was in total control of the space. The stares made Persephone stumble, but his arms tightened and no one noticed her misstep. Gradually the itchiness and the weight of being watched faded. She could enjoy being so close to him, the way his muscles moved under her hands, the way his eyes stayed on hers, as if they shared a secret.

Well, they shared many secrets, but he made this one feel delicious, private.

She found she was sorry when the dance ended and he escorted her back to the grandmother. She looked vaguely like an éclair tonight, all cream-colored lace and chocolate-brown velvet. "You do make a fine pair," her grandmother fluttered her fan. "So handsome."

"He is, rather."

"I meant you, my dear." Persephone hugged her grandmother tightly. She patted Persephone's arm fondly. "I like to see you dancing."

Someone opened one of the terrace doors and the night ruffled through the room, touching flowers and ribbons and painted fans. The beeswax candles from the chandelier above dripped wax onto Persephone's glove and the edge of the table. Her grandmother clucked her tongue and moved them aside. One of the candles gutted out, spitting smoked and tiny bits of burning wax. They landed on the table, burning through the lace tablecloth. A footman darted forward, slapping at the sparks with his gloved hands. "Never say a dance is a dull affair," her grandmother remarked.

Now safe against the wall, Persephone couldn't help but

watch Conall as he accompanied another lady onto the floor. He was so graceful, so fine-looking. And she wasn't the only woman watching him tonight. How could she be? His eyes glittered like spring leaves under the candlelight. But she fancied she might be the only one to notice the sudden tension in his shoulders when he joined a group of gentlemen near the refreshments table. He tossed back the contents of his glass in one swallow, his throat tense. His jaw was too tight.

The acrid smoke reached her corner of the ballroom, stinging her nose. She thought she might understand what had caused the sudden stiffness in Conall. During the fireworks, he'd mentioned it wasn't the sounds so much as the smell of the smoke that had distressed him. He'd known to hide himself away in the shadows then but there was no schedule for a tablecloth catching fire.

She approached the knot of fine gentlemen, her own nerves vanished. She had a mission, and they could eat their starched cravats if they thought to keep her from them. She curtsied and smiled like the newly betrothed lady she was meant to be. "My lords, if I may steal my fiancé?"

She ignored the winks and hearty laughs, though they were preferable to the slow blinking stares down the end of the nose. It was terribly gauche to seem enamored of one's betrothed. Sod them. Better they think her backwards than what they would think should Conall lose the very brittle grip on his calm. She couldn't think how no one else noticed the way his smile was all wrong, the way his nostrils flared when he breathed, as if the air was too thin.

"Gentlemen, if you'll excuse me," he bowed, too sharp, too abrupt. No one noticed that either.

She slipped her arm into his and steered him into the hall where the light was softer, and the sounds muffled. He attempted to pull free. "I'll be fine," he said.

"I'm sure you will," she agreed, lightly. "Now come with me."

She led him past the other drawing rooms, the dining room being cleared by footmen, the duke's library. She didn't stop until they had reached the music room, filled with plants, a fine pianoforte, a harp, and several violins. Paintings of bucolic forests with attendant nymphs frolicked along the walls. Conall watched her light the oil lamps. "Persephone, go back to the dancing. You don't have to worry about me."

"I'm not worried," she said, though in truth she wasn't keen on the waxy sheen to his brow. He flinched when a footman dropped a tray and the sudden clap of sound seemed to reverberate through the room. "I would simply like to hear some violin music."

He blinked. If she had to confuse him out of being beset, she would. "Violin?"

"Yes, please."

"Percy, I haven't played in years. Not properly."

"Well, I can't play at all, so it hardly signifies." He opened his mouth to argue some more. "Is it not my right as your fiancée to request a serenade? At our betrothal dinner?"

His expression was wry. "And here you thought you wouldn't be able to pretend well enough to convince anyone."

She flashed him a grin. "I'm practicing."

"I can see that."

He went to the nearest violin case and took out the bow, tightening the horsehair and covering it with rosin. Only then did he raise the instrument into place. The knot of muscles along his shoulders softened. He took the bow in his other hand. "Hello, there," he murmured, as if greeting an old friend.

He tested a few notes and then suddenly they were strung together to turn into music, like beads in a glittering necklace. It was soft and melancholic, tickling the tiny hairs on the back of Persephone's neck. Her throat itched, as if she might cry. He played on, eyes finally closing, fingers working easily and confidently. She saw the old Conall, the one who had lost himself so utterly to his music that Tamsin had once managed to sneak close enough to dump a bucket of water over his head. She'd been thirteen and he'd been coldly furious, concerned only about possible damage to his violin. They'd had to make a pact not to involve musical instruments in any prank after that.

He'd still snuck spiders into Tamsin's clothespress the very next day.

While Persephone sifted through memories of Conall playing at midnight in the ballroom, or in the nursery when guests visited with their children, she could tell that he was remembering nothing at all. The memories that gripped him too tightly had faded. There was only the music in his ears. She knew she had disappeared too, as well as the painted nymphs and the vases of hydrangeas, the plush carpet underfoot. All of it until the last note shivered and he opened his eyes again.

"Another, if you please," Persephone said. "Something jaunty."

"I know what you're doing," he replied drily.

"Is it working?"

He shook his head ruefully. "Aye, it might be at that."

WHEN THE CELEBRATIONS tapered off enough for Persephone to escape, she darted back to her chambers. She checked under the bed, inside the dressing room and the cabinet. No one nefarious hid inside, waiting to do her in. She might finally unclench the muscles in her spine.

The fire popped, sending sparks up the chimney and light flashing over silver candlesticks and gold framed paintings of hills and stone circles and a single confused looking sheep. It was familiar, comfortable.

She sat at the table in the corner and put pencil to paper on the writing desk. It was sloped, wood worn to a satiny finish with tiny flowers along the edge. She started the list she had promised Conall of the guests who were still happily ensconced at Lady Culpepper's house party. It was then that she noticed a letter next to the inkwell; thick parchment and a wax seal she recognized. The British Museum.

Finally, something normal. A forgery which did not have a life hanging in the balance, or some new item they might consider lending last-minute to the duke for his exhibition. She had tried to convince them to share one of the Elgin marbles, even just a piece, but to no avail.

The letter, once skimmed, had her eyes narrowing.

"Conall Hunter, you *sneak*."

He was trying to keep her out of the investigation. He'd contacted the museum and asked them to send them their most competent forgery expert. And they were sending *her*.

Serves him right.

How dare he work behind her back? He might have saved her life, but it hardly gave him the right to now make autocratic decisions with it.

A noise at the balcony made her skin prickle. She rose slowly, gown swishing over the carpet as she reached for a candlestick. It was reasonably heavy, certainly heavy enough to do some damage. She ought to scream for help, but the other guests were still below stairs, laughing and drinking through yet another parade of champagne. The duke did like to celebrate.

She could hide behind the curtains or slip out the door.

Or she could take her assailant by surprise and knock him about the head until he agreed to leave Henry out of his plots.

She found she had a rather bloodthirsty urge to do the latter.

"Percy?"

The voice was soft, husky. Recognizable.

Unfortunately, her body was already moving and the adrenaline coursing through her veins made her brain a little slow to catch up. She shrieked like Boudicca on the battlefield, the silver candlestick overhead as she rushed the intruder.

Conall.

He was faster than a man who spent his evenings dancing in ballrooms or playing the violin had any right to be. He caught her wrist tightly, stopping the candlestick before it could collide with his head. Instinct had him following through with the movement, turning her abruptly so that her back was against the wall. It was so fast, too fast. She was pinned before she could instruct her feet to kick or her knee to jam up. His expression was hard, focused. Gone was the charming earl; someone else stood in his place. Her breath caught in her throat.

Then he caught her gaze. His stance relaxed though he did not let her go. "Persephone?"

She blinked back, adrenaline tingling through her. It made

her thighs feel hot and heavy.

Possibly not adrenaline.

"Who else did you expect in my bedroom?"

"Our traitor." He glanced down at her, noting the flush of her cheeks, the rise and fall of her breasts, pushed by her stays. "I'm sorry if I frightened you," he said, suddenly abashed. "I'm still on alert, it would seem."

"I'm sorry if I frightened *you*," she returned. Her voice sounded odd, breathy. To compensate, she tugged at his grasp on her wrist.

"You did, rather," he nearly grinned. "But it serves me right. I ought to have thought it through." Mollified, she stopped pulling at her arm, trying to free herself. "You're rather fierce."

"Not that it did me much good," she grumbled.

"Next time don't shout when you attack," he suggested. "And you're a little…petite… for the overhead strike."

"Are you saying I'm short?"

"Are you saying you're not?"

She wrinkled her nose. "Continue."

This time he did grin. It was boyish, appealing beyond measure. Damn it. "Not that you'll have need of it, but next time, go low. Being shorter than your opponent gives you an advantage."

"Such as?"

"Such as a lower center of gravity."

"Show me."

"As I'd prefer not to have my nose broken tonight, I'll only say that if you smashed your head back into my face, it would hurt enormously. More, it would cause my eyes to water, my grip to loosen. At that moment, you go low. Wrap your hands around my knee and pull up with all your might. I would stumble, or outright fall, and then you could run."

"After stomping on your throat."

He raised an eyebrow. "Ouch."

"Precisely." She sounded smug, especially for someone still trapped against the wall who had yet to move a single muscle. Embarrassing, really. Particularly when fear turned to an entirely different sort of heat. It sparked and hummed in her throat, in her fingertips, the back of her knees. She ought to feel anxiety, or at the very least mild consternation. She only felt excited, alive. Seen. "You haven't let go."

"No, I haven't, have I?"

He didn't seem inclined to. She smelled the bergamot of his soap, the night air still clinging to him, cool and green. There was an ivy leaf caught in the folds of his cravat. "You do have a thing about climbing through windows," she said.

"We haven't had an unchaperoned moment to ourselves in two days," he grumbled. "Violin concertos notwithstanding. How else was I to see you?"

Pleasure followed the heat. He'd wanted to see her.

"We have much to discuss," he added, releasing her abruptly.

Fool. Again.

She took the opportunity to get a hold of herself when he turned away to set the candlestick down. She was thinking about the breadth of his shoulder, the strength in his hands, the grey of his eyes and he was thinking about a traitor. Not only was he right to do so, but she was utterly idiotic in thinking someone like him might be interested in someone like her. A pretend betrothal was just that. *Pretend.* Honestly, she was embarrassing herself. And possibly all of womankind. She had a goal. And that goal was not kissing or being kissed by Conall Hunter, Earl of Northwyck.

"You're pink," he said, frowning lightly.

Botheration.

"I really am sorry to have frightened you. But you needn't worry. I'll make sure you're safe. You won't have to break anyone's nose." He paused, amused. "Not unless you want to."

It would help immeasurably if he could stop being so charming. She could only repeat the truth to herself: *he's not for you.*

"Thank you for the lesson," she said, only sounding a tiny bit strangled. Why was it so hard to breathe? Where was the air? Why did he have to burn so bright? "I am a part of this too."

"You shouldn't be. Henry ought to be horse-whipped for putting you in danger."

She narrowed her eyes, reminded that Conall had already contacted the British Museum behind her back. "He trusts me."

"This isn't a matter of trust."

"It's entirely a matter of trust," she returned, nettled. "And anyway, as I *am* involved there is no sense in pretending otherwise." He watched her steadily. She lifted her chin. "Regardless, I am more concerned for my grandmother."

"She will be protected. There is a man at her door even now."

"But won't that be a little obvious?" she wondered. "Might the traitor not realize we are onto him if he notices burly footman at her beck and call?"

"You're right." Conall looked at her then and she wondered that her gown did not simply melt away. It was like he was touching her everywhere. "You are even more clever than I thought."

She had to swallow. The appreciation in his gaze was tangible. She wanted to lean into it. "Thank you."

"We'll put it out that is feeling unwell, and you are merely being overly solicitous," he said. He took her hand. "She will be well cared for, I promise."

His fingertips brushed her palm. Neither of them wore gloves. She thought she saw him swallow, as though he'd noticed. But she must be mistaken. He was accustomed to sophisticated widows and hungry debutantes who had left fleeting touches of the hand far behind them. Not to mention that her hands were not the soft perfumed hands of a lady of quality. They were the hands of an antiquarian who dug in the dirt. She snatched them back, curling her fingers into her palms. She would not be ashamed, she told herself sternly. Not about something she loved.

He was like a magnet and she had no experience with this kind of pull. She was out of her depths. Best to focus on what she did know: Cleopatra's eye powder was made of powdered malachite and lapis lazuli. Ancient Egyptians used a paste of salt, mint, dried iris flower and pepper to clean their teeth.

She didn't know what to say or how to stand, alone in a darkened bedroom after midnight with a handsome man and nothing more to say on matters of state. It seemed ridiculous to mention the weather. He was too striking in his evening clothes and the firelight glittering on the silver thread of his waistcoat. He was all juxtaposition, beautiful colours and fabrics, easy compliments, but then that hungry darkness. The glimpses of it should have frightened her, but they didn't. They were thrilling. He was letting her see parts of him no one else saw. He was being uncovered like a treasure buried under gold and silk, instead of earth and barrow. It spoke to her in a way nothing else could.

"Oh, I nearly forgot," he said abruptly when she began to wonder if the silence was stretching on too long and if he would think her dull and addlepated. "Wait right there."

"You don't—." She was about to tell him he needn't make excuses to return but he was already gone. A man such as him, with the people he knew, would hardly find her diverting. She was part of a bigger mystery; she wasn't the mystery herself. And yet, he returned in moments, a wicker basket in hand. She stared at him. "You climbed the trellis holding a picnic basket?"

"You hardly ate at dinner."

"Oh." He'd noticed. That meant something, didn't it? *Stop it, Persephone.* "I don't enjoy being the center of that kind of attention."

"Who does?"

"Lots of people do. I would have thought you were one of them." She tilted her head. "But you don't either, do you?"

"Not particularly. But it's a means to an end."

She nodded. "That makes sense."

"Does it?" He knelt on the thick carpet by the fire and began to unpack the food.

"I've been trying to reconcile the Conall I knew years ago with The Earl of Northwyck, coveted by hostesses, matchmaking mamas and widows alike."

"Any luck?"

"Only when we're alone." His head came up, eyes glinting. She shouldn't have said that. It sounded too…intimate. She cleared her throat. "That is…" She trailed off when he smirked gently, eyebrow arching. "Oh, be quiet," she muttered.

He laughed and it wasn't his polished, courtly laugh of the ballroom; it was smoky, quiet. It made her want things she should not want.

It made her feel like fire.

"Come and eat," he said softly.

She licked her lower lip nervously as she sank onto the carpet beside him. His eyes tracked the tip of her tongue and she felt suddenly powerful; adrift but also completely anchored. "I've never had a picnic indoors," she said.

"Does it offend your sense of decorum?

She laughed. "I usually eat nuncheon in a hole in a field." That was hardly the seductive image she'd wanted to present him with. If she'd wanted to present him with any such thing. Which she didn't. *At all.* A little bit.

A lot.

He built a plate for her, adding a little bit of each dish: roast beef, cheeses, cucumber slices, raspberries, sugar biscuits flavoured with orange, and sugared grapes. And a crumpet from a basket absolutely stuffed with them.

"I did promise you crumpets," he grinned. She grinned back. "And I always keep my promises."

"I'll remember that." She nibbled on a crumpet with a bit of cheese, followed by a plump, tart raspberry. It tasted better here, with him, in the silent shadows than any food on gilded porcelain plates. He filled a delicate blue teacup with lemonade from a bottle. "You thought of everything."

He'd clearly done this before. She refused to let it needle her. He was a man grown, for God's sake. Of course, he'd done this sort of thing before. That she hadn't, only made it more special, not less. "Thank you," she whispered.

He shrugged a shoulder. "It's nothing."

"It's not," she insisted, surprised and mortified by the stinging behind her eyes. She was being a goose.

"Percy?"

She forced a smile.

"Don't," he said. "Tell me what you're thinking."

"Only that this might be commonplace to you but it's not for me."

"Do you think I make of habit of scaling walls with picnic

baskets?"

She wrinkled her nose at him. "Courtesy is not something I am often offered," she said carefully, trying to explain herself without sounding like she was drowning in self-pity.

Conall's jaw clenched. "Yes, about that."

She winced. "I expect you received…comments about our engagement. I did warn you."

"That everyone has lost their minds? You never mentioned that part." The fire touched his strong jaw and she felt true jealousy then. Her fingers itched to do the same. "I nearly launched several gentlemen into the fishpond. A few ladies too."

She giggled without meaning to. He glanced at her out of the corner of his eye, satisfied. "That's better."

"I don't mean to sound as though I am feeling sorry for myself," she hastened to clarify. "Self-pity is useless. It gets absolutely nothing done except to give one a stomach ache."

He shifted so he could face her. She wasn't expecting the true delighted smile on his face. It was the same smile he'd given her when she'd asked for crumpets directly after nearly being murdered. "The men here are imbeciles. But I'm glad I do not have to fight them off."

She snorted. "Hardly."

"Was it Henry?" he asked casually; casually enough that she toyed with the idea of not answering him, of pretending she did not know what he meant. But she was beginning to realize that anything he did casually was a mask. "Is he the reason behind the loss of your reputation? Of courtesy, as you call it?" There was darkness in his voice now, an edge. She found she liked it very much. It was honest. It spoke a truth even when he couldn't.

"It wasn't Henry," she answered, more awkwardly than the worldly lady she was supposed to be would have answered. "He was away."

"Who then?"

"No one from these parts."

"Do you protect him, Percy? Even now?"

She smiled a little. "Are you trying to protect *me*, Conall?"

"Of course, I am. Does he need a bruising? I'm happy to

oblige. Delighted, in fact."

"It was a long time ago." She ate a sugared grape because she didn't know what else to do with her hands. "I planned it, you see."

Conall blinked.

"Do you think less of me?" she asked.

"Don't be daft." A quick, harsh answer. Truth again, not flummery.

Her smile widened. He narrowed an eye. "Are you remembering him, fondly, then?"

"Good Lord, no. He was a prat."

He choked on a laugh. "I see."

She shrugged. "But he was handsome and useful." She shifted. It was strange to tell her side of the story finally, especially here, now, with the wind coming through the open balcony doors, full of roses and starlight. "He thought it was his idea. He plied me with poetry and flattery and never noticed the whole thing was my idea."

"Naturally." He shook his head. "I can't give young men glowing recommendations in that regard, I'm afraid. I like to think most of us outgrow our own sense of self-importance."

"We both got what we wanted so it does not signify."

His jaw ticked again. "Did he, now. And you? What was it you wanted? Love? Pleasure?"

"Freedom," she said, simply.

He looked surprised. "Freedom?"

"I was in danger of being permanently on the shelf, you see. But I didn't mind. My parents, however, minded quite a lot. They worried I was too enamored of digging in the fields. It was all right for my father, but not for me. Not for a young lady who ought to be swoony over young men in starched cravats and counting proposals instead of bones. They wanted me to stop digging."

"What happened?"

"I did turn down three marriage proposals." She half-smiled. "I wasn't always like this."

"I like you like this," he said easily. Warmth spread under her collarbones. "But I liked you then, as well. I assume all of this happened while I was away?"

"Yes. Two of the offers were from men more than twice my age and the other, while only a year older, was obviously planning to carry on as if he wasn't married."

"Not unusual."

"No. But not good enough, either. If I'm to give up everything, I deserve something in return. And more to the point, he had already suggested several hobbies more appropriate than collecting and studying the past."

Conall's smile flashed. "I bet you set him right."

"I did."

"I'd have loved to have seen it."

"It wasn't enough though. So, I made a choice. An exchange. Ruination for freedom." It hadn't been easy, and probably a bit more impetuous than it should have been. She didn't regret it though. Well, not most of it. "It worked well enough though my parents were furious." She paused, remembering her mother's shock, her father's face, white lines etched around his mouth. The shouting. And then worse still, the silence. "And then they died a year later, and it was for naught."

He took her hand. "I'm sorry." His thumb rubbed gentle circles over her knuckles. She'd had no idea knuckles could be so sensitive. "But he left you Halcyon House. Your father might not have thought of it if you hadn't forced his hand."

"Perhaps."

"You're very brave."

She pursed her lips. "Hardly. I scandalized a few aristocrats. Not even scandalized for they've all done far worse than I. But it was my refusing to hide what I'd done which infuriated them. *You* went to war. That's brave."

"I went to the battlefield, after the fact. It's not the same thing. They don't generally let earls fight. Anyway, there are many ways to be brave. You decided what it was you needed, and you took it. Even if it meant turning your back on society. Very few people have the nerve to do that."

"Henry said I was a pea-brain, not brave."

"Is that why didn't you choose him for your plans? Would you have, had he been here?"

"Henry?" she asked, surprised. "Definitely not. He's like a brother."

"I find myself relieved to hear it."

"Y-you are?" Conall lifted her hand to his mouth, brushing his lips over her knuckles again. It tickled, awakening a responding ticklish feeling in her belly. When he looked up at her, eyes flaring, she felt suddenly like a banquet, lush and desperately needed. It was intoxicating.

He rose to his feet, tugging her up with him. Her breath caught in her throat. "I should go," he whispered against her skin, eyes still locked on hers.

He was *going? Now?* Was he trying to turn her inside out?

He bowed sharply and turned away, striding toward the balcony.

"Wait," she said, surprising herself.

He froze but did not turn back. The light gilded his strong legs and back, the curl of his hair at his nape. "Don't."

"Don't what?" she asked, not understanding. Then it hit her. He was too much of a gentleman to want to have to turn her away. Being brave and being wanted were two entirely different things. It was a meaningless flirtation. It only sounded true because she wanted it to be. A hard ball of hurt and humiliation stuck in her throat.

"If you ask me to stay, I won't be able to say no," he added softly.

"I understand," she said, trying to sound calm, unruffled. "I don't expect anything from you, Conall. And I did warn you. My reputation is hard to ignore."

He turned his head slightly, enough that could see his profile, the line of his jaw. "That's not it, at all. If you ask me to stay, I'll stay because I want to. But it wouldn't be fair to you."

"Conall."

"Yes, love?" The endearment hummed through her.

"Did we not just agree that I know who I am and what I want?" He was trying to protect her. It was sweet. Annoying at the moment, but sweet.

"Yes."

"Then what if I want you to stay?" Did she? Was she really going to do this? It might hurt when he said goodbye, when the need for their sham engagement was over, but surely it would hurt more if she went on forever without being touched. For the right reasons. By someone who clearly knew what they were about. She was already on the shelf, already ostracized. So, what did it matter?

And she'd nearly died. There was a traitor out there possibly still willing to murder her. He hadn't changed his mind, after all, or made penance. He'd only missed. So, if there was a better time to take your own joy in your own two hands, she couldn't think of it.

"Persephone."

"Yes?" His voice was dark, raw. It lit fires in the darkness of her body. There were frozen rivers deep inside her, all turning to thaw. It was a sudden riot of need.

"Be sure."

Chapter Nine

"I 'M SURE."

He moved so swiftly that one moment he was still as a shadow and the next, he was coming for, advancing over the plush carpet, his profile lit by firelight, like something out of a story. Her throat went dry and she had to swallow hard. He half-smiled and it was knowing and amused and utterly devastating. She faltered back a step before she could stop herself. He kept coming and it was thrilling, down to her toes. He stopped mere inches away. His gaze roamed over her, hot and hungry. It was as though he was already touching her.

"Still sure?"

She nodded silently. He dragged his fingertips up her bare arms, tickling, awakening every nerve. He threaded his fingers through her hair, dislodging pins, scraping her scalp lightly until she wanted to purr. Her bones were already melting and he'd barely touched her.

And then his fingers tightened, suddenly, enough to send another thrill down her legs. He tilted her head back to better take her mouth with his. Gone was the veneer of carefree aristocrat, even the hunter seeking retribution and justice. There was only Conall. And herself, the center of his gaze. He deepened the kiss, licking her lower lip until she opened to him, a small sound escaping her.

She'd never made a sound like that.

She wondered if she should be embarrassed.

Later.

Much later.

The sound seemed to wake something in Conall. He kept kissing her, urging her to respond until their tongues tangled and their breaths ran ragged. One hand steadied her at her lower back, warm and big and strong as he moved her backward. Her shoulders pressed against the silk wallpaper. The room whirled around her, blues, firelight, moonlight through thc window. It was a kaleidoscope. She was a kaleidoscope, all colours, fire, want. She wanted to laugh but it would have required her to pull away and she had no intention of doing any such thing. She honestly didn't think she had the physical or moral strength to do so. If the traitor had come strolling through the door, she was very much afraid she would not have noticed. Especially when Conall dragged open mouthed kisses along the curve of her neck. When he reached her shoulder he bit down, gently. Heat jolted through her. He laughed softly, pleased. "That's it, love."

She absolutely would not be the only one turning to fire.

Which was fine in theory but altogether different in practice.

She wasn't sure what to do. She did know she wanted to peel away the layers that kept him so contained, so earl-like. The coat, the patterned waistcoat, the fine lawn shirt. Starting with his cravat. She wanted the strong column of his throat, wanted to see if his pulse was as frantic as hers. She fumbled at the knot, wilting the starch that kept the complicated twist in place.

Conall eased back, eyes heavy-lidded and breath not entirely steady. It made her feel strong. Joyful. He was affected, just as she was. It wasn't up to her to keep the mood polite or pleasant, to agree with historical mistakes because they were spoken by an earl, to pretend she was in on the joke when she was the reason for it. This was for both of them, a conversation of hands and tongues and desire. She wasn't alone in this. And it made it all that much sweeter.

The cravat knot, however, could go straight to the devil.

"My valet will be put out."

"Good. He's made this entirely too difficult," she muttered.

"And I'm strong from digging. I'm sure I could best him in a fight."

He grinned. "Of that I have no doubt."

She grinned back and the fire was still there between them, but so was a curious kind of comfort, of ease. She kissed him because she could. Because she wanted to. And then she unravelled the cravat and tossed it aside. She brushed her thumb over his skin, feeling his pulse as it jerked under her touch.

"I may not survive you," he groaned. When she couldn't smother a tiny smug smile, he leaned down to whisper in her ear until she felt his voice everywhere, in her belly, in her thighs, in all the secret places. "You like that, don't you?"

"Yes."

"How much?"

"More than I care to tell you. You already have all of the power."

He shook his head. "Love, you have that backward. Every ounce of power is yours." His mouth moved lower, tracing the edge of her neckline, dipping into the gap between her stays and the top of her breasts. "And that's exactly how I want it."

He licked along the line of lace until she clutched at his arms and he slid his fingers under her gown and lifted her breast free. It was both shocking and perfectly natural when he lowered his head to suck at her nipple until she squirmed.

"Tell me what you want."

She wanted more. Just more.

She couldn't find the words, but it didn't seem to matter. He knew what her body wanted before she did. He licked and sucked at her like she was the sweetest of sweets. She gasped again, cool shivers on the back of her neck, fiery tingling between her legs. She didn't know how she stayed standing, had the sneaking suspicion it was only because he was holding her up. His knee slipped between hers, pressed up. The contact and pressure were unexpected, delicious.

"Shall I tell you what I want, then?"

She nodded, tugging at his shirt until he pulled away long enough to divest himself of the offending thing. "I want to taste you on my tongue." His tongue tickled her earlobe. The sound of his voice and his breath rumbling in her ear had her shivering. "I want to hear all of the sounds you make."

She flattened her palms over the warm ridges of his chest and abdomen, the soft skin, the brush of hair. He was magnificent. Strong. When she tentatively traced the line of his breeches, the way he had her gown, he made a sound in the back of his throat. Now she understood what he meant. It was music, primal and empowering and she wanted more of it, more the way his breath hitched, more the way he had to force his words past the other things he was doing with his mouth. There was no hiding, no wondering which version of Conall touched her, which version she touched.

She fumbled with the buttons until he reached down to help her, his lips never leaving her skin; on her neck, her collarbone, tracing the blue veins inside her wrist. She closed her fingers around his length, and he stilled, eyes blazing. He was soft and hot and hard. She stroked him and when her palm grazed the tip of his manhood, he jerked. She worried that she had hurt him.

The expression on his face said otherwise.

Some dam inside him seemed to break. "I'm going to make you come until you're weak from pleasure."

He swept her backwards, lowering her gently to the floor, his hands eager and demanding. The carpet was soft on her skin, warmed from the fire. She could smell the raspberries, and smoke. Her skirts were bunched around her knees and then at her waist, a froth of offending lace he had to stop himself from tearing. He kissed around her belly button, dragging his mouth over her stomach, and then just inside her thigh. Her muscles quivered instinctively, and he chuckled against her. When he reached the juncture of her thighs, tongue dipping into the heat gathered there, she gasped. He licked at her, gently, softly, then with increasing pressure. He slid a finger inside of her and it was nearly too much and at the same time, not nearly enough. It was torture. Perfect, beautiful torture.

She squirmed and he grasped her hip with his big hand, keeping her still. "Ah, ah," he murmured.

"I can't..." she couldn't bear it. There were too many sensations racing under her skin.

"You can," he crooned. He licked a stripe along her folds, then stopped. Abruptly.

She lifted her head. He grinned at her from between her legs and it ought to have been awkward, but it wasn't. "Did you want me to stop?" he asked.

"You..." She might have called him names if she could tear any part of her from the sensations coursing through her, retreating like a river in high summer. "Don't you dare stop!"

He bent his head, taking the little nub into his mouth and sucking on it until she had to bite her lip to keep from crying out. A second finger moved inside her and her back arched. Pleasure built, tingling in waves up her thighs, finally cresting until she had no choice but to let it carry her away.

When her lower back touched the carpet again she was out of breath, and he was smug.

A clock chimed somewhere down the hall. A bird answered from the gardens, now pink and grey with the mists of morning. "The maids will be coming around soon to see the fires," he said. "I should go. Regrettably." He moved up her body to kiss her again. "You are as delicious as I'd imagined."

She blushed from her ears down to her collarbones and it made him smile. She sat up, pulling her skirts down around her. It was ridiculous to feel shy now, but she did. "You...," she tried to force herself past her bashfulness. "You didn't..."

He kissed her again, swift, hard. "All in good time."

He fixed the buttons of his pants where they sat low, showing an expanse of skin and muscle and a trail of dark hair she very much wanted to follow. He winked and turned away, toward the balcony. "You can use the door," she said, still feeling dazed.

"I've a guard outside."

"You do?"

"Of course. And outside your grandmother's rooms. As I told you I would."

Something softened inside of her, something too important to inspect too closely. Here was a man who was steady, strong. And careful. Someone who *saw* her and still kept his promises even though she was an inconsequential wallflower in the eyes of the world.

"It hardly matters if someone sees you," she said. "We are engaged, after all, and I'm already ruined." She shrugged one shoulder, trying to appear debonair, sophisticated. Women with her reputation generally came with a great deal more experience.

He scowled. "I won't have them looking down their noses at you." He bowed and the was gone into the cold grey shadows of the morning.

He was sweet. It was a surprise, though it shouldn't have been.

PERSEPHONE JOINED THE other guests for breakfast at half past ten. She ought to have been exhausted on so little sleep, but she only felt hungry and happy. A little fatigue was a small price to pay. Although she'd woken from strange dreams of a house filled with baskets of raspberries, the color too bright and too red. She put it down to being fed berries in the dark by a handsome earl.

Her grandmother looked well and safe, happily wearing a wig in a disconcerting shade of lilac. Persephone smiled at her fondly over a plate of coddled eggs, trout, and sweet rolls. She helped herself to coffee and a disapproving glance from a lady at the other end of the table. Persephone shot a toothy grin at her, raising her cup in a silent toast. If only she knew how disapproving her glare ought to have been. A little coffee in mixed company was nothing.

Conall was not at the table which was just as well. She wasn't sure how ladies acted after a night like last night. Just thinking of it made her blush.

"Lady Persephone?"

She turned to Holly. "I'm sorry, what was that?"

"I only asked if you will you be married in Town?"

"Oh. Um. We haven't decided yet."

"Town?" the duke scoffed. "Why would you go there when I have a perfectly good chapel? It was built in 1215, you know. Robin Hood himself might have passed through it."

"We are a ways from Nottingham," Persephone smiled.

"Bah."

Some of her smug pleasure dimmed when the duke set his newspaper down near her elbow. He thought she pored over the pages for news about archaeological discoveries, but really, she was searching for Henry's name. And every time with the same prayer in her head: *not today, please, not today.*

She skimmed the announcements section, articles on the war and then indulged in a small sigh of relief. Nothing about Henry. No ships run aground or lost at sea, no shouts of treason.

Except.

Her blood ran cold so abruptly she fumbled her teacup and nearly ended up wearing the contents. "Easy on the reins," the duke said amiably.

There was a name she recognized. Peter Oliver. She knew him from Henry's letters. He'd been a friend, a confidant. As well as being the other man who knew the traitor's name and the details of his plot.

And now he was dead.

Found floating face-down in the Thames. No suspects, no motive given, only that every item in his pockets had been taken by the mudlarks. Not just the mudlarks, she'd wager. The traitor too. Had he traveled to London? Did he have accomplices? Had Henry been with him?

When Persephone caught a glimpse of Conall striding down the hallway, she turned to the duke, newspaper in her hand. "May I keep this, Your Grace?"

"Of course."

She nearly bowled over the footman stationed near the door in her haste to reach Conall. He paused down the hall and turned to look at her over his shoulder. He smiled slightly. He thought she was chasing him because of what he'd done to her the night before. Because of what they'd done to each other. "Idiot," she muttered.

He blinked, nonplussed. "Percy?"

She nudged him out of sight and out of earshot. He let himself be herded. "I have an appointment, I'm afraid. I cannot linger."

An appointment with her, in point of fact.

She waved the newspaper at him. "Have you read this?"

"I haven't had the time yet." He frowned at her pale face and her flushed cheeks. She probably looked feverish. Fear made her skin hot, her blood cold. "What is it?"

"Peter Oliver, whom Henry mentions in his letter, was found in the Thames last night."

Conall cursed once, viciously. Then his hands closed around her upper arms, firmly. His grey eyes snapped onto her. "Which means Henry is still alive, or he'd have been found there as well."

It wasn't precisely true—anything could have happened to Henry—but it was true enough that she found she could catch her breath again. If anything could have happened, then it went to reason that anything *good* was therefore also possible. He might be in hiding, or still on a ship. He might right now be on his way home. She took another breath.

"Better?" Conall's voice was soft, even the edges were comforting. He might have different motives, but he was as determined to find Henry. That helped too. She nodded.

"I apologize," she said.

"Don't," he replied. "Don't ever apologize to me for being honest. Don't hide from me."

The timbre of his tone should not have felt like a caress.

But it most certainly did.

"Unfortunately, I really must go," he said. "I'll find you as soon as I can."

She narrowed her eyes. What was good for the goose, was good for the gander. Clearly, he needed a little reminder. She widened her eyes again, trying to look innocent. "Of course, my lord," she said, sweetly.

If he'd been paying attention, he might have been terrified.

"I'll walk with you a while," she added. "There is a book I have been wanting to borrow from the duke's library."

His jaw clenched. It might have escaped her notice if she hadn't been looking for it. Even had the British Museum not suggested she meet the very discreet Earl of Northwyck in the library, if she was comfortable revealing herself. He had been vetted, of course, but she generally worked anonymously.

In this instance she was definitely comfortable with being seen.

Vengefully eager, in fact.

She felt him vibrating with suppressed frustration as she dallied throughout the enormous room, trailing her fingertips over the gilded spines of leather-bound books. Conall glanced at the door. She hid a smile. "I can't seem to find the volume I was looking for," she said. She pointed to the shelves that reached the ceiling, to the second-floor balcony framing yet more books. The duke had separate exhibition rooms for his collections. Here were books, and more books. A muscle ticked in the earl's jaw. "This could take some time," she added. "I'm sure I'll be perfectly safe here. I see John in the hall there, no doubt waiting for me."

Conall looked as though he were about to say something but couldn't quite figure out what it was. He bowed politely instead. "Of course."

He marched away, the clipped sound of his boots echoing over the marble floors. Persephone grinned and sank into the blue chaise tucked into the corner behind a small army of ferns to wait, as requested by the British Museum.

She was still grinning when Conall returned, no doubt relieved to find her away. She was well tucked into the leaves. There was a pause long before she saw him, before his shadow even reached her. Not quite as well hidden as she'd thought. "You're the consultant," he said ruefully.

"Courtesy of the museum, yes," Persephone replied when he finally stepped into the green shadows.

"You might have said."

She rose from the soft chair. "You ask me that?" she snapped. "Truly?"

He had the grace to look mildly abashed, slightly hunted. She mimicked his voice. "Don't hide from me."

"Percy…"

She poked him in the chest, incensed. Not so incensed as to not notice the warm strength of him under his shirt but incensed enough. "You lied to me."

"I didn't …lie."

"You went behind my back. You tried to keep me out of this investigation."

"I was trying to protect you."

She made a thoroughly unladylike sound at that. "Bah."

He blinked, tried another tack. "Henry would want you to stay safe."

Persephone wondered if the top of her head might actually blow clean off like a tea kettle. Steam was surely hissing out of her ears. "Don't you dare, Conall Hunter. Not only is Henry *my* oldest friend, but your best leads in this investigation have been through me. *Me.*"

He paused. "True."

"And if I'm good enough for the museum, I don't see why I'm not good enough for you."

"You are. Of course, you are." When she returned his steady gaze without a word, he sighed. He wasn't the only one who had perfected the art of seeing without being seen. "You're right."

"Bloody right, I am."

He flashed a half-smile.

"Don't smile at me."

He stepped closer. "Why not?"

"I know what you're doing." The scent of cedar soap enveloped her.

"And what's that?" His hand slid over the nape of her neck, fingers digging gently into the tense muscles at the back of her skull. He massaged until they released and pleasure tingled into her scalp.

"You're trying to distract me." She nearly moaned when he leaned down to press his mouth at the base of her neck where her shoulder started. His mouth was warm, soft. A gentle scrape of teeth. "It won't work."

She pinched him hard. Very hard.

"Ouch!"

"You are not going to leave me out of things again," she said, emotion tightening her throat. She felt helpless enough as it was.

She wouldn't fail Henry.

And a traitorous part of her heart did not want Conall to fail her. Sham engagement or not.

"I won't," he said softly, and it took her a moment to realize he wasn't responding to her fleeting wish but to her spoken demand.

"I am too used to being left out," she said. "Discounted. So, I'll know if you do, Conall."

He caught the truth of it, the weight behind her statement. His hand slid down her arm, fingers squeezing hers. It was no longer a fleeting flirting touch. It was serious, firm. A promise. "I'm sorry."

"Thank you." She narrowed her eyes. "I am going to magnanimously assume that you have not found a forgery you were ferreting away for a secret consult."

"No."

"Good, then I might not have to hide your body in one of the barrows."

He didn't look particularly concerned to be threatened with murder, rather amused. Impressed. Fond.

Damn the man.

"I only thought to be prepared and waste no time once we find it. I've people combing London collections though I understand, of course, that thanks to you and the duke, the vast majority of all Egyptian artifacts in this country will be right here in this house."

"True," she said, with no small amount of pride. "So, let's at it, shall we?"

ANCIENT EGYPT TRULY had arrived and taken up residence in the duke's ballroom. With a bit of sand on the ground, they might have thought themselves transported. A giant sphinx towered in one corner, watching with an enigmatic smile. Meg had completed a mural of papyrus reed, ibis birds, with the pyramids in the distance.

There were dozens and dozens of items sitting in crates, waiting for Persephone to sort them; a painted hand mirror, a blue tambourine, bone-handled daggers and swords, a funerary barge carved of wood and painted green and complete with a replica of a mummy, a priest with his head shaved, and several attendants. A small box filled with flies made of gold. "These are curious," Conall remarked.

"They were awarded to soldiers who had done well in battle," Persephone explained. She gave a small gasp which made him think of a hundred things he could do to her to elicit the sound again. Starting with the inside of her left knee.

"These are shabti figures," she said softly, stroking one of the painted figures.

The look of longing on her face, the sweep of her fingers, made him think of the previous night again. He hardened instantly. He knew how those fingers felt, stroking him as though he were as fascinating as her Egyptian artifacts. He fought the urge to shift from foot to foot like a green lad. It took concentrated effort to focus on what she was saying. She was in her element, standing with confidence, cheeks pink with pleasure, eyes shining. He wanted to hire an artist to paint her exactly like this.

He wanted her to look at *him* just like that.

"Aristocrats and priests and priestesses didn't want to have to work the fields or sweep the floors in the afterlife," she was explaining. "So, they made replicas of servants and prayed to Osiris to bring them to life to do their chores." She tore her gaze away, caught his expression and misread it entirely. "I apologize. I know I go on and the duke is the only one with the stomach to listen." She gave a small self-deprecating laugh that kindled a rage inside his chest. The world at large, even her own world of antiquarians, had created that laugh.

"I'm interested in anything that interests you, Persephone."

The pink in her cheeks deepened, reminding him of the pink elsewhere on her body.

He forced himself to nod to a squat ugly statue. "Who's this fellow?"

She circled the statue thoughtfully. The open jaws offered rows of heavy sharp teeth. "A guardian of some sort, possibly."

She glanced at him out of the corner of her eye. "Have you ever seen a hippopotamus in your travels?"

"I'm afraid not."

"They are quite ferocious. Enough that the Goddess of childbirth, Taweret, also has the head of a hippopotamus."

She continued to move through the ballroom, checking boxes, stopping to admire artifacts, nodding to familiar faces. John, the footman, stood stoically to the side, eyes alert. Conall had confirmed with the duke that John was indeed more than the average footman. Conall took note of the other footmen, the villagers who had agreed to work for the duke, the goddaughters trailing in and out to investigate. Nothing seemed out of place.

Until Persephone said his name.

"Conall," she said quietly. He turned his head, saw the fiery glitter in her eyes.

She'd found something.

She stood facing a shelf with unpacked items. There was a parchment with one of her endless lists in her hand. He crossed the floor toward her, unhurried, stopping to help a footman with a crowbar and a particularly stubborn wooden crate lid. "Which one?" he asked quietly when he'd reached her side. Her breath trembled but her expression was calm.

"The flask."

It was an earthenware jar with a rounded belly, two handles, and a narrow neck. It looked old enough, with the same reddish sandstone hue he had come to associate with ancient Egyptian findings. Blue lotus flowers were painted in a ring around the mouth. "How can you be sure?" She glanced at him, one eye narrowed. He lifted a hand. "I'm not questioning your talents, I'm honestly curious."

She made a smug little sound in the back of her throat which he should not have found adorable. "It's a fair forgery," she said. "But see these birds here, along the bottom?"

"Yes."

"They are meant to be Ibis birds, which were sacred and therefore common as decoration."

"But?"

"But an Ibis has a very distinctive curve to its beak. See the ones Meg painted there? Nothing like this sad example." She clicked her tongue like a disappointed governess. He couldn't help but grin.

She picked up the flask as casually as she could, which would have been more casual without the tense line of her shoulders. "Easy," he murmured. "No one here has any cause to suspect anything."

She nodded. She tilted the jar, peering into the opening. It was dark and not especially forthcoming. She cursed. It was vicious enough to have him lift an eyebrow. "I had no idea your vocabulary was so extensive."

"I can't reach inside," she said. "It's too narrow. I need a pair of tweezers."

"You're in luck," he said, nodding to the next shelf down. A set of tweezers sat in a box with several needles and a collection of glass beads.

She stared at him. "Those are probably three thousand years old," she pointed out, truly horrified.

"They look sturdy enough."

"Absolutely *not*."

The clock by the door assured him it was nearly teatime. By the time he returned, the ballroom should have emptied, especially as the crates all seemed to have been opened. He already knew, without being told, that the only ones allowed to touch the artifacts from here on in would be Persephone or the duke. John was at hand and Persephone would be safe. "I'll fetch something more suitable," he assured her.

"Thank you," she replied primly.

It took no time at all to secure tweezers from his valet and a sewing kit from an upstairs maid. As predicted, the lure of tea and cakes had cleared the room. Only Persephone remained, making notes on her lists, and John in the hall. When he reached for the flask, Persephone stopped him. "I'll do it," she said. "My fingers are smaller."

The way she bit her lower lip when she concentrated made him want to bite it too.

"Almost there," she breathed. A lock of hair fell into her face and he brushed it away. He was gratified at the small hitch in her breath when he let his fingertips trail down her neck. "Got it."

She pulled a soft piece of paper out and it tore, ragged edges releasing. Cursing, she fished out the remains and spread the pieces out on the floor. He crouched beside her to examine them. They were ruined. Sodden, ink running, disintegrating even as she smoothed them down.

"Botheration," she muttered.

"Can you make out any of the words?" he asked.

She peered closer. "Ship," she pointed. "And this looks like a name."

"Which name?" Everything snapped into focus as if he could will the ink back into place.

She shook her head. "I can't make it out. It's too smudged. But it *is* Henry's writing, of that much I am sure." Her mouth turned down with disappointment. "We were so close."

"There's one more letter."

"It's like looking for a needle in a haystack. Anything could have happened to the forgery. It could have been broken or stolen or fell behind a stack of crates."

"Or it could be here." He put the tatters of the letter into his pocket. He didn't want the traitor searching Persephone's rooms, as he'd searched her hermitage, and concluding that she knew more than she did. If he wished to reach such conclusions about Conall, Conall welcomed them. He hoped for them in fact.

Let the traitor come at him.

He was ready. Eager, in point of fact.

Not just for the men lost on that battlefield, but for her.

For Persephone.

Chapter Ten

PERSEPHONE AND CONALL met Priya in the late duchess's private parlor in the family wing. The duke opened it for his goddaughters' use, as long as they did not change the décor. It still had the silk wallpaper patterned with spring-green leaves and the footstools with the gold fringe that Persephone had loved to play with as a child. She had only met the duchess a few times before a fever had claimed her. While her husband loved all things ancient, the duchess had been enamored of...hedgehogs. Crystal and china hedgehogs lined the mantlepiece and marched along the windowsills. They were a cheerful addition, as cheerful as Lady Pendleton had been.

Persephone wasn't sure what she would have thought of her personal morning parlor being converted to a war room. Needs must.

"Meg is fussing with her paintings and Tamsin is trying to get a game of cricket going, thank God," Priya said. "We'd never be able to keep her out of this if she saw us congregating so privately."

"I made a list of everyone at Lady Culpepper's house party," Persephone said as Conall went to stand by the window. It was difficult not to notice the way the morning light gilded his profile and flashed off his coat buttons. "And especially everyone on the terrace the day of the accident."

Conall perused the list. "Very comprehensive," he said.

"The ones on the row on the left were on the terrace when the urn fell," she said.

"Four collectors and two antiquarians. And they match my own recollections. Not a bad place to start.

"I'll start inquiries," Priya said.

"Henry did mention it was a peer of the realm," Persephone added. "So we know that, at the very least. And indeed, only another peer could wield the power to seriously testify against him." She glanced at her list. "We have Lord Darrington, Lord Snettisham, Lord Fairweather, and Sir Barton though I'm not sure he'd have the clout for spy work. Or to take on Henry. He is an earl's son, after all."

"They were on my list as well when we came here," Priya said. "And several others but they've only now arrived so we can likely count them out."

"Not entirely," Conall said. "But they can certainly wait. What do we know of Snettisham?"

"He likes to race his curricle," Priya offered. "Only he's not very good at it. He owes a substantial amount to several earls and to two gaming hells in London."

"Is the amount enough to risk his life and reputation in a scheme to pay them off?"

"Ten thousand pounds."

Persephone couldn't stifle a small gasp. "That much? On wagering?"

Priya nodded. "It's not unusual. He's very kind, so most of his creditors are willing to wait. That part *is* unusual."

"Anything else?" Conall pressed.

"If it wasn't for me, he'd have spent a fortune on a bust of Aphrodite made right here in England and nowhere near Athens," Persephone put in. "He's passably good at knowing the provenance of an Egyptian piece but dismal when it comes to marbles."

"Noted. And Darrington?"

"He is on the market for a countess and popular with the ladies. He has two mistresses."

"He sounds expensive."

"He is. And he also takes very good care of his younger sisters who are both away at school. They want for nothing. He bought a second house strictly to decorate in the Egypt fashion."

Persephone felt a stab of envy. "He does have a grand collection, nearly as good as Lord Fairweather. And Lord Darrington was in the barrow that morning I went down to have a closer look around," Persephone remembered. "It was also the day I found the flask from the burial in the Culpepper library. Someone took it out of the burial I'd opened."

"Perhaps they thought you'd found something inside it," Conall suggested. "Such as a letter."

"Perhaps. But it could just have easily been a well-meaning footman."

"I would be more inclined to believe that if it hadn't been followed closely by your own collection being tossed and an urn falling on your head."

"Fair point."

"Fairweather is *persona non grata* in this house," Priya said. "He *might* be allowed to visit the exhibit but that's it. He'll never be invited to the balls or any soirees. Pendleton is nursing a grudge."

"That might push him to be reckless," Conall said. "As the best of the Egyptian pieces are reserved for the house ballroom, correct?" Persephone nodded. "Do we know why he's been banished?"

"The duke maintains he stole an artifact out from under his nose."

"Do we believe him?"

"It's possible. But it's just as likely Fairweather was simply faster."

"Egyptian piece?"

"No one can remember," Persephone said when they both looked in her direction. "Sumerian? Pompei possibly?"

"The city where that volcano hardened all those people to ash?" Priya asked.

"The very one."

She wrinkled her nose. "You antiquarians are rather ghoulish."

As she wasn't particularly wrong, Persephone didn't bother to argue.

"Are any of these gentlemen so obsessed with Egypt that they would stoop to treason?"

"Yes," Persephone said. "I'm afraid so. But then on paper, so am I."

Priya snorted. Persephone caught the very pointed look she sent her brother. "You suspected me!" Persephone realized.

Conall's cheeks went ruddy. "Not entirely."

Priya rolled her eyes.

"You *investigated* me," Persephone clarified from that reaction.

"I had to."

He looked abysmally uncomfortable. It was strangely endearing. She might have teased him further if Henry's life wasn't depending on the very dogged, stubbornness that had made him add her name to his list. She could appreciate that kind of thoroughness. Especially when it might save her friend. And had already saved her own life.

"Never mind," she said. "You were only doing your duty."

"Well, that was no fun at all," Priya muttered. "You didn't even make him sweat."

Something about the way he glanced at her from the corner of her eye made her struggle not to blush. He was remembering when she had, indeed, made him sweat. And now she was too. She cleared her throat. "I wish we had more to go on."

"I've gone further with less," he assured her. "We will figure it out."

"And if I can ferret out that Fairweather has a secret passageway and two secret rooms in his house, surely I can find out something incriminating. It's only three men, after all," Priya said dismissively.

"And the festival starts tomorrow with a series of lectures on Sixth Dynasty Egypt," Persephone said. "It will attract the Egyptologists in particular."

Conall glanced at the tall clock in the corner, with brass

hedgehogs for hands. "Forgive me, ladies. I have a previous engagement." He bowed. "Percy, don't you dare leave this house without me."

She tilted her head. "John is at hand, should I need to."

"No," he said very decisively. "It's not safe." His eyes burned into hers before he turned on his heel and left. He fair smoldered. She felt like patting the hem of her dress to be sure she wasn't on fire.

"Oh yes," Priya remarked, dry as toasted bread. "Definitely just a sham betrothal."

"It is."

"Mm-hmm." Priya set down her teacup. "I'm worried about Meg."

"Are you? She *is* looking a little peaky." Were her friends in danger even now? Would it be safer to tell them or keep them in the dark? A headache throbbed in her left temple.

"I don't think her uncle is treating her well."

Iron marched through Persephone's voice. "What shall we do?"

"I'll see what I can find out."

"We could ask her."

"She'd never tell us. She wouldn't want us to worry."

"That does sound like Meg."

"But I don't worry," Priya said as they left the parlor. "I act."

There was a soft sound, like a slipper sliding over the wooden floor. Hastily. Persephone caught the hem of a dress, the flutter of a ribbon. By the time they had made it around the corner, the hall was deserted.

"Someone eavesdropping?" Priya wondered grimly.

"Seems that way."

"I didn't see who it was. Did you?"

"No," Persephone said. "But she was wearing a yellow and pink ribbon. So, I know exactly who to ask."

A CONVERSATION WITH her grandmother confirmed that she had given a Miss Ivy Jones a particularly cheerful ribbon because the girl looked so "woeful".

"She keeps herself apart," Lady Blackwell sighed. "And lurks in the corners. She may need a tonic, something to balance her humours. An excess of sanguine, I expect."

There were many reasons why Ivy might have traded her corner-lurking, to hallway-lurking outside private parlors, and most of the ones which immediately sprang to mind were untoward. Did she know the traitor? Was she working with him?

Persephone did not have time to track Conall down. Some things must be dealt with head-on. Especially as Ivy had been in conversation with Persephone's grandmother. The thought of the possible danger made her belly turn sour. Obviously, nothing had come of it, but it was like a shock of cold water down the back of her neck.

She located Ivy taking tea in one of the drawing rooms with the other guests. Holly and Lady Louisa were there, which gave Persephone pause. Holly wore a necklace of garnet that gleamed like raspberries. There was something familiar about it; the color perhaps. She searched for the Lords Darrington, Fairweather, and Snettisham, but they were absent.

"Percy, I'm so glad you've come to join us," her grandmother exclaimed. She'd added tiny birds to her old-fashioned wig for the afternoon. "You need a spot of tea. You haven't stopped in weeks."

"The festival opens tomorrow, Grandmaman," she said, bending to kiss her cheek. She was immediately enveloped in the scents of honey and rose powder. Chartreuse, happily ensconced in her lap, gave a small bark until she received a scratch behind the ear, as was her due. Persephone stepped back and dipped a quick curtsy to everyone assembled on settees and chairs, balancing painted cups and plates of cake. Her grandmother did like cake.

Persephone waited until the conversations resumed before taking her seat next to Ivy. "Good afternoon, Miss Jones."

Ivy forced a smile. "Lady Persephone."

Her grandmother was right. She did seem out of sorts and melancholic. Were there plans afoot? Before she could prod the other lady for information, Lady Louisa gasped theatrically. Her voice carried the soft-loudness of false whispering. The kind that never meant anyone well. "I hear Henry Talbot is wanted for questioning," she said. "Something about misconduct during the war."

Persephone felt the blood drain from her face. Her mouth went dry. It took every single ounce of her willpower not to leap to her feet and toss Lady Louisa straight into the seven-tiered cake on the table behind her. An over-reaction would be suspicious. But not reacting at all, also strange coming from Henry's oldest childhood friend. Persephone got to her feet, slowly.

"Lady Louisa," Persephone's grandmother snapped before she could say anything. "I shan't have the grandson of my greatest friend and *your hostess*, denigrated. Is that quite under-stood?"

Lady Louisa turned red. Holly, showing an unexpected burst of wisdom, abandoned her friend, slipping quietly away. "Of course, we don't believe the gossip, Lady Blackwell," Lady Louisa rushed to explain. "It's only…"

"If one doesn't believe the gossip, one ought not share it."

Persephone allowed herself a brief smile at the sight of Lady Louisa realizing just how formidable of an opponent her grandmother was.

"You're looking flushed," her grandmother continued ruth-lessly. "I believe some fresh air would do you good."

"Yes, Lady Blackwell." Lady Louisa knew herself to be evict-ed. The others didn't make a single comment. Lady Blackwell's stance had been made abundantly clear.

As Louisa slunk away, Persephone caught Ivy slipping out of the drawing room through a side door, only noticing because of the virulent ribbons catching the light. Bless her grandmother. It took her a moment to track her down, tucked inside the music room.

She knew something was amiss. Ivy's furtiveness and nerv-ousness were palpable.

Their reason, however, was not quite what Persephone was expecting.

She imagined one of the first rules of espionage might have something to do with expectations.

Less about two women locked in a passionate embrace.

Ivy was definitely hiding something. But it had nothing to do with Henry. Or the crown.

Perhaps she ought to have been shocked, but she only felt a mild embarrassment for having intruded on a private moment. There were always ladies who had affection for each other, or who lived together and called it practical. But love wasn't practical. She knew that, if nothing else. The feelings she had for Conall burned in her chest and there was nothing she could do about it. They were anything but convenient.

And at the end of the day, who Ivy Jones kissed simply wasn't any of her business. It would not save Henry or falsely condemn him. Persephone eased back around the corner, her heart hammering in her chest. She'd been so certain she was onto something. And she had been, in an accidental roundabout way. It hardly spoke to her skills of deduction and reconnaissance.

And more to the point, it wasn't *her* secret.

It was a kiss that spoke volumes. There was clearly love and devotion between the two, certainly more honesty than there was between Conall and Persephone's pretend engagement and yet Ivy had to hide, fearing for her reputation. And her dignity surely if her odious brother discovered them. Which he might yet do, seeing as he was heading in their direction even now.

"Sir Jones," she said, loudly. Very loudly. "Are you not joining my grandmother for tea?"

"Eh?" He stopped abruptly, blinking at her. "Have you seen my sister?"

"Yes," Persephone replied. "As a matter of fact, I have." She heard the softest scuffle of silk slippers and took Sir Jones's arm hastily. "She was taking tea in the drawing room. You may escort me."

"It's like that, is it?" He puffed up his chest. His cologne was eye-watering.

"Yes," Persephone replied, trying not to choke on either her words or his scent. "Shall we?"

PERSEPHONE TOOK ADVANTAGE of the last moment of solitude she was likely to see for at least a week and padded quietly down the carpeted stairs. The festival started first thing in the morning and excitement found a small space to put down roots, even in a garden fraught with worry over Henry. The new gossip was concerning. It meant either he had landed on British soil and was even now trying to prove his innocence or else it meant… she couldn't even think it.

She must hold onto hope with both hands. It would serve him better than giving into black moods and despair. As tempting as it may be.

Thousands of years ago, women hired themselves out to funeral processions as professional mourners. They ripped their clothes and smeared ashes in their hair and wailed as proof of everyone's grief.

Definitely tempting.

But hardly practical.

She stepped out into the hallway where John stood outside her grandmother's door. "Do you not sleep?" she asked him.

He shrugged one shoulder. "We take shifts, my lady."

"Can I get you some tea? I've just had a tray brought up. It's still hot."

"No, thank you," was his predictable reply.

She narrowed one eye affectionately. "One day, John. Mark my words."

"As you say, my lady."

She darted back into her room and brought out the tray with the silver teapot and a clean cup. There was also a wedge of lemon and a dish shaped like a castle filled with sugar. "I'll leave this here then," she said, putting the tray down on the table between her door and the one he guarded. "With these biscuits."

He nearly smiled.

Strains of violin music interrupted them before she could latch onto her success. It swirled and swelled from under Conall's door. It was beautiful, fervent before ebbing to gentle and fainty melancholic. He had not lost the knack of playing. The sound of it still sent tiny shivers across the back of her neck. John very carefully did not look at Conall's bedroom door, nor at herself. He likely thought she'd been about to sneak into his room. Hardly unusual for a betrothed couple. She decided she would not blush.

Someone forgot to tell that to the red splotches on her cheeks.

"I'll leave you to it then, John," she said, lifting her candle and hurrying down the hall, *away* from Conall's bedroom. His music followed her, tempting.

She made her way down to the ballroom and set her candle down on a pedestal table inside. The shadows softened, edged with gold. The light gleamed off polished glass and waxed floors and the deceptively demure quality to Meg's painted nymphs. Much like their artist, a soft cheek hid a will of iron. If you looked close enough one of the nymphs appeared to be holding a knife instead of silvery flowers.

Persephone wandered along the exhibits, admiring the coins, the carved marbles, the statuary. The duke was well pleased with the effect. They had done what no one else had yet to do. He ought to be proud. And her, as well. She allowed herself a tiny beat of pride. She was a good antiquarian. She had not upended her life in vain, despite her feelings for Conall. She had traded one passion for another. It might not feel fair, but there were far greater injustices.

Her reflection in the glass of a cabinet partially obscured the funerary mask of a noble Egyptian lady. Her elegant braids replaced Persephone's hair and she shared her gold circlet willingly. Persephone took strength from it.

When the light of a candle angled into the ballroom from the doorway, Persephone moved without cognisant thought. She ducked behind a group of potted ferns, prodded by the events of the last week. She might be safe here in the duke's country house, but she was not a fool. The click of a gentleman's shoes echoed on the marble in the hall and a long shadow fell into the room.

Lord Darrington.

Interesting.

Persephone stayed still, watching as he peered hurriedly into the cabinets. He looked nervous as he opened one of the doors by breaking the glass, muffling the sound with a cravat wrapped around his hand.

Outrage exploded under her skin. He was tampering with her exhibits.

He reached inside, plucking something from a velvet case and dropping it into his pocket.

Correction. He was *stealing* from her exhibits.

She'd known he was dodgy from the morning he'd expected her to climb out of the barrow because it wasn't suitable for ladies. She'd just had no idea how dodgy.

Certainly dodgy enough to be a traitor.

She knew the shelf he was rifling through didn't hold any forgeries. But he didn't know that.

She gave serious consideration to tackling him where he stood. She had the element of surprise. She might even be able to take him down. She was about to launch from the shadows when Conall filled the doorway. He spotted her at once, his gaze sharp and full of warning. He shook his head once, nearly imperceptible. Persephone hesitated, staying hidden among the leaves.

"Darrington," he said lazily, as if he hadn't a care in the world. "I thought you'd have found better entertainment by now."

Darrington jumped, making a squeaky sound that he tried to cover with a cough. "Northwyck."

"None of the ladies to your liking?"

"Fancied a walk," he said.

"That's not all you fancied, is it?"

"What's that now? I really must be off to bed," Darrington said quickly. "Big day tomorrow with the festival and all."

"Oh, I don't think so," Conall said, still blocking the exit. "Let's have a chat, you and I?"

"Can it wait?" Darrington tried another tactic, a wheedling boys-will-be-boys chuckle. "Bedsports, as you said. Can't keep the lady waiting. Frightfully rude."

Conall, clearly bored with the game, whipped his arm out, grabbing Darrington's shirt in his fist. He lifted the surprised man off his feet. Darrington gurgled. "Here now!"

"Empty your pockets," Conall demanded.

"Is this a joke?"

"Empty your pockets," he repeated coldly. "*Now.*"

Shaking, Darrington complied. Gold tumbled onto the floor at his feet.

There was a beat of silence. "These are coins."

Persephone frowned. Coins? How did he expect Henry to smuggle a letter inside coins? She stifled a sound of frustration, much like the one Conall appeared to want to make. Darrington wasn't a traitor. He was a thief.

Well, not *just* a thief. Persephone still considered that reason enough for a proper smack. Preferably with a big stick. *How dare he?*

"You were stealing coins."

"A bit of a lark," Darrington said, sweat beading his brow. He tried to smile. Nothing about Conall's stance or expression invited a smile. Of any kind.

"I'm sure I don't need to mention that should anything else go missing, anything at all, the magistrate's irons will be nothing to what awaits you when I find you, Darrington."

"See here, I'm an earl, same as you," Darrington sputtered, bravado wavering.

"Yes, but you didn't steal from *me*, did you? You stole from a *duke.*"

Darrington paled. "Meant nothing by it."

"I am sure."

"Are you…going to tell him?"

Conall paused, waited for more sweat to bead on the other man's brow. "Of course, I am."

"But…no harm done. You have the coins!"

"Being a poor thief does not absolve you from the theft in the first place." He shoved the other man away, releasing his shirt. "Off you go."

Darrington fair galloped from the room. Persephone expected he might try running all the way back to London.

Conall locked the doors carefully behind him. "You can come

out now, Persephone."

"Priya's right, you do have a preternatural ability to see where we are," she grumbled.

He smiled faintly. "And as I told her, when the fashions change to less frippery on the hemline, you will find hiding to be much easier."

She glanced down at the lace wafting around the bottom of her dressing gown. "Noted." She stepped out of the leaves. "Do you think Darrington is still running?"

"Definitely."

"Good." She hurried forward and plucked the coins from the floorboards. "What did he take? Did he harm them?"

"A handful of Roman coins," Conall explained.

She beamed at him. "You knew they were Roman."

"They were sitting next to the figurine of an armless Vestal Virgin. Hardly remarkable detective skills."

"Still." She examined them carefully. "He left a fingerprint." She wiped it off gently. "And he calls himself an antiquarian."

"Shameful," Conall agreed.

She heard the teasing in his voice as she placed them carefully back where they belonged. "There."

"All right with the world?"

She stepped back and surveyed her borrowed domain. "I think so. I am going to have to lock the rest of these cabinets myself and move the artifacts from the broken shelf. I assumed the duke had seen to it. A shameful oversight on my part. Not that it excuses Darrington in any way."

Luckily, she had the keys in her pocket. She'd been carrying them with her since the crates had first been delivered. She went to each door, found the right key from the ring, fit it into the lock and turned it, then tested it. On and on she went. Conall watched her patiently, with a little smile.

"Better?" he asked, when she had finally finished.

"Yes."

"All done?"

Something in his voice alerted her. "Y-yes."

"Good."

He was kissing her practically before she saw him move. He pressed her back against the cabinet, lips slanting over hers. The case behind her rattled. She pulled back, horrified. "The artifacts!"

He chuckled against her mouth, even as his hands encircled her waist and lifted her up, taking her weight. She clamped her legs around his hips and his hands skimmed lower, clasping her bottom. His kiss deepened and it had her head swimming, especially when he stalked away from the delicate exhibits and pressed her to the wall behind the ferns. They were alone. Frantic, heated. Desperate.

She'd never felt like this before. The juxtaposition of the press of his warm body against hers and the hard wall behind her was intoxicating. She kissed him back hungrily. He yanked at the ties to her dressing gown until it fell open and then he pulled away, enough to lower his head and suck her nipple into his mouth. She moaned. "Shh," he said, sucking harder, then swirling his tongue around the tight bud until she tingled. "Someone will hear you."

She tried to bite back the sounds, squirming against him until he groaned. They taunted each other, teasing, competing to draw out needy keening sounds, husky gasps, something that sounded suspiciously like a purr.

He skimmed his thumbs under her nightdress and along her folds, while sucking at her collarbone. She wasn't just on fire, she was drowning too. She ran her hands down his sculpted chest, warm muscles contracting at her touch. She followed the trail of hair, dipping under the waistband of his trousers. She managed to undo the placard and his hardness sprang into her hands. "We should find a bed." His breath was ragged. "Before I take you against a wall."

"Do it," she whispered, biting his earlobe, marveling at her own demands. "Now."

He pulled back, eyes blazing into hers. She wasn't sure what he was looking for, but he must have found it. He ran the tip of his cock along her heat, then pushed into her, slowly. With such agonizing, delicious slowness that she clutched at his shoulders, gasping. "Conall."

He withdrew, pushed forward. Heat gathered in her belly; a

tingling softness washed up her thighs. *"Conall."*

Her orgasm built, like the tide flooding through her, waves pushing deeper and deeper inside her until they crashed the shore and she fell apart. As her cries intensified, he put his palm across her mouth, muffling her. The pleasure sharpened, threatened to pull her under. She went willingly.

When she bit into the pad of his thumb, he followed. He pulled out, careful not to leave her with child, but it was a mere second's work and he still came as if she had found a sudden secret switch. She felt powerful, pleased, desperate for more of the way he groaned against her. His muscles tightened, shoulders rigid, and his head dropped against her neck. His breath was warm, sated.

He grinned, lips tickling her skin. "I begin to see why you love these exhibits so much."

Chapter Eleven

THOUGH THEY HAD eliminated two suspects, the next morning did not offer much time to celebrate. Not even with her muscles feeling soft and deliciously sore from the previous night's exploits and a plate piled with crumpets, crannies filled with melted butter and honey. The tea was hot and sweet, the excitement for the dawning festival palpable—and the daily newspaper from London unwelcome. She did not manage to read it until she was in the duke's study, summoned from a table swelling with whispers.

The house was full near to bursting now which put her on edge. Conall had not come to breakfast again. Lord Darrington had fled the house, and the village, as expected. She admitted to a small thrill of justified vindication at the news. It served him right for trying to steal precious artifacts from the duke. But at least he wasn't actively trying to get anyone hanged. That was in his favor.

The duke was drinking strong coffee with cream, the tray placed haphazardly among piles of paper. Mrs. Hastings bustled past Persephone. "See that he eats something, dear."

"I'll do my best."

The duke, being a duke, did not take orders. He was, however, somewhat more susceptible to his goddaughters. He was also the tiniest bit contrary. Persephone reached for the toasted bread next to his cup even though it was monstrously rude to steal from a duke. And she'd already had her breakfast. "Hey now, that's mine," he tuttered and took a large bite of the next piece.

She hid a smile. "Good morning, Your Grace."

"We're well in hand, are we?" he asked, reaching for the elderberry jelly. Mrs. Hastings was clever; she'd brought him all of his favorites.

"Well enough. The exhibits are secured." She debated telling him about Lord Darrington. He'd be cross if she kept it from him, as she would have been. She explained his absence briefly. His scowl was so fierce she wondered he wasn't giving himself a headache. "That blackguard!" he roared. "And to think I admired his mummy case." He thumped his hand down on the oak table, rattling his cup. "I'll have him barred from every good antiquarian society."

"I believe Con—that is, Lord Northwyck, may have put the fear of God into him."

"Good lad," the duke approved.

"How go the preparations for the opening ball?" she inquired. He still looked put out, but he did eat a handful of raspberries with his bread, so it evened out.

"Mrs. Hastings informs me the circus troupe has arrived and their caravans are digging up the back lawn. She is quite cross over it"

"And you still won't tell me why you have hired acrobats?"

"It's a surprise, my dear. You've worked yourself to the bone on my festival, you ought to have a lovely surprise like everyone else."

She smiled. "Thank you, Your Grace."

"Now where's your young man?"

She stifled a wince. How she hated lying to him. "I have not seen him this morning."

"Lying in bed like a lazy good-for-nothing. I'm glad he'll have you to set him straight. I don't mind saying his rakehell days were beginning to be a concern to me. Very unlike him."

She couldn't disagree. She couldn't explain either.

"But that's not why I summoned you here," he slapped at her hand when she reached for the berries. "Nor to nibble on my breakfast like a rabbit in the carrot patch."

"If you won't eat it, I shall. Pity for it to go to waste."

"I'll eat it." He pointed a toast corner in her direction. "And don't think I don't know what you're doing."

She sank into a chair and grinned. "I'm sure I don't know what you mean."

"Hmph." He brushed crumbs off his hands. "Have you read the newspaper today?"

Her grin faltered. "I haven't."

He pushed it toward her, opened to the relevant headline: *Earl's son vanished and wanted for questioning!*

She skimmed it, a chill creeping under her skin. Henry Talbot, heir to the Culpepper earldom mentioned by name. It wasn't merely gossip any more. The traitor had launched his attack on Henry. Printed in black and white.

Hot rage licked up her chest.

"Balderdash, of course," the duke said, and she could have kissed his weathered cheek. "I've known that boy since he was in swaddling clothes. You wouldn't happen to know what this is about, would you? He never did get into scrapes without you."

That was true. She blinked back the sting of tears. No time to fall apart. Cleopatra didn't weep all over Marc Anthony. "I fear for him," she said through the constriction of her throat. "He should be home by now."

"Try not to fret. A peer is not so easily maligned."

Unless it was by another peer. Another reason to suspect the traitor was well-heeled and well-connected. Lord Darrington might be guilty, after all. She had the sneaking suspicion that Conall had already set a man on him, just in case.

"Lady Culpepper must be beside herself," he added.

"I imagine so. She will attend every event though, I am certain of it," Persephone said. "She won't give an inch to the gossips or the naysayers."

"Good. What's left to do then?"

"Tending to your acrobats," she said, trying to sound calm. Adrenaline sizzled through her. She realized she was still gripping the newspaper and wrinkling it beyond the repair of a hot iron.

She set it down carefully. "The artifacts have all arrived, the lecturers are secure and comfortable in their lodgings, the hall is clean and ready."

"You are a treasure, Percy."

"It was my pleasure, Your Grace."

"One day you'll run a museum to rival Bullock's Egyptian Hall. To rival the British Museum even!"

"If only, Your Grace." Right now, she would settle for clearing Henry's name and having him safe at home. Having the funds to open her own museum was a distant dream.

"You'll see," the duke winked. "Why do you think I've asked you to help me with this festival? Now you have the experience and the stage on which to prove your skills to the world."

"Is that why you're doing this?" she asked, surprised. "Sneaky."

"It's *one* of the reasons. I want my Cinderellas happy and well taken care of. We need to show you off to all of the eligible young men."

She groaned. "You're not matchmaking, are you?"

"It worked well enough for you, didn't it? I knew how it would be. Conall always did have a soft spot for you."

She looked at him dubiously.

"Always made sure you were nearby when he played his violin. Never noticed that, did you?"

She blinked. "No, I didn't. I'm sure that was a coincidence."

"Ha! But there is also the side benefit of having the others gnashing their teeth in envy over my festival." He rubbed his hands together. "And Snettisham might finally sell me that blasted gold torc he won't stop gloating over."

PERSEPHONE FOUND CONALL in the music room, a violin perched on his shoulder. She wondered if the duke was right. Had he really played near enough to her that she might hear him, all of those years ago? He called forth a few notes now, long trembling sounds that set the hairs on her arms to prickling. He had discarded his coat and rolled up his sleeves. His forearms were strong, lightly dusted with hair. She would have let herself be momentarily distracted if he hadn't been frowning.

"Is the violin misbehaving?" she asked, stepping inside.

He tensed, hardness in his eyes, alertness in every line of his body, before realizing it was her. He smiled faintly. "I've been away a long time. She wants me to prove myself."

"As she should."

The storm cleared from his face if not the edgy vigilance. "You are looking well this morning." He dropped his voice. "No soreness?"

A blush crept up her neck and into her face so hotly she half worried her hair might catch fire. "I am well." In truth, she was a little bit sore, but it was a delicious soreness. The kind you earned with pleasure. He knew it too if the look on his face was anything to go by. "Oh, stop it."

He chuckled softly and reached for her hand. She wasn't wearing gloves again, they interfered with pencils and quills and there was too much to do. "But I don't want to stop," he said, pressing his lips to the inside of her wrist. He nipped gently and heat shot between her legs, as if he'd lit an invisible candlewick. She caught her breath. "You are delightful," he grinned against her.

"And you're teasing me."

"Every chance I get, love."

She was flustered and overly warm and had the ridiculous urge to giggle. Honestly, he was far too powerful. She could get drunk on him, like a port wine.

Later.

She held up the newspaper. "There's news."

His spine straightened immediately. "Tell me."

"Henry is now mentioned by name. They are already casting doubt on his honour."

He took the paper from her. "Anything specific?"

"No."

"That's something in our favor."

"Do you think so?" She wanted him to be right. Wanted the comfort of it. But she needed it to be true. Platitudes were not enough. Not now.

"Yes. If they had any kind of proper evidence, they wouldn't hesitate to print it. To use it against him. I'd know about it. This is our traitor, chumming the waters." He started to pace.

"What's chumming?"

"Fishermen will agitate the waters with blood and fish parts to lure in the bigger fish they mean to catch."

She watched him for a moment. His shoulders were tense, the tendons in his neck standing out against his skin. "You're worried."

"I'm restless," he admitted. "Prickly."

"Is that why you were playing the violin instead of eating breakfast?"

He nodded. "It helps. I never would have thought it could. I have you to thank for that."

"I'm glad."

"It's more than that today, however," he added. "That night of the fireworks, I was reacting to memories of the past. But this is different. I've had this feeling before, during the war. As if my body knows something my brain has not yet realized."

"What does that mean?"

"It means I think we need to draw out the traitor."

"I have been thinking the very same thing. If we wait much longer Henry might be lost."

"More importantly, I don't want the traitor to grow any more desperate and come for you."

She swallowed. "I suppose he might."

"He won't reach you," Conall said darkly. "But we must flush him out. It's becoming more and more obvious that we can't wait for an artifact that may or may not come to a little English village all the way from Egypt."

She lifted an eyebrow. "I could make one. A forgery."

He lifted an eyebrow back at her. "You could at that."

"A better one."

"Naturally." It felt good to have a plan, an objective that did not rely on chance. "I'll start at once."

He caught her hand before she could dart away. His expression was serious, practically solemn. "Persephone."

She froze, the scowled. "What? If you tell me to stay in my rooms and let you handle this, I will brain you with that violin."

He half-smiled, quick, fleeting. "I shouldn't dare."

"Good."

"But this is dangerous business. I need you to be careful. Don't think to leave *me* out in the cold while you try to handle this alone."

"I wouldn't." She squirmed. She would. She absolutely would.

"I made you a promise, not to leave you out of your own life, as you put it."

"Yes."

"I need the same promise from you."

It was only fair. She didn't like it, but it was just. She met his eyes, that sea-grey. "I promise."

"Thank you. This man has already proven that he will do anything, including hurt *you*, to keep his secret."

She frowned. "Do you know, it occurs to me that we are *assuming* it is a man."

He blinked. "Are you suggesting a woman is behind these plots?"

"It's possible."

"I hope you're wrong."

"Because a woman couldn't have the shrewdness to do this?"

"No," he said, wryly. "Because it would make me an idiot who only investigated half of the possible culprits."

"SHE'S SMILING AGAIN," Priya sighed.

"It must be the ague," Tamsin put in. Meg only smiled at Persephone sympathetically and made herself comfortable in a well-worn chair in the corner of the room.

They had descended on the hermitage to keep her company and keep each other safe. Conall had posted John, who still refused to take tea, and another footman in the rose garden while he went about some other bit of investigation, something about doing his own chumming of the waters. It was noon, the sun was high, there were armed men patrolling outside her window and several fierce women at her side. She was safe as houses.

And it was deeply comforting to be back in the hermitage, even if some of her artifacts were still in pieces. One of the shelves had yet to be affixed back to the wall where it had been torn away. But it was still hers, down to the painting of Cleopatra on the far wall and the baskets of flints she'd been finding in the fields since she was seven years old. She could breathe here, could think properly.

Conall had balked at telling Tamsin and Meg the truth, but Priya agreed it was safest. Tamsin would start poking about if she realized something was afoot and she could easily make things inadvertently dangerous for herself. She was already asking pointed questions. Persephone wasn't convinced that any traitor who was willing to put her in his sights would also not be willing to turn his ire on her closest friends, should he think it an advantage. Her grandmother, however, remained blissfully unaware. An elderly lady wearing marzipan fruit in her hair and waving a pistol on the front lawn was surely to no one's advantage. Although a fine back-up plan, should it be required.

She would feel better when this forgery drew out the traitor.

"We'll find him," Priya said. Persephone must have made some sound.

"And we'll clear Henry's name," Tamsin agreed. "I always liked Henry. He never tried to talk me out of climbing trees when we were little."

Persephone smiled at that, and her resolve hardened. They would bring this affair to an end. She would not wait like trout in the pond for the fisherman's hook. "Conall did not say where he was going?" she asked Priya again.

Priya shook her head, also frustrated. "You know how he is. Infuriating."

"You don't need Conall," Tamsin scoffed. "You have us."

"But maybe Conall needs *us*," Persephone said softly. She turned her attention back to the clay in front of her since there was nothing else to do. She had decided on a scarab beetle, large enough to fit in the palm of her hand. It formed the lid of a small dish, both fired in the small kiln locked away in the secret room.

She used blue paint, though it rankled not to use crushed lapis lazuli as would have been proper. Gilt shone on the lines of the body, contouring the legs and the partitioned curve of its back. She could picture something similar sitting in Cleopatra's boudoir, for lotus root sweets, or powdered kohl to line her eyes.

It was simple soothing work, so familiar under her hands that her mind wandered.

To last night.

She could scarcely believe that she, plain and slightly odd Persephone Blackwell, had done such things. In a ballroom. With an *earl*.

She could still feel his mouth on her neck, his hands on her thighs, pushing gently at her knees, sliding into the heat of her.

Tamsin leaned her head back, feet swinging. "I will say this subterfuge business is surprisingly dull."

Persephone jumped. She'd nearly forgotten where she was.

Tamsin slid Meg a sideways glance. "And Meg has eaten all of the biscuits."

Meg did not look up from her novel. She had embroidered small red birds all over her dress, especially along the hem where it threatened to fray. "The crumbs on your dress prove otherwise."

"I was hoping someone would give me a pistol," Tamsin added, wistfully.

Priya snorted.

"And oversight," Tamsin continued, pointedly. She pulled a small pistol out of her reticule. "One I rectified immediately."

Meg did look up at that. "Try not to shoot off your own foot."

Tamsin rolled her eyes. "I daresay I'm a better shot than that footman currently traipsing through the foxgloves. Father started taking me hunting when I was in pigtails."

Meg nodded. "That's true."

Tamsin sat back, mollified. No one mentioned that her father had not taken her anywhere since he married Lady Chester, the summer Tamsin turned thirteen. Tamsin, being Tamsin, had kept practicing. Hoping.

"There." Persephone wiped her hands on her work apron. "That should do it. It will need to be fired and then to sit awhile. But it will be ready by tomorrow evening."

"Just in time for the opening ball," Priya murmured.

"Finally," Tamsin said. "A ball with the promise of some excitement."

THE FIRST MORNING of Little Barrow Antiquarian Festival dawned cloudy and wet, because this was England, after all, not Egypt. Even a duke could not control the weather. But it hardly signified as the day started with lectures located inside several buildings well stocked with carafes of tea and towers of elegant sugar biscuits in the shape of pyramids and Roman columns. Excitement thrummed through Persephone, eclipsing all other worries, if only for a moment.

Men gathered, removing their tall-crowned hats and ladies slipped between them in pelisses trimmed with braid. The duke sat in the front, nodding and smiling and clearly enjoying the spectacle. A footman stood nearby, ready to bring him refreshments. The duke had been very clear that all women, from the dairymaid to the dowager countess, should be admitted to all of the events, should have they have even a modicum of interest. The baker's wife sat in a chair in her best dress, having made so many pastries and cookies in the shapes of ancient buildings that Persephone now considered her an architectural expert. This morning's new display of the Parthenon had been carefully carried inside the hall to be admired by all and sundry. Pride stained her cheeks red.

"You've done well," Meg said.

Persephone surreptitiously wiped her hands on her dress. "I hope so." She could have done without the heads turning in their direction, and the whispering. But it was worth it.

"They are impressed with what you've accomplished here," Conall murmured, stepping up behind her. He bowed to Meg. "Lady Meg." When he bowed to Persephone his eyes glinted wickedly. She felt it like a streak of heat running down the back of her legs.

She cleared her throat. "Lord Northwyck."

His eyes laughed at her. She narrowed hers back at him. "You look fetching as always, love."

"Mm-hmm."

He turned his head suddenly, focused on the trio of ladies on the front step: Lady Dorcas, Lady Louisa, Miss Richardson. Rain pattered softly on the street behind them. "Just the ladies I wanted to see," he said under his breath.

Persephone blinked. "Really?"

He filled the doorway, suddenly imposing. There was none of the carefree charm he usually showed in public. "Ladies, I regret to inform you that the lecture hall is full."

Lady Dorcas drew herself up. "I beg your pardon?" The flowers on her bonnet bobbed indignantly.

"Lady Persephone has done such an admirable job that there are simply no spots left."

"Conall," Persephone murmured but he ignored her.

Meg nudged her gleefully. "Oh, let him."

"Do you know who I am?" Lady Dorcas asked sharply.

"In fact, I do," Conall replied blandly, before shutting the door in her face.

It was magnificently rude.

"My sister told me how they treated you," he said to Persephone as her mouth dropped open.

And deeply touching.

"Don't you dare let them in," he said.

"I won't let her," Meg promised, her usual quiet smile rather bloodthirsty at the edges.

"Good," he said, before walking away as if nothing particularly out of the ordinary had happened.

Persephone felt warm all over. "What just happened?"

Meg slipped her arm through hers. "Oh, I do like him."

"Still, I ought to let them in."

"Certainly not," Meg returned. "The first lecture is about to begin. It would be rude to interrupt."

THE DAY PASSED in a blur. Persephone was thrilled and exhausted by the late afternoon, as people dispersed to discuss what they had learned or to rest for the duke's ball. Persephone had learned that the wall around the Pyramid of Djoser had 15 doors, but only one that opened. The other fourteen were reserved for the pharaoh's spirit's private use in the afterlife. She also learned that Sobekneferu was the first lady pharaoh, Hatshepsut the longest ruling lady pharaoh and that her new shoes pinched. That last discovery was unlikely to make it into the journals. She was grateful to step into the carriage the duke had sent to fetch her as John leapt up to sit next to the coachman.

She was even more grateful for the picnic basket filled with food and bottles of lemonade, offered to her by a smug Conall. Burgundy embroidery covered his waistcoat, and his cravat was a silvery gray, simply yet impeccably tied. He exuded strength and calm confidence. She found herself craving it almost as much as the food her stomach grumbled for. "I thought you might be hungry," he said, handing her a piece of soft bread smothered with fresh butter.

"Starving," she admitted. "There was very little time to eat once the schedule really got going."

"You must be proud."

She wiggled her feet out of her shoes with a small sigh. "I'm grateful it's gone well so far."

"Well, I'm proud of you, if you won't be."

"Maybe a little proud," she said as the horses were urged into a walk. The carriage swayed slightly.

"That's my girl."

She really should ask him to stop saying things like that, especially with that fond smile, the secret quiet one she remembered from years ago. It was going to make things so much more difficult for her when they had to part ways. And yet she couldn't bring herself to ask him to stop. She may as well have a secret well of memories to keep her warm when the inevitable came. She took another bite of bread and cheese to stop herself from saying something untoward. Something embarrassing. "Is the duke pleased?" she asked, after swallowing.

"Strutting and swaggering like a man just out of short pants."

She grinned. "I'm glad." She tried to stretch her ankles surreptitiously. Conall glanced down when she accidentally nudged his leg. "I'm sorry. I should have known better than to wear new shoes. And there's dancing yet to do." There would be precious little time to rest before the ball.

Conall touched her knee and let his hand slide down her shin, lightly. His finger hooked around her ankle, lifting her foot into his lap. She blinked. "What are you doing?"

"This." He ran his knuckles firmly along her instep and she nearly purred. *Did* purr if she were honest. Out loud. "Oh my."

He smiled. "Poor love, you've had a day. I don't think you sat down once. I saw John trying to catch his breath just following you."

"It's been brilliant." She nearly moaned when he increased the pressure of his ministrations. "This is the best part. Even considering I learned about Thutmoses."

She leaned her head back and closed her eyes. She might have fallen asleep if the intense pleasure of having her feet rubbed wasn't making her feel inappropriate. She shouldn't have her feet in a man's lap in the bright daylight. But it felt so good.

"Percy," Conall whispered against her ear. "Sweetheart, we're here."

Her eyes popped open. He was caging her against the cushions. The gleam in his grey eyes was devilish, amused. "Did I fall asleep?" she asked.

"You did, love." He kissed the tip of her nose.

She blinked. "I did not."

"You snored a little too."

"I did not!"

He grinned and it was the grin of a well-pleased man who had been able to forget they were hunting a possible murderer, if only for the length of a carriage ride from village to country house. "Come on," he said, leaning back as John opened the door. She slipped her shoes back on though her feet protested. "They'll have a proper meal waiting for you inside."

She curled her hand around the handle of the picnic basket. "I want this meal," she said. He'd brought it for her. She would take cheese and hand pies and currant buns over goose in cream sauce with asparagus from the hothouse or the rarest of pineapples. No insult to the duke's chef. She didn't want blancmange set in a mold shaped like a peacock. She wanted this.

"As you like," Conall said when she tightened her hold as if he might take the simple feast away. "But let me carry it up for you."

"I can manage."

"Percy, let me help. I don't know anything about the pyramids or how to catalogue Greek marbles, but I can do this."

She relinquished her hold and stepped down onto the gravel drive. The house bustled, stableboys ran back and forth to the barn as guests arrived from the village, more guests strolled in the last of the sunlight and yet more shared tea in the drawing room. Mrs. Hastings rushed past with a basket of beeswax candles, followed by several housemaids with armfuls of fresh flowers or tea trays for the bedrooms. Conall led the way between throng, Persephone behind him. She wanted only a meal and a moment of quiet before the preparations for the ball truly got underway. Conall left the basket inside her door and bowed. "Until tonight."

Something about the way he said it made her feel like blushing.

She wished she could think of a reason he might want to stay engaged after they found the traitor out. But a girl like her did not become a marchioness. She might be an earl's daughter, but she was hardly trained for regular household management. She knew how to make a replica of a Grecian urn, but little about the kind of social navigation the wife of a marquess needed to know. No one would accept a supper invitation from her, even if she wished to issue one. And truthfully, she'd rather be digging in the fields.

"We've been through this before, Percy," she muttered to herself. "Don't be a ninny."

She ate more cheese than anyone ought to and three currant buns with icing and felt better equipped to deal with the evening. The duke had already expressly forbidden her to plead a headache or fatigue. She was to attend and dance and flirt like a lady who knew how to do those things effortlessly.

Even if she didn't feel like one.

She did feel warmth though, lingering in her cheeks and her belly, from the way Conall had turned Lady Dorcas and the others away, from the way he noticed when she was tired or hungry and always seem to have the remedy on hand. She was beginning to look for him every time she entered a room, to wonder if he was playing the violin when he wasn't there, to smile when he caught her eye from across the room and winked.

It would be hard to say goodbye.

"Stop it," she added, since she didn't seem to be listening to her own earlier scolding. She had her grandmother, her friends, the duke, a lovely house and a full larder. She had more blessings than most. It wouldn't do to sulk.

Sarah helped get her into an ivory gown with a thin burgundy mesh overdress. She'd added a bright pink ribbon under her breasts and pink flowers in her dark hair, to make her grandmother happy and to save herself from yellow or orange festoons. Her gloves were the same pink and reached to her elbows, tied with little white bows.

"Oh, you do look fine, my lady," Sarah said.

"Thank you, Sarah."

Persephone met her grandmother in the hall. She wore a dress that resembled nothing so much as limes and champagne, al brightness and lace froth. Her wig was the same green, fresh as spring. She'd wrapped silk leaves and flowers around her cane. Persephone hugged her fondly. "You look like springtime."

Lady Blackwell smiled. "Thank you, dear. You look very well, yourself. I do like that pink ribbon." She looked askance at John, stationed between their doors. "This fellow is always outside our door."

Persephone met John's gaze quickly. "Yes, Grandmaman. In case you need anything."

Her grandmother snorted. "He's here because Henry's troubles have found us."

Persephone blinked. "Oh. Um." Clearly, she would not have made a brilliant spy. She couldn't fool her own grandmother.

She rolled her eyes. "I'm old, Percy, I'm not stupid."

"I've never thought that!"

"I know." She patted her hand. "You're a good girl. Now, I expect you to dance and make merry. Henry won't be helped by your hiding behind the potted plants. And you have a fiancé, now."

"Yes, Grandmaman."

She pursed her lips at John, in his dark livery. "Young man, you could do with some brightening up. Have you considered a red ribbon for your hair?"

John looked decidedly nonplussed.

"Or around the buckles of your shoes?"

"I don't think the duke allows trimming of the livery," Persephone jumped in. John looked relieved. Possibly. For a man with so few facial expressions, it was difficult to tell. But she was nearly positive the mention of a red ribbon had caused a tick at the corner of his left eye.

"Hmph," her grandmother said. "I shall talk to him about that."

Chapter Twelve

T HE DUKE OF Pendleton had outdone himself.

Guests and gossip columnists would talk about the Little Barrow Antiquarian Festival opening ball for months to come. The ballroom glittered with candelabras set with beeswax candles, and oil lamps that heated and scented the air with honey. Music was provided by an orchestra hidden behind a screen. That was where the similarities ended. For one thing, the screen was painted with mummies and turquoise scarab beetles.

Meg had finished her murals and the stunning artwork reflected the Roman countryside and mythical figures on the right and the pyramids and Nile and mysterious hieroglyphs of Egypt on the other.

The footmen were outfitted with leather tunics such as centurions might have worn, causing more than one appreciative murmur. The costumes did not end there. The female dancers hired by the duke wore traditional sleeveless chitons, caught at the shoulders with fibulae brooches. They were ornamented with gold snake armbands and gold-painted sandals. They stood between columns decorated with flowers, holding yet more candelabras. At some secret signal known only to them, their postures would change, like living statues. They offered bowls of wine like Vestal Virgins, fainted upon couches as though at a feast, stayed still as the marble columns of the Parthenon. They were paintings come to life.

On the other side of the room, more dancers posed: Isis with her wings, Cleopatra with her golden hairpiece and kohl-lined eyes, Anubis in a dark kilt with the plaster-head of a jackal. Persephone could all but feel the hot sand under her feet, and the sun on her head. She couldn't stop smiling, even though she knew one was supposed to act with casual ennui at all times. It simply wasn't possible, not with such a feast for the eyes. They were unique and breath-taking and quite pulled focus from the excellent canapes circling on silver trays and the glitter of diamonds and pearls and gold pocket watches. Elegant gowns and starched cravat points seemed so very dull in comparison.

"This is madness," Tamsin said, popping up behind her. "Beautiful, brilliant madness. I think Julius Caesar just offered me an onion tartlet."

"Never mind that," Meg added, joining them. Her gown was embroidered with vines of delicate green leaves and lush red peonies. Her cheeks were rosy and already less gaunt than when she'd arrived a week ago. She'd woven a green ribbon in her hair in case Persephone's grandmother forced one on her again. "Isis nearly poked me in the eye with her wing."

"It's even better than I could have imagined," Persephone sighed.

"If you walk down there, perhaps a goddess will poke out your eye too." She handed Tamsin a yellow ribbon. "Lady Blackwell instructed me to give you this."

Tamsin groaned. Persephone wrinkled her nose. "You know how my grandmother is."

Tamsin tied the ribbon around the top of her left glove with a rakish bow, muttering under her breath all the while. Persephone searched the stylish and sophisticated crowd for a glimpse of Conall. She saw oiled hair, flounces of lace, flashes of jeweled hair bobs. Older men with whiskers, younger men with spots. "I'm too short," she muttered. "Meg, can you see Conall?"

"Conall, is it?" Tamsin teased at her casual use of his given name. "How scandalous. The old men will choke on their cravats."

Meg, being the tallest, rose on her tiptoes, surreptitiously scanning the guests. "I don't see him."

Persephone told herself not to worry. He'd survived the war. Traitor or no, he'd survive a summer ball. John stood behind, sharp-eyed. She turned to ask him if he knew where Conall had gone, but he shook his head before she could open her mouth. He didn't look worried. Of course, he never looked worried so that was hardly telling.

As her grandmother led the first dance, a cheerful round lime on the arm of the dignified duke, Persephone accepted a flute of champagne. A viscount in a red coat asked Tamsin to dance the quadrille and she accepted. The viscount would have to work to keep up with her. Meg's time was claimed by an older gentleman who smelled like clove oil. Persephone watched the dancers whirling and laughing. She couldn't suppress an anxious feeling that tightened her muscles and made bones her feel itchy. She circled the room, trying to enjoy the attention the exhibits were receiving. A conversation between a small group of guests floated toward her.

"An earl's son, can you imagine? Written up in the newspapers."

"His father won't even vouch for him."

"Henry always was a little odd, you know. Hated life in Town."

"That hardly makes him odd." The last was delivered by Persephone, in a tone generally reserved for pharaohs and annoyed governesses. The gentlemen straightened and blinked down their noses at her. "Have we been introduced?" One asked in a tone he likely thought was cutting. It did not hold a candle to her pharaohs and governesses.

"No," she replied blandly. "Thank God."

She was rewarded with three identical sniffs of surprise.

"Percy, there you are?" Priya interrupted. She was beautiful in a white gown and gold braid wound through her hair. She curtsied at the gentlemen and drew Persephone away. "Do you know who they are?"

Feeling mulish, Persephone shook her head.

"The worst of the gossips."

"They were talking about Henry."

"I hazarded as much." She tugged Persephone until they were promenading, two genteel ladies with nothing to worry beyond the state of their slippers and if the weather would be fine enough for riding in the morning. It was an illusion Priya was adept with. Persephone wasn't used to being seen at all and it still took her by surprise. "Let's have a glass of canary wine."

As she accepted a glass of the amber wine, Persephone's temper cooled. "I'm worried about your brother. I haven't seen him."

"He can look after himself," Priya assured her. "I promise you."

"I suppose."

Priya's smile gentled. "Truly, Percy. There's nothing to worry about."

She forced a return smile. "I'm being a ninny."

"Hardly. These are trying times."

"They certainly are," Tamsin agreed as she and Meg joined them from the dancefloor. "Someone's eaten all of the almond cake already."

"Call the militia," Meg said.

"I just might."

Her companions' banter put her at ease, as it was meant to. She twitched at every glimpse of dark hair and strong shoulders, but the tension began to relinquish its hold on her muscles. She was less likely to snap at every gossip. She'd never done that before. The worry had clearly gotten to her.

She had her chance to snap again, if she wished, almost immediately.

"That's her," a lady tittered loudly from behind them. Persephone knew that particular tactic well, a volume loud enough to be overhead, not quite loud enough to be confronted with outright rudeness. The perfect weapon of Polite Society. "I can't believe she caught Northwyck. Imagine her as a marchioness, my dear."

"I don't dare." They shared a snicker. "There will mud and bones in the drawing room."

"Introduce him to our Petronilla," the woman returned. "She's much prettier and she has a fortune. Surely he'd reconsider."

"Capital idea."

Tamsin turned the colour of plums and made to whirl around. Persephone touched her arm. "Don't bother, Tamsin."

"I want to bother. Violently."

"I don't care what they say about me." She didn't, she realized. Not nearly as much as she had previously. "And anyway, they're right about the mud and the bones."

"You cared what they said about Henry," Priya pointed out.

"That's different. That kind of gossip might actually see him hanged. This is nothing."

"I can't wait until you're a marchioness," Meg said darkly. "You can watch them simper and grovel."

"I do like it when you are vengeful," Tamsin grinned.

Persephone was about to remind them that she was not going to be a marchioness, not really. Another reason to keep to the quiet shadows. Despite her earlier outburst, it would be easier to weather the smug reactions when her engagement was called off, if she didn't rely on it too much now. Conall was trying to save her life, and Henry's. She wouldn't repay him by embarrassing him.

"There's my brother," Priya said, nodding in his direction as he made his way toward them, smiling his charming earl's smile. He wore a burgundy waistcoat picked out with silver thread glinting under his dark grey coat. It made his eyes seem lighter, more piercing. Men called out his name, ladies curtsied and glanced at him from behind their fans. He barely noticed. His eyes were on hers as he made his way through the crowd. It was intoxicating, that kind of regard, that kind of focus. It should have made her uncomfortable, but the others fell away and it was only him, only her, and the strains of several violins.

The family who had been whispering about her jumped in his path. "Lord Northwyck, you've not met my daughter, Lady Petronilla. Allow me an introduction."

Conall paused, but barely. "A pleasure, I'm sure. If you'll

excuse me, my betrothed is waiting for me. Never keep a lady waiting, Horace."

"Oh, um, of course." Horace's laugh was forced, strangled. Conall had already left him behind. He stopped in front of Persephone and bowed.

"Lady Persephone. You are breath-taking." His voice carried, frankly appreciative. More heads turned their way. She felt herself blushing as he held out his hand. "May I have the pleasure of this dance?"

Tamsin nudged her when she took too long to answer. He was so handsome, so caring. It befuddled her sometimes. "Oh," she said, finally. "Of course."

They had danced before, of course. But it was different tonight, knowing even as he gathered her close that they'd been pressed even closer, skin to skin. Heat and want burned in him, despite his polite smile and the perfectly ordinary way he held her waist. She could see it in his eyes, feel it in the lines of his body. It made her feel powerful in a way she'd never felt before.

"Do you know what I'm thinking?" he whispered, his breath tickling her ear.

She smiled drily though every part of her reacted, burning hot. "I can guess."

He laughed softly. "I look forward to a time without distractions."

Persephone could count on one hand the number of times she had danced since her scandal and all but one had been with the duke, intent on showing his support. The other had been Conall when Priya insisted. But never the waltz. She had little experience, but he held her firmly, supporting her in the turns, leading effortlessly. She barely had the chance to worry about stepping on his toes. The candlelight and the jewels and bright dresses went by in a blur of glowing colours. They danced between Rome and Egypt until Persephone was breathless. It was magical. And far more primal than she would have thought. Perhaps it was because she could feel the heat of him against her, the play of his muscles. And she knew exactly how those muscles felt under her hands, how he looked when he crowded her against the wall in a different sort of dance.

By the time the music stopped Persephone was grateful she hadn't embarrassed herself by licking his lower lip.

Clearly all of the stress was getting to her.

He offered his arm and they walked slowly toward the supper room, as though he were proud to have her by his side, as though she might one day truly be his marchioness. They ate roasted quail, potatoes in butter and herbs, and tiny marzipan flowers. Conall's gaze never stopped tracking the others around them and yet he still smiled and acted the gallant. No one would have realized he was on the hunt, not if they didn't truly know him.

"Have you spotted him?" she asked quietly, over the rim of a glass of ratafia she did not want to drink. It offered her something useful to do with her hands that did not involve touching him.

He shook his head. "I put it out that I'd found a forgery in the assembly hall. I expect to be cornered by tomorrow."

"Is that safe?"

"Safer than waiting." He rose. "Let's dance, shall we? We must not give him the chance to feel suspicious. I want the trap to shut tight before he even realizes it."

IT WAS FOUR o'clock in the morning before the last of the guests found their carriages or their beds and the house settled into soft silence. Dawn waited on the horizon. Persephone stayed back from the procession to private chambers, lingering in the empty ballroom. The servants would clear away the glasses and the lost hair pins and detritus of the celebration in the morning. For now, it lay scattered about, the air heavy with the scents of melted beeswax, perfume, and wine. The flowers were wilting, but still lovely.

She had wanted a moment with the artifacts. Everything was about to change. The trap was baited, it was only a matter of time now. The artifacts were old friends, offering her assurance that some things lasted. Some things did not fade, like the lilies in the vases and the candles dripping away. And despite the worry, it had been a beautiful night. One she would remember until she was an old woman tottering about her hermitage. She was smiling as she padded quietly up the staircase.

Her smile died when she stumbled over John sprawled on the landing.

There was blood in his hair, and he was slumped in an awkward position. She knelt beside him. "John? John, can you hear me?"

He did not answer. His eyelids did not even flicker. She fumbled for his pulse. His arm was too loose. "John?" She finally felt his pulse, strong under her fingertip. "Oh, thank God."

The blood dripping down his face was her next concern. She was still dressed in her ballgown and tearing off the tulle flounces would do him no good at all. She undid his neckcloth, which luckily consisted of more material for the formality of the evening. She pressed it hard to his wound and he groaned. "Yes, do wake up, John. I'm a terrible nursemaid."

He struggled to open his eyes. "Lady Persephone?" He mumbled but was still coherent. Relief flooded through her.

"Yes, it's me."

"I'm sorry."

"For getting hit in the head? Hardly your fault. Can you sit up?" She helped to prop him up. He was pale but steady. He winced when she pressed harder with the cloth and reached up to take over her ministrations. "Is it too much to hope you had a fall down the stairs?"

"Someone coshed me from behind," he muttered darkly.

"My grandmother!" Persephone leapt to her feet.

"I left a man at her door," John said, trying to stand up. She slipped an arm under his shoulders when he listed to the side. "I was hit while coming down to find you." He blinked at her. "You're very strong."

She smiled slightly. "I have an unladylike habit of digging in the fields. You should stay here and rest your head. I'll fetch Lord Northwyck."

"I'm not about to loll about on the main staircase," he said, affronted. "I should have used the servant stair in the first place. But I was worried you were alone."

"Well, I am glad you used common sense instead of protocol.

And I shall say so to anyone who dares harangue you over it."

"No need, my lady," he said gruffly, holding tightly to the wall with his free hand.

"You're going to be stubborn about this aren't you?" She paused, noting the grim, slightly green, determination on his face. "Of course, you are. Come on, then. Let's take you to Conall," she added. "I admit I'm not sure what else to do for a head wound. We'll have to call for a doctor."

"Don't need a doctor."

"I'm afraid that's not up to you," she returned tartly. "I found you, you're my patient now." She chattered at him as they moved up the rest of the steps, slow as treacle running uphill. When he paused, disoriented, she asked him about his family, and whether or not he had enjoyed the festival so far. Anything to keep him tethered when he started to drift. It seemed to help. At her question about the festival, he snorted. She sent him a side glance. Blood had dripped down to stain his collar. "I see your point," she added.

She was sweating by the time they made it to her bedroom door. The footman at her grandmother's door leapt forward. "Nay," John barked. "Don't leave your post. Any troubles?"

"No, sir. Lady Blackwell called for tea for her room and yours, Lady Persephone, not a quarter of an hour ago. Her dog tried to chew on my boot."

"He does that." The footman reached out to open her door. "Thank you." She hauled John inside while he was too off balance to fight her and pushed him down into the nearest chair.

"I can't be in your bedroom, my lady!" he squeaked in alarm. "'Tisn't proper."

She nearly grinned. "You're worse than the dowagers. Who would have thought it?" She saw the tea tray on the table and poured him a cup. "It's nice and strong. It should help." She forced his fingers around the warm porcelain. "I told you you'd take a cup from me, didn't I?" She saw the tightness around his mouth. "Your head must be throbbing. Let me fetch Northwyck and some willow bark powder."

Nerves hit her in the hall, once she realized the wound was

bleeding less and she didn't have to put up a front for John. Her hands trembled when she knocked on Conall's door softly. No response. Perhaps he was sleeping too soundly to have heard her. She knocked loudly, firmly. Chartreuse barked once, followed by her grandmother's shout from her chambers: "Stop that banging!"

At least her grandmother was safe. Whatever was happening now had not touched her. But still no response from Conall. The worry that nibbled at her turned to large, toothy bites. She pushed the door open. "Conall? That is, Lord Northwyck?"

A single oil lamp burned on the window ledge. His bed was empty, coverlet still perfectly tucked. A dreadful feeling uncurled in the pit of her stomach, even as she tried to tell herself that there were dozens of perfectly good reasons why he might not be here. The footman hadn't heard anything unusual, after all. Still, he might have found a clue and gone off alone. She darted back across the hall to her chambers. John was slumped over, having lost consciousness. He jerked up as she reached him. Right. Priya could send for the doctor without awakening the household or worrying the duke while Persephone sat with John and tried to think what to do next. And she might know where her brother was. It wasn't much of a plan, but it would do for the next five minutes.

She ran down the hall, grateful that Priya hadn't been housed in a different wing. She knocked once and then burst through the door. "Priya, come quick."

Priya, bless her, was on her feet and coherent in moments. Her hair was thickly braided down her back, her eyes barely bleary. "Who's on fire?"

"We need a doctor for John," Persephone explained as Priya grabbed her dressing gown and followed her. "And do you happen to know where your brother is?"

Priya paused before quickening her steps again. "If he's not with you and he's not in his bed…."

"That's what I was afraid of." Back at her rooms, she knelt in front of John. "John, wake up."

He lifted his head. "Not sleeping."

"Good."

"What happened?" Priya asked.

"He was hit from behind."

"I see." They exchanged a look of worry and forcibly restrained panic. Priya examined John's head and the bloody gash. "You won't need a doctor," she said. "When my husband was ill, he lost his balance frequently. He hit his head a lot." She smiled faintly. "Head wounds always look worse than they are, and they bleed like the dickens. You'll have a goose egg and a sore head, and you'll need to rest. An ice pack wouldn't go amiss."

"I'll get some," he said, making to stand up.

Priya pushed him back down. "You will not. I will fetch the ice."

"But… you're a lady. You can't."

Poor John. He was learning rather quickly about the not-so-hidden autocratic nature of the Cinderellas. "Priya will fetch the ice and I will start searching for Conall. Perhaps the footman at the front door saw him go out. He may have wanted fresh ai—."

She froze, going hot and cold all at once so that all of her skin prickled painfully.

A letter lay on her bed.

She approached it cautiously, feeling as though it were more akin to a venomous snake than a simple piece of parchment. She didn't want to touch it. She snatched it up all the same and broke the seal. There was no design to it, no helpful family crest, only a blank circle on red wax.

"What does it say?" Priya asked sharply.

Persephone swallowed hard. "He's got Conall."

Priya rushed to her side to read over her shoulder. "Does he say who he is? A ridiculous question," she added immediately. "Of course, he doesn't."

"He wants me to bring the third letter. Or he'll kill Conall."

Priya straightened her shoulders. "I think not."

"He thinks I already know who he is," Persephone said, her brain running in wild circles like a ferret with a burning tail. "That I have the letter. Conall's ruse worked too well." She crumpled up the letter and tossed it to the floor, striding toward her wardrobe.

"What are you doing?" Priya asked.

"I might not have time to change out of this ballgown," she replied grimly, reaching for a pair of boots. "But I can't very well run off on a rescue mission in dancing slippers."

"Begging your pardon," John put in, alarmed. "You don't mean to say you're going yourself."

She yanked savagely at the laces. "Of course, I do."

"We need to tell the duke. He has an army of footmen."

"We don't have the time for that," Persephone said. "By all means, let them follow, but I can't wait for them."

"I'll talk to him," Priya assured her. "I can convince him not to send too many footmen willy-nilly. It might set the traitor nervous where he'll do something rash if he spots them."

"He wants me to leave the letter at the Avenue, at the statue of Jupiter."

"And then he'll tell you where Conall is?"

They exchanged a short-charged glance. "Not likely. Which is why I have to go now. I know the area better than anyone. If I can hide myself, I can follow him."

"You'll take Tamsin and Meg."

"If they can catch up." She reached for a shawl, tying the ends of the raspberry-red wool at the small of her back so it would stay secure. The colour distracted her for a moment, reminding her of dreams of raspberry bushes scratching her arms until they bled. Of that *something* hiding in the back of her mind that she couldn't quite access. And then suddenly, a wash of understanding. Puzzle pieces clicking into place.

Raspberries.

Raspberry jam.

"Holy hell," she muttered, staring at the shawl. "I know what I was missing." Priya looked at her expectantly. "*Holly* is involved in this somehow."

"What? How? She's a mouse."

"It's been bothering me for days. We had lists of the guests and we knew who was on the terrace when the urn was pushed off the roof. But Holly wasn't there. I'd passed her going back up the stairs. She was fussing over a stain of raspberry jam on her dress. I didn't think anything of it."

"And why think something of it now?"

"What if the traitor was on the terrace, after all? You said it yourself, you couldn't get anything out of the servants or the other guests, and your brother questioned them thoroughly. To say the least. Holly Carter wasn't questioned because I'd just seen her on the staircase. I thought she was upset over the raspberry jam on her dress. Now I wonder."

"And the ladies were unlikely to be questioned as thoroughly as the men," Priya added. "You think Holly was a distraction then?"

"Maybe. So he could hide in plain sight. Do you think it's possible?"

"Yes. And it's clever, which I do *not* like. But there is one way to find out," Priya said darkly. "She's sleeping in the east wing. Let's ask her, shall we?"

THE BLIGHTER HAD come at him from behind.

Conall's head ached like the devil. He was dizzy, blurry.

And tied up.

He blinked, trying to get his eyeballs to work. He was outside, that much he could make out. The summer air was cool, and he thought he heard the paddling of swans, the soft murmur of water. Where was he?

More importantly, where was Persephone? Was she here? Was she hurt?

"Persephone?" He was still befuddled from the blow to the head. His voice didn't sound like his own. His only reply was from a disgruntled swan. With any luck she was safe in her bed. He'd kill the bastard if he hurt her. Treason demanded justice from the crown. Harm to Persephone demanded murder.

He strained against the ropes that bound him, but it only served to set his head to a vicious nauseated throb.

IT DID NOT take long for Priya to return with Holly, dressed in her nightgown and wrapper. Persephone had used the time to pen a letter in Henry's handwriting. She knew it well enough for it to be no trouble to forge. Priya pushed Holly ahead of her. The other woman looked nervous and miserable. Her eyes darted back and forth. "So it *was* you," Persephone said.

Holy blinked rapidly. "What was? It's very odd to pull me from my bed in the middle of – why is this man bleeding?" She gasped.

"This is what happens when you have dealings with a traitor, Miss Carter," Priya said. "People get hurt."

"I never!"

Persephone did not have time for this. Conall did not have time for this. And she was fairly certain Priya was only seconds from tossing Holly to the ground and pummelling her. Which might only send Holly into histrionics and delay this longer.

"If you don't tell us immediately who you have been helping, you will be implicated in the death of an earl. Do you know what they do to murderesses, Miss Carter?" Persephone said. "Furthermore, since you very nearly killed *me*, I believe I am entitled to answers. *Now.*"

Holly lifted her chin as though she meant to fight back and then promptly burst into tears. "He said it was a harmless prank!" she wailed.

"*Who* did?"

"He told me to go up to the roof and wait for his signal. That he would tell me when it was safe to push the urn. No one was supposed to get hurt."

"*Who*, Holly?"

"L-lord Fairweather," she sobbed.

"Lord Fairweather," Priya repeated in the tones of a woman with enough secrets to ruin half of the Ton. "Is that so?"

"He said it was a prank," Holly repeated.

"What kind prank of involves pushing things off a roof onto people? He is a grown man, not a child."

"I don't know," she mumbled. "He was very...forceful. He spilled jam on my dress so I would not get into trouble. I thought he was being solicitous, in his way."

Persephone didn't wait to absorb the impact of the confession. She knew his intentions, even if Holly didn't. He had begun to worry she knew more about his transgressions than she had; that she might know his identity even. And now he had Conall. She turned toward the door.

"Wait," Priya stopped her.

"No."

"We need more information."

"We have enough. You take Holly to the duke for a full confession, and I shall go to Lord Fairweather and keep him distracted until the others come. If I have to follow him, I will try and leave a trail."

"Give me a moment," she insisted. "Let me see if I can remember anything useful about Fairweather. We need any advantage we can get."

Persephone felt as though she were vibrating with impatience. As if her blood had turned to lightning inside her body.

"He has a mistress, of course." Priya began.

"Two," Holly put in. Priya raised her eyebrows. "My mother hoped he would make an offer for me. She didn't want me to be shocked and put him off over it. She was insistent that I do whatever it took to marry him."

"I see. He has atrocious debts."

"So does my father," Holly said glumly.

"Fairweather also has one of the most impressive collections of Egyptian artifacts in Britain," Persephone added. "None of which he deigned to add to the festival exhibits, by the way."

"He does not like to share attention," Priya guessed. "He's arrogant, and obviously selfish. Those are weaknesses." She snapped her fingers. "And he cannot see well out of his left eye. He lost peripheral vision in a hunting accident. Not many people know that since he is sensitive about it."

"How do you know about it?"

"It's my business to know," she sniffed. "He once tried a rather backhanded business deal with my husband." She bared her teeth in a smile that was more wolf than maiden. "It did not go well." She hugged Persephone. "I know you won't wait, even if I make you promise. I'll send Tamsin and Meg to you as soon as possible. And then I'll take Holly to the duke."

"Thank you."

"Be careful, Percy. Fairweather has everything to lose."

"I know. But without a letter, I would have no evidence. And he knows I could not give testimony in court. No magistrate would take me seriously, not against him. And he might be more squeamish about killing a woman." She paused. "I hope."

"Perhaps you could hide and wait for the others."

"Perhaps. But he won't be squeamish about killing Conall, I don't think."

"Be careful." Priya hugged her again. "This is madness," she added before rushing from the room.

"He's a snake," John said, trying hard to stand. Blood dripped onto the carpet. "I can't let you go alone."

"You have to." She tried to smile but her face felt stiff with fear. "You're still bleeding and wobbly as boiled pudding."

"Take this then," he said gruffly, sitting back down hard and pulling a knife from his boot. "Stab him hard if he comes after you."

"I intend to."

Chapter Thirteen

PERSEPHONE KNEW IT was madness to set off on her own in the shining grey light of dawn, but she was physically incapable of waiting a single moment longer. Conall had already saved her life and she intended to save his right back. It was only fair, after all.

Never mind the terror clawing at her throat that she might already be too late.

Fairweather would think he had the upper hand. The pity of it was that he was right. Still, she had a few surprises of her own. For one, he had abducted Conall, even if Persephone was smaller and easier to grab, because he assumed that she would crumple, that she would do anything to save him. And she would. But she was made of sterner stuff than that. She had a brain. More, she had the Cinderella Society at her back. He would never see them as a threat. It would not occur to him that an earl's daughter might come as armed as any earl. Another advantage, surely.

She ducked into the stable for a horse, careful not to wake any of the stableboys. Hay tickled her nose. "Shh," she murmured to the nearest horse as she tossed a saddle over his back. He snorted sleepily. "We're going to be brave."

She didn't feel brave. Not now that she was alone on horseback in the thick shadows, closing in on a murderer. She really was mad to think she could do this. But she had to try. She had thought Conall leaving Little Barrow for his real life without her would be difficult. She would take being left behind any day over him being injured. Or worse.

She loved him. It was that simple and useless to deny it, alone on horseback with the reins shaking in her hands.

The sky burned pink and orange on the horizon, staining the sky. Birds sang in the hedgerows and burst into the air when she passed by, cutting across the estate's extensive lawns. The horse hooves left a clear track through the glittering dewy grass. The statues of the Avenue glowed in the quietly, slowly, building light.

She spotted Lord Fairweather, keeping to the shadows at the other end of the Avenue. He thought he was well hidden, and he might have been for someone who had not spent as many hours as she had studying the marbles. Meg had sketched each one ten times over. The duke held picnic teas here for Persephone's birthday. Tamsin challenged them all to foot races over the grass. Persephone knew perfectly well she was looking at the shape of a man, not another statue or an odd bush. And as the light changed yet again, it caught on his gold buttons. As well as the weapon in his hand.

She needed a new plan.

One which preferably did not involve being shot with a pistol.

She hesitated behind the sheltering trunks. She had hoped that shooting an unarmed woman would give him pause. Apparently not.

Blast and damn.

Nothing for it. She was going to have brazen through. If he was already armed, there was no telling what he might do to footmen coming over the lawns. They could be shot before they even knew the danger. She edged closer, finding a spot that offered some protection with both trees and a huge statue of Artemis, moon carved into her hair. She was the patron goddess of hunting and a protector of women, known for turning Acteon into a stag and letting his own dogs devour him as a punishment for spying on her. Persephone hoped she might lend her a little luck.

She was fairly certain she was going to need it.

"Lord Fairweather," she called, wincing as her voice carried clear as a bell. Birds fluttered off of branches, wings snapping a scolding.

Fairweather turned in her direction, pistol swinging. "Lady Persephone. So good of you to come."

She hoped he shot his own foot clear off.

"There's been a change of plans," she said.

There was a pause, a huff of stunned laughter. "I think not."

"Indeed, as I have no wish to be shot."

"I assure you," he said, stepping closer. She could see him peering through the greenery, trying to pinpoint her exact location. "This is merely for my own protection."

"And for my own protection, I have left another letter written by Henry hidden away."

He saw the fury contort his face, even from a distance. "You're bluffing."

"Certainly not," she said with a crisp authority she was far from feeling. She tried to imagine what Queen Boudica might have done in her place. How Cleopatra might have argued her way to safety. But her palms were sweaty, and her mouth was dry. At least she *sounded* calm. "Should my return to the house be delayed or something untoward happen to me, I have left instructions for the letter to be read. In public. And then printed in the London Times."

He swore under his breath. "Damned interfering gel."

"Just so. I have a proposal." Her horse snorted and she nudged him back behind a more substantial tree, keeping to his left side as Priya had advised. There was less chance of him spotting her through the foliage. And shooting her. "You will tell me where you are holding Lord Northwyck and I will leave this letter for you. We will go our separate ways."

"What's to stop you from blabbing after you get your way?"

"Nothing at all, I suppose." Her voice cracked slightly. "But your choice is a possible accusation later or a definite accusation very much sooner. Say, within the hour."

He cursed again. "Then I suppose we have a deal, my lady. It seems I may have taken the wrong person captive."

"Where is he?"

"Give me the letter."

"You'll tell me where he is first."

"He's down in the folly across the pond."

"Is he alive?"

"I suppose you'll have to wait and see. Give me the blasted letter."

She tossed the letter into a tangle of blackberry bushes. "It's in the berry bushes," she said, wheeling her horse and urging him into a gallop. She tried to keep the trees between her and Fairweather. He was a blur as he dashed for the letter. She had to cross into the open to circle the side of the pond. Her spine prickled in warning. She flattened herself over the horse's back as mud flew from under his hooves. *Please let him be alive. Please, please let him be alive.*

The folly stood like a Roman temple, all white columns open to a circular rotunda covered in mosaics. Conall was currently lashed to one of those columns.

"Conall!"

There was a long moment when he did not respond. Her heart felt like one of those fireworks, whizzing around inside her body, in great danger of burning to a cinder and turning everything to ash.

And then he stirred, lifted his head. "Percy?"

Relief flooded through her, making her feel light-headed as she slid from the saddle. She ran, the mist from the pond tattering around her knees.

"Goddamn it, woman, what are you doing here?"

She laughed, because she could. He was alive. There was blood in his hair and on his collar, much like John, but he was alive. Thick ropes kept him immobile, raw flesh gleaming red where he had been struggling. There were bruises on his face. He'd never looked more beautiful. She kissed him quickly, to reassure herself that he was, in fact, real. He nipped at her lower lip. "You daft woman," he said, emotion thick in his voice. "Get out of here before Fairweather returns."

"Not without you." She found the knots that secured him

around the back of the column. The rope bit at her fingers. She pulled John's knife from her boot and started to saw through it.

"Don't you know I'm supposed to rescue you?" Conall asked, gently.

She grinned. "We rescue each other, remember?"

"I'm afraid that's no longer an option." Lord Fairweather's voice was at her ear before she even realized he was there. The butt of the pistol pressed against the back of her head. She froze. "I won't be organized like your damn festival."

Conall swore, pulling viciously at his bindings. "Fairweather, if you hurt her, I'll disembowel you."

"Yes, yes," Fairweather returned. "As a threat, it would be improved if you weren't already tied up. By me." He leaned closer to Persephone and she shrank from the feeling of his breath at her cheek. "I've decided I don't like your proposal, after all. I am sure I can both find that extra letter and have you out of my business permanently. Move."

He pressed the pistol into her flesh until she felt a bruise forming. Luckily, he didn't think to look down at her hands. She didn't have the width of movement required to stab him from this angle, but she could wedge the knife into the knot in the ropes and against the column. Conall might be able to saw his way free.

Fairweather pushed her forward. Conall strained against the ropes again, fury in his eyes. She saw the flicker of recognition when he realized what she'd done. Fairweather yanked her back with one arm banded across her chest. His fingers dug painfully into her arms. He was stronger than he looked. "You have been a nuisance, Lady Persephone. You and that damned Henry. Couldn't leave well enough alone."

"Where is he?" Persephone asked. "What have you done to him?"

"If I knew where he was, this would all be over much quicker."

"You betrayed your country," Conall spat, trying to draw his attention. "And caused your fellow countrymen to be killed in droves. For what? Pieces of old rocks found in a pyramid."

"Regrettable." Fairweather shrugged. "But they ought to have been better soldiers."

"You can't mean that," Persephone said.

"Of course, I do. And the material point, my dear, is that precious historical artifacts have been given into my care. You of all people should understand that. We certainly can't trust the French, can we?"

"I'd trust them over you. You're the one who's the traitor."

He shook her when she pushed against his hold. "Stop struggling."

"Fairweather," Conall snapped, cold as a winter pond. "Let her go."

"Not quite yet. You are my insurance against each other. And I need to think. You've made a mess of things."

Conall caught Persephone's eye. He glanced down. She blinked at him, bemused. He glanced down again and moved his knee deliberately. He'd told her once that her lower center of gravity was an asset. That she could use it against an attacker.

And he'd told her exactly how to do it, bless him.

She bent her knees slightly, throwing off Fairweather's steadiness. Then she kicked back, hard, aiming for his groin. He grunted in pain, choking on his breath. It wasn't quite enough to have him release his hold, but he did drop the pistol. And Persephone could now bend down, wrap her hands around his left knee, and yank his foot forward with every ounce of her strength. Still dealing with the pain she'd inflicted, he wasn't able to plant his feet or fight the momentum. He toppled, letting go of her and landing with a great thud. Persephone darted out of reach, her breath burning in the throat, adrenaline shivering through her. She kicked the pistol hard, sending it into the pond.

Conall's muscles bulged as he pulled the rope against the dagger's blade. "Run, Percy!"

As if she would leave him. As if her legs hadn't also turned to water. She stumbled forward to finish untying him. He pulled the rope against the knife and it shredded, finally cutting loose. But Fairweather had already gotten to his feet. His face was red and he was panting, but he was hardly incapacitated. In fact, he turned and ran, cutting across the grass. Conall roared angrily, pulling at the rope around his feet. He was nearly free. Fairweather closed the distance between him and his horse, waiting under the tree.

"I've got him!" Tamsin suddenly shouted, racing across the marbles of the folly. She had a rock in her hand, dripping with pond water. She stopped, wound her arm back and released it like it was a cricket ball, turning her body into the throw. Having played cricket since she was a girl, the rock flew true and hit Fairweather in the back of the neck with a fair punch behind it. He sprawled in the grass, as Meg darted out of the bushes and took hold of his horse's reins.

Conall fought free of the last of the ropes and as Fairweather struggled to push to his hands and knees, he thundered forward, vaulting over a decorative wall and bearing down on him like a summer storm. He punched down, cracking his fist into Fairweather's jaw. Fairweather slumped. Conall held him up by the shoulder for another punch to the face. The other man went flying again and this time, stayed still.

"Bring me the rope," Conall said.

Persephone and Tamsin hurried forward. He wrapped the rope around Fairweather's wrists. "It's too short now that it's been cut," he said. "It won't hold him long when he wakes. Damn it."

Persephone looked at her friends, bejewelled and beribboned from the ball. She pulled the pink ribbon from her bodice. Tamsin grinned and yanked at the offending yellow ribbon around her upper arm.

"I think I have the solution," Persephone murmured.

THEY BROUGHT FAIRWEATHER back to Pendleton House, trussed up like a Christmas package in pink, yellow and green ribbons. He lay folded ignominiously over the saddle of his horse, who was more interested in nuzzling Meg's hair than anything else. Persephone's horse had wandered back to the stable in search of breakfast. Conall's bruises were already darkening, the blood dry on his shirt. He kept stealing glances at Persephone. "Are you sure you're not hurt? We'll have the doctor look at you regardless."

"I'm fine," she assured him again. She felt odd, as if she was floating and all the colours were too bright. The sun too intense, the grass too green, the sky pulsing like blue fire. Her teeth chattered. "Not this again," she muttered, recognizing the same sensations of shock she had felt after the urn had shattered beside her.

Conall smiled faintly though his eyes were uncivilized, warrior-like. "I'll have them bring as many crumpets as you like."

She smiled back.

"She's a Cinderella," Tamsin said. "It would take more than a coward like Fairweather to take her down." She sounded blasé but she squeezed Persephone's hand the entire walk back to the house.

Footmen ran toward them, wigs askew, muskets and daggers in hand. Conall shook his head. "The cavalry has already come," he said.

They stared at Persephone, Tamsin, and Meg uncertainly.

"'Gor," the tallest one said.

Conall handed him the reins. "You can take this sorry excuse for a man to the stables. Do not untie him. Do not take your eyes off him for even one minute. Am I perfectly clear? And I'll need a carriage. Immediately."

"Yes, your lordship."

The duke was waiting on the gravel drive for his horse to be brought to him. Priya was beside him, arguing. They both turned at their approach, relief screaming from their postures, even at a distance. "I am only seventy-two, I can certainly shoot a blackguard with a hunting rifle," they heard the duke grumble as they approached.

Priya ran to hug her brother hard. "I was so worried." She squeezed Persephone's hand. "For both of you." She stepped back, eyeing Conall. "You've blood in your hair. I hope it's his."

"Alas, it's mine." He crooked a smile. "But I'm fine. No need to fret."

"I don't fret."

"Liar."

The duke reached them; his face pinched with worry. He drew Persephone into a tight hug and shook Conall's hand. "I am very cross with you both." He scowled at Priya. "And this one who thinks I am too old to do anything of consequence."

"Stuff and nonsense," Priya shot back.

"She forgets I am the duke and I give the orders."

"No one could forget *that*, you remind us daily."

"Impertinent."

"You taught me everything I know."

Persephone drew her arm through the duke's. "Your Grace, could I trouble you for some tea," she said. "With brandy, preferably. I'm feeling rather tired."

He patted her hand, distracted from Priya who rolled her eyes. "Of course, my dear. We'll all go inside. I've already summoned the constable."

Conall nodded. "Thank you. I'll wait in the stables."

"You won't," the duke argued. "You will come fortify yourself and clean yourself up before you head off to London. The lads can watch him for an hour."

"Let me secure him with proper rope first," Conall said.

"Fine, fine. I have breakfast waiting in the library. I thought we could avoid the guests and keep the fuss to a minimum."

The duke strolled back into the house surrounded with ladies in various states of disarray but still dressed for the ball. "My pigeons," he said, mistily.

Tamsin rolled her eye. "First doves, now pigeons."

"Swans then."

"Swans? Honestly."

The duke smiled at her. "You have no idea how vicious swans can be under all those pretty feathers."

PASTRIES, FRUITS, AND pots of tea, chocolate and coffee had been brought to the library. Silver serving dishes kept the eggs warm as well as bacon, ham, and trout. The Cinderellas fell on it with the kind of furor generally reserved for bears in springtime. "Goodness," the duke said, amused as a grape rolled across the table and onto the floor. "Did I say swans? Surely I meant vultures."

Persephone ate another pastry and put too much sugar in her tea. It helped with the shaking of her hands and the light-headedness. Eggs and cheese took care of the rest of the agitation.

"I didn't know crime made one so hungry," Tamsin said, attacking a thick slice of ham.

"You were all brilliant," Persephone said. "Thank you." She pushed her plate away and drank more tea, this time with a splash of brandy. It warmed the chill threatening to take up residence in her bones.

"What happens now?" Meg asked. "I didn't think earls could be arrested."

"Not generally," the duke replied. "They make an exception for treason. He'll be tried by the House of Lords. And I'll be there," he added darkly. "To add my verdict."

"As will I," Conall added, joining them at the table. The bustle from the hallway muffled as the door closed behind him. The housemaids would be running up and down the stairs, the footmen filling the dining room sideboard with food and folded newspapers. Conall sat next to Persephone. "Have another crumpet," he said softly, placing one on her plate before helping himself.

She smiled. "Is this our tradition, then? Crumpets after crime?"

"It would seem so." His smile was warm if a bit distracted. "Let's stick to crumpets alone next time."

She wanted to lean into him, with his hair wet from washing and the energy that radiated from him.

"Is he well secured?" the duke asked.

"Yes, as well as can be. He woke up, so I gagged him."

"Good.

They ate until only crumbs and the bitter traces of tannin in the teapot remained. "We fair demolished that," the duke said. "We must keep up our strength. We've a festival to run, after a good rest."

"And I should go," Conall said, rising from his chair. He bowed to the duke and then to the table at large. They turned discreetly away as Persephone followed him to the other end of the library. She felt suddenly and oddly shy. He was leaving and she might not see him for a long time. They had accomplished what they had set out to accomplish. Henry was vindicated and the men Conall had found lying on that battlefield had some justice. It would not bring them back, but it might make it easier for their families.

"It may be a while before I can return." Conall took her hand. "So, before I go, thank you, Percy."

She forced a smile, annoyed with herself for feeling so abruptly melancholy. "Thank you as well." It was all so formal, polite. She hated it. "I will call off the engagement once you've gone, as agreed."

"Will you, now?" She couldn't read his tone or his eyes, it was a confusing mix of fondness and exasperation and something harder.

"Of course. I'm hardly suited to be a marchioness."

"What rot."

A knock sounded behind him and Basil bowed. "The constable has arrived, my lord."

"Thank you, Basil."

She searched his face, but the mask had already fallen, that charming gallant smile, the twinkle in his pale eyes blinding to anything else lurking beneath the surface. She wanted to memorize him nonetheless, the leanness of him, the strength, the quiet calm that he carried everywhere. She already missed him, and he was standing right in front of her.

He lifted her hand and kissed it, mouth grazing her knuckles softly. "Goodbye, Lady Persephone."

PERSEPHONE TRIED TO rest but it was impossible. She kept bouncing from the feel of her ballgown as she raced across the fields, to the pistol against her neck, Conall's blood smeared over the column. It helped to focus on little tasks: changing her dress, petting Chartreuse when her grandmother barrelled into Persephone's bedroom to assure herself her granddaughter had suffered no serious ill effects. She prescribed cupcakes and canary wine and a handsome fiancé.

Her grandmother was more upset about the broken betrothal than she was about having dined with a traitor.

Meanwhile, the festival went on. Word got out that there had been some excitement and murmurs followed her wherever she went. She barely noticed now. It wasn't important. Lady Culpepper found her in the village the next day and embraced her right there in the middle of the street. She didn't speak but her eyes glittered, and she patted Persephone's shoulder with such feeling that Persephone was nearly propelled into a display of Roman statuary. They rattled alarmingly but regained their balance. Persephone chose to see it as a sign. She too would regain her balance.

She saw to her duties, attended lectures and dinner parties with a smile but inside she longed for the solitude of her hermitage. For Conall. He hadn't written to her, had only sent a brief word to the duke assuring everyone that the War Office had everything in hand. She missed him. It made her morose and then annoyed that she was morose. She was a woman grown. She had had no illusions. She had hoped that would protect her from heartache somewhat better.

Henry had not yet come out of hiding, or at least not into the public eye. The newspapers devoted pages and pages to his story. Etchings and cartoons were sold in London shops painting him as a war hero. On the third day, she couldn't go three feet without someone stopping her to ask her about him. Tamsin was particularly put out about the whole thing and was spectacularly rude, even for a duke's daughter.

And then, after an especially long day packed with lectures, Persephone begged off the formal dinner and borrowed a carriage. All she wanted was to go home, to eat Cook's custard tarts, and not have to wear a practiced, borrowed smile. Not to be stared at with that knowing smug look that said they had all known the engagement couldn't last. That Conall would see sense soon enough. That, of course, there had to be extraordinary circumstances. They'd all known it from the start.

The tension started to melt as soon they turned onto the

familiar drive, with its oak trees and rose bushes. She had always found strength here. By the time the horses pulled to a stop and the coachman opened the carriage door, she already felt miles better. She was a founding member of the Cinderella Society, after all. They'd chased a traitor across a field and bound him with dress ribbons. They could do anything.

She alighted from the carriage as the last of the setting sun nestled behind the trees. Oil lamps cast a warm glow on the gardens. She was home.

So was Henry.

He stepped out of the shadows of the recessed doorway, grinning like a fool. She knew exactly what kind of foolish grin he wore because she wore it too. "Henry!"

The coachman scrambled back a step to avoid being run over by either of them. Henry caught her around the waist and swung her around like he had countless times when they were children. She laughed when her feet left the ground. He finally set her back down and they held each other up, still grinning. "I've missed you, Cleopatra," he said, falling back on her old nickname.

She noticed the shadows under his eyes, the gauntness and hardness of his frame. He was still handsome, even with that new edge. He'd left a boy, barely a young man, and now returned a new version of himself. She wondered if he had trouble with certain sounds and memories the way Conall did. Now was not the time to ask. Now was a time to celebrate. "I wager Cook has some of those lemon biscuits you used to love so much."

He ran a hand over his head, his dark hair cropped too short. "I could eat a crate of them."

They went inside where Mrs. Bell greeted them with a shriek of welcome. She dabbed at her eyes. "Welcome home, my lord. We feared you were gone forever."

"I didn't," Cook barked, having run up the stairs with a butcher knife to investigate the fuss. "No one could take down our lad, certainly not the French."

"It was an Englishman who nearly did," he said wryly. "The French only wondered what we were all doing in those muddy fields, same as we did."

"Hmph. You need lemon biscuits."

Persephone laughed. "That he does."

They sat in the drawing room and drank tea and ate sweets until dinner was laid out for them. There was a new stillness to Henry, a wariness in his movements, the way he seemed to hear every sound, saw every shadow. "Have you seen your grandmother?"

"I have. You are suddenly her favorite person. All that terrible gossip about you couldn't *possibly* be true."

"But alas, it is."

He scowled. "You do get into an awful lot of trouble when I'm away."

She snorted. "I think you have that backwards." She paused. "Are you safe now? Truly safe?"

He nodded. "I'm not sure when I'll feel safe but yes. The evidence against Fairweather is iron clad."

"Bastard."

"Quite."

"How was London? I hear you are feted wherever you go."

"Yes," he said. "It's annoying."

"You brought a traitor to justice, at great personal cost. You should let yourself be adored a little. You deserve it."

"Speaking of which. I thought I told you not to get involved."

She sat back in her chair. "When have I ever taken orders from you?"

He grunted. "True enough."

She touched his hand. "It is so good to see you, Henry."

"You saved my life."

She shrugged one shoulder. "I only did what any friend would do."

"No, Percy," he said, seriously. "You are a marvel."

"Oh stop," she blushed. "If you keep flattering me, I really will think you're ill."

They went outside to lay on the flagstones, still warm from the sun, as was their custom. The moon rose in a bed of stars. Henry loved stars as much as Persephone loved Egypt. He turned his head slightly. "You won't ask about him?"

"Who?" He raised his eyebrows. She wrinkled her nose. "Oh, very well. How is Conall?"

"Conall, is it?"

She poked him in the side. "Don't tease. Is he…well?" Has his head healed cleanly? Has he asked about me? Does he miss me? Is all of London worshiping him?

"He's fine," Henry replied. "He barely sleeps, he's either at the War Office or the House of Lords. I can't think of the last time an earl was ever accused of treason. It's a complicated business."

"I'm so glad your part's done."

"I expect I'll be needed again but they agreed to send for me here instead of having me wait in London."

"Good."

They watched the stars come out, serenaded by industrious crickets and grasshoppers. "If you could hear the way he talks about you," Henry said quietly.

Pleasure stole through her before she could convince herself not to feel it. "Really?"

"Yes. And I can see by that blush that you feel the same about him. So, what's the trouble?"

"I can't be a marchioness."

"Why not, you goose?"

"Henry. Despite recent events, society and reality has not changed that much."

"To the devil with them. I mean it," he insisted when she opened her mouth to reply. "I've seen too much in the last few years. I'm finally free now and I won't sell my freedom to the gossipmongers and the bullies. And I won't let you do it either."

"If only it were that simple." But he had a point. Hadn't she thought the same?

Although, Conall hadn't written to her. He wasn't exactly here professing his love.

Of course, she *had* told everyone their engagement was a sham.

"Do you love him, Percy?"

She nodded without hesitation. Not only was Henry the

person she could always be honest with, but the truth of it rushed out of her before she could stop it. "Of course, I love him."

"Then be brave," Henry said.

"I don't feel brave."

"You were brave enough to chase down a traitor in order to free him. But you're not brave enough to tell him you love him?"

When he put it like that, it was ridiculous.

IT WAS ANOTHER two days before the festival was over and Persephone could finally leave for London. She shared a carriage with Priya, Tamsin, and Meg. Tamsin had wheedled a luncheon basket and a bottle of champagne for the trip.

"We deserve it," she insisted when Priya questioned the wisdom of delicate flutes in a bumpy carriage. Persephone took a glass gratefully. She hadn't thought she'd be this nervous.

"To the Cinderella Society," Tamsin announced, lifting her glass. "Anyway, we foiled a dastardly plot, didn't we? We deserve champagne."

"To the Cinderella Society," they chorused back, clinking glasses. The carriage wheel found a pothole and champagne sloshed over the rims. They laughed.

"We were able to help clear Henry's name and save Conall because no one takes us seriously," Tamsin added. "Think of what we could accomplish with that."

Meg raised her eyebrows. "Such as?"

"Fairweather is hardly the first or the last gentleman to use a lady, or two, for his own nefarious purposes. We are overrun with such men. They use us because they can get away with it."

They all knew what she was thinking: the mysterious man Priya never spoke of but who had been the reason behind her surprise marriage to a much older man, the way Tamsin's family neglected her because she was not the male heir, Meg's uncle who had inherited her family estate but declined to pay Meg the annuity she was owed. The choice Persephone had made to ruin herself in order to free herself.

"Not any more. If we can take on a bloody traitor to the crown, fortune hunters and libertines should pose no challenge at all."

"A tiny taste of violence and she's unstoppable," Priya murmured.

"But she's not wrong," Persephone added. "If we can help, shouldn't we? If I hadn't had your help, and Conall's, I might not be here today."

"Don't say that," Tamsin shivered.

"It's true. And lots of women aren't as lucky as I am."

"Not yet," Meg put in. "Give us time."

"WHERE ARE WE?" Persephone asked, hours later. She hadn't been to Tamsin's family townhouse in more than two years, but she knew Mayfair when she saw it. The streets outside were far too crowded. "Is this Piccadilly?"

"It is," Priya confirmed. "And if we're going to be a proper Society, we're going to need someone with a bit more clout."

Tamsin opened the door.

"Someone like a marchioness," Meg added, shoving Persephone bodily out of the carriage. The door slammed shut.

The carriage pulled away.

"But..."

Persephone stood, bemused. They'd left her here. Without a chaperone or a footman. It was odd, even for them. She turned on her heel, trying to get her bearings.

She was standing in front of Bullock's Egyptian Hall. It was as magnificent as the drawings she'd seen. It was a partial replica of the Temple of Dendera, with lotus columns flanking the door. There was a winged sun disk, the sacred uraei serpents. Even though the voices around her spoke English and the air was scented with coal smoke and the Thames, it was a beautiful mirage of Ancient Egypt dropped squarely between two perfectly ordinary London buildings. There were no crowds jostling for entry which she found strange.

Two statues perched above the door, watching her approach. Her belly fluttered with nerves. Meg's parting remark had not been subtle. The door opened before she could reach for the handle. A man smiled at her genially. "Lady Persephone, we've been waiting for you."

She stepped inside because so many different types of curiosity had gripped her, she could no more have stayed out on the stoop as she could have learned to fly.

"This way, if you would."

He led her past a truly impressive collection of fossils. There were plants waving fronds over her head, large rocks with patterns of curled creatures embedded on the surface and amber with insects frozen inside. Her guide moved at a fast clip, proceeding to the entrance of the main hall. He bowed and left. She hesitated, peeking inside. Her breath caught.

This was the replica of Karnak, with its towering columns with lotus designs and hieroglyphs painted top to bottom. They soared up to a gilded ceiling. Even knowing they weren't authentic, her fingers itched to reach out and touch. What a gift to be able to visit Egypt, even when one could not leave London. She hadn't realized she'd even moved by the time she found herself in the center of the space.

"That is the most beautiful smile I have ever seen."

She started. Conall stepped out from behind one of the pillars, pale eyes warm.

"You brought me here?"

"I want to make you smile like that every day of your life." She stared at him. He tilted his head, amused. "I was hoping for more of a reaction, I admit."

She shook her head, as if it could realign her brain with the excited fizzing in her blood. He was so handsome, so patient.

Cautious.

She read it in the slant of his smile, the real one, not the one he wielded in society. She stepped closer, leaning her head back. "I've never visited the Egyptian Hall before."

"One day I'll take you to Egypt, if you'll let me."

She felt like laughing. There was too much bubbling inside her. "I thought I might not see you for a long time."

"You broke off our engagement."

She winced. "I thought it was what you wanted."

"You know, for such a clever woman, you have the oddest

notions. I never wanted that."

"Truly?"

"You're the one who ran scared."

She made a face. "I suppose I did."

"And now?" He was so close, his lips brushing her cheek, lightly, gently. It sent shivers up her spine. "Do you love me, Percy?"

She turned her head, trying to kiss him but he grinned and moved away. He nuzzled her ear instead. "Ah, ah." Frustration nipped at her when his hands ran up her arms. "I need wooing."

She nipped at the corner of his mouth in happy retaliation. His fingers dug into the hair at her nape, sudden, strong, but still gentle. "Tell me you love me."

She met his eyes, slipping her hands inside his coat to feel the warmth of him. The fierceness of his expression flickered. "I love you," she whispered.

"Good god, woman. Was that so hard?"

She was laughing when his mouth finally closed over hers. He teased her with his tongue before pulling back slightly. "Say it again."

"I love you."

"Enough to marry me and be my marchioness?"

"Enough for that even," she said softly. Why shouldn't she take her happiness with both hands? They had already rescued each other, why stop now?

Conall kissed her again, hard and deep and joyful. "I love you, Percy. I love the little wrinkle you get between your eyes when someone has miscatalogued an artifact, the gasps you make when you've discovered something in the dirt. Your…other gasps," he added wickedly. "I've never felt happier or safer than I do when I'm with you. Marry me?"

He pulled a ring from his waistcoat pocket. It was a blue scarab beetle sitting on a band of gold. She swallowed hard against happy tears. "I can get you something else!" He hurried to say. "A diamond, or pearls."

"No, don't you dare," she said, slipping it onto her finger. "It's perfect." She couldn't stop looking at it. He understood her. "I'm going to make a terrible marchioness."

He shrugged. "I don't care."

She slid her arms around his neck and pressed against him. "I will absolutely marry you."

He gathered her closer and smiled against her hair. "Tell the truth, it was the trip to Egypt that did it, wasn't it?"

About the Author

Alyxandra Harvey lives in an old stone house with her husband, multiple dogs, and a few resident ghosts who are allowed to stay as long as they keep company manners. She likes chai lattes, tattoos, and books. Sometimes fueled by literary rage.

Author of The Drake Chronicles, The Witches of London, Haunting Violet, Red, Love Me Love Me Not.

Twitter: AlyxandraH
Instagram: alyxandraharveyauthor

www.ingramcontent.com/pod-product-compliance
Lightning Source LLC
Chambersburg PA
CBHW070929190726
48292CB00004B/1159

* 9 7 8 1 9 5 6 0 0 3 9 5 6 *